THE OTHER MRS COLLINS

MICHELLE MORGAN

Print ISBN: 978-1917705530

For Hannah and Adam.
This book could not have been written without your
encouragement, support and love.
Thank you for everything! I love you both! Xx

Oft have I heard that grief softens the mind,
And makes it fearful and degenerate;
Think therefore on revenge and cease to weep.

Henry VI, Part 2 – William Shakespeare

CHAPTER ONE

2014

The rain thrashes against the window as I make Charlie his favourite breakfast. Pancakes, syrup, and a glass of orange juice. It's Thursday. Book publication day for me, and rugby final match day for Charlie. A big day for both of us, and yet in spite of that, the rain has decided to piss down.

"Mum! Have you seen the weather out there? How am I going to play rugby in all this rain?"

I laugh, and ruffle my son's hair. He might be fifteen years old now, but he'll always be my little baby. He swerves his head from my grasp, and fiddles with his hair, using the back of a knife as a mirror.

"Don't worry, you look fine. And I'm sure it will all have changed by four pm. That's eight hours away. Besides, you've played in all kinds of conditions before, what's so different about today?"

He shrugs.

"Jennifer Craig said that she might watch me, if she gets out of cheerleading in time."

"Ahh, now it all makes sense."

I place Charlie's breakfast on the table, and then stick some bread in the toaster for myself.

"Are you not having pancakes?" Charlie asks.

"No, I'm saving that treat for the weekend. You're only having them now because you've got a big day ahead, and I want it to be the best day ever. Happy Charlie, happy life as they say."

Charlie rolls his eyes and grimaces.

"Another mum joke," he says. "Just don't be saying stuff like that when you're watching me this afternoon. Especially if Jennifer is there!"

I throw up my hands in mock horror.

"As if I would! Now eat up, I've got to get you to school, and then be back here by ten. I've got a podcast to record, a blog to publish, and then an interview with someone at the *Daily Mirror*. And that's just this morning!"

"Oh, that reminds me. Here you go. Happy publication day, Mum!"

Charlie pulls out a card from his rucksack, and thrusts it into my hand. It's pink, with a cute teddy bear on the front, holding a four-leaf clover.

"Aww, this is lovely! Thank you. Let's see what you've written inside... 'To Mum, have a great book day, love Charlie'. Oh, this is beautiful. Beautiful!"

"Don't cry, Mum! You'll embarrass yourself!" he says through a mouthful of pancake.

I can't believe my beautiful boy took it upon himself to buy a card to celebrate my big day. This is my tenth novel, but this is the first time Charlie has thought to buy me anything.

"I'm not crying," I sob. "My eyes are just sweating."

"Yeah, well I was going to buy you flowers too, but they were a bit expensive. I only had money to buy one or the other, so I picked the card because you can keep that as a souvenir. Flowers go in the bin eventually."

He has a point. I stare over at the huge bouquet of flowers that Scott gave to me before he went to work this morning. He's bought me blooms for every book I've written, but Charlie's right, they end up in the bin after a couple of weeks. But this card... I'll treasure it forever.

"Will Dad be back in time for my match?" Charlie asks. "I hope he will."

"He said he would try, but he's got back-to-back meetings today, so don't be too disappointed if he doesn't."

"More meetings. Shocker."

Charlie sticks a big forkful of pancake into his mouth, and the syrup leaves a sparkly trail on his lip.

"He'll be there in spirit," I say, trying to play down Scott's probable absence, "and I'll definitely be there in person. I made sure that no book interviews were scheduled after three, so that I can get down there in time."

Charlie sniffs, and goes to wipe his nose on the sleeve of his school shirt.

"Oi! I just washed that yesterday. Use a tissue, for heaven's sake." I hand him a piece of kitchen roll, and he rubs it roughly along the bottom of his nose. "Right, come on. Eat up, go clean your teeth, and then I'll get you to school."

I kiss the top of Charlie's head.

"Mum! Do not do that in front of my friends this afternoon! Promise?"

"I can't promise anything," I say, laughing. "If you win, I might be so overcome with joy that I run onto the pitch and plant a smacker right on the top of your head."

"You would as well."

Charlie rolls his eyes, picks up his rucksack and goes out of the door.

"Teeth!" I shout. "Cleaning teeth would be good here!"

We arrive at school, in time to see Charlie's friends getting off the school bus. They all live at the other side of town, so travel in together, which is something that has really annoyed Charlie in the past. In fact, for years he begged us to move house so he could go to school with his mates. Scott would joke that we should move to the moon, so that he could take a rocket to school instead.

"There's Harry, and Luke. Don't give me a kiss, Mum, they'll think that's hilarious."

I lean over and wave to the lads through the rain-soaked window.

"Hey, boys!" I shout. "Have a great day. I'll see you later!"

"They can't hear you. The window is closed."

"Okay, smart arse, but they saw me wave at least. Now have a beautiful day, and I'll see you on the rugby pitch at four."

I kiss my fingers and touch them to Charlie's shoulder. He squirms as though I've just placed a gigantic kiss on his cheek, but he doesn't wipe it off. I know that little peck will be invisibly imprinted on his school blazer for the rest of the day. A secret moment between a mum and her precious son.

"Bye, darling," I say as Charlie exits the car. "I love you."

He leans close to the door, sheltering his head from the rain with his rucksack.

"I love you, too," he whispers. "But don't tell anyone that!"

I cross my heart, and assure him that I'll keep it a secret between the both of us. Then I watch as he runs to his friends, and then they all sprint through the wet tennis court, and into the school.

The day disappears in a haze of blogposts, podcasts, social media, and interviews for my new book. I've been a full-time, bestselling author since Charlie was born, and I always tell him that all my dreams came true because of him. It's the truth. Before he arrived, I had worked as a secretary at a greetings card manufacturer, and despite trying every day to become a full-time writer, I was rejected at every turn. When Charlie came along, I took almost a year off for maternity leave, and then went back part-time. Both of those things gave me the opportunity to work on my writing (mainly during naptimes and after Charlie had gone to bed) and before long I had completed a rom-com novel, which an agent decided to take on. He sold it shortly after, for a considerable advance, and I couldn't believe it.

At first, I didn't know if I'd be able to support myself financially with one novel. It was before social media and being able to spread the word online wasn't that easy, but I persevered, and with the help of my publisher, friends, family, and local media, I found a readership. Not a small one either. My book became something of a bestseller, and I was bombarded by readers with requests to write more. By the time my first royalty payment came through, it was big enough that I was able to give up the day job once and for all. After that I won a lucrative two-book deal, and I was astounded.

And now, here I am, fifteen years later and still going strong. It hasn't been easy at times. Some books have done much better than others, and I've had to change editors several times, as they move on to other jobs and lives. However, my readership has remained faithful, and I receive emails and letters from all over the world, spurring me on to write more.

For several years after my first novel was published, I was concerned that something might come and take the success away from me, so when I was offered another job working on children's activity books, I took it. Since then, I've turned my hand to many different areas, such as TV tie-ins, articles, the odd celebrity biography and even a psychological thriller. This flexibility has enabled me to remain a full-time author, and has provided me with a regular income, but my heart will always belong to my rom-coms. That's why publication days are always a highlight in my world. Not only do I get to celebrate the novel itself, but I am reminded how lucky I am to be here, and to be doing what I love.

As I log onto Skype to talk to another interviewer, my phone pings. It's a WhatsApp message from Scott.

> Hey! Hope everything is going well today. Hope the new book sells a million copies! Then I can retire! LOL! So proud of you! I'm probably not going to be able to get out of the office in time for Charlie's rugby match. The guy who was supposed to be here to present the lunchtime meeting has had to postpone until 3.30, and it's due to run for about an hour. If I can get away on time after that, I'll try my hardest to get there, but if I'm not, tell Charlie I'm there in spirit, and I'll see you both this evening. Love you! xxx

I groan. Charlie wanted so much for Scott to see him play in the game. My son was so proud to be chosen for the team, and made a huge deal about us both going to see him. Even though we both knew that this might happen, Charlie will be gutted that Scott has to work late, but what can I do? Scott loves his job, and has worked hard to become Head of Department at The Norfolk Marketing Company, so I have to accept the fact that sometimes the hours are not particularly flexible. Certainly not as flexible as mine anyway.

I hit reply.

> No! That's such a shame. Charlie was really
> looking forward to seeing you there. But I
> guess it can't be helped. Maybe we can get a
> pizza (or two!) tonight, and have a little
> celebration for Charlie's first match. I'm sure
> he'd like that. xxx

I press send, and thirty seconds later another message arrives.

> Not sure if I'll be hungry after all the meeting
> snacks at work today. Maybe tomorrow?

Tomorrow. Always tomorrow. I love my husband more than anything in the world, but sometimes his obsession with work takes precedence over general family affairs and it drives me crazy. Ironic really, since years ago I briefly put my fledgling career over our relationship, and I soon learnt how much he didn't appreciate it. Now Scott does the same thing, with far more at stake. I click to reply, but before I can type anything, a voice booms out of my laptop.

"Hi, Olivia! This is Teresa from the Gigantic Romantic Books Podcast. How are you?"

I tuck my hair behind my ears, and smile.

"Hi. I'm doing good, thanks. Thanks so much for inviting me onto the show, I'm looking forward to speaking with you!"

"Great. I'll press record, and we'll get on with it."

My publication day has gone well, and I leave the house, knackered but happy. Every interviewer claimed to have loved the book, and whether they really read it or not is none of my business. They gave it time on their platforms, and that's really all I need. Added to that, my publisher called to tell me that the book will be featured in this weekend's *Sunday People*, and that first-day sales in Tesco and Asda have been through the roof. This is the first of all of my books to find their way onto two supermarket shelves, and I am ecstatic. Absolutely ecstatic.

I turn on the car radio, and Madonna's "Ray of Light" blasts out of the speaker. I am in such a great mood that I turn the volume up, and sing all the way up the road. Today has been a good day, and all being well, my book will go onto the bestseller lists, and I won't have to worry about money for a while.

I turn into the little road that leads up to Charlie's school, and I'm surprised that there are about twenty cars in front of me, trailing all the way from where I am, up to the gate. Nobody is moving anywhere, and I figure that someone must have broken down at the front of the queue. Shit. I send Charlie a WhatsApp.

> I'm here, but I'm not in the school yet.
> Someone is holding things up, and nobody can
> get through the gate. But I am here! I will see
> you soon. Love you! xxx

I press send, and watch to see if Charlie reads it, but he doesn't. He must be in the changing room already, waiting to get out onto the pitch. I open the window and crane my neck to see what the hold-up is. It is only then that I see the tiniest flashing blue light in the distance, parked outside the main school entrance. An ambulance.

Blood rushes through my ears. If emergency services are at the school, that must be the reason for the delay in getting in. A dad who I recognise gets out of his car, walks closer to the gate, talks to another parent, and then trudges back toward his vehicle. I open my door and he comes over.

"What's going on?" I ask.

"My kid just texted and said that there was some kind of accident in the sports department. It's all closed off apparently."

An accident in the sports department? But that will be where Charlie is at this moment. I say goodbye to the parent, close my door and retrieve my phone. My son still hasn't seen the message, and hasn't been online for the past thirty minutes. My fingers fly across the keyboard, trying to control my shaking long enough to send a message.

> Charlie, is everything okay? One of the parents
> at the gate said that there had been an
> accident. Let me know you're all right. Love
> you lots. xxx

Two seconds after I press send, my phone rings. It's the school reception.

"Hello? Is this Mrs Collins?"

"Yes, speaking. Is everything okay?"

"I'm afraid there's been an incident in school. Are you able to get here?"

Oh God. A sour taste pours into my mouth, and I have difficulty swallowing. Why would the school be phoning me, when there were dozens of other parents here? Why?

"I'm... I'm... outside now. I can't get in because the gate is closed. What's going on?"

"Stay there," the receptionist says, completely ignoring my question. "We'll send somebody down to get you."

I hang up the phone, and sit back heavily into my seat. Chills invade my shoulders and despite it being mid-September, my fingers are freezing. All around me, parents get out of their cars to see what the hold-up is. There are shrugged shoulders, scowls, and much talking on phones. There are muffled, confused conversations, and some stilted, nervous laughter. And in the middle of it all is the sight of a policewoman, marching steadily down the driveway, staring at each and every number plate.

I want her nowhere near me. I want her to go to the car in front, or the car behind, or better still, no car at all.

But she does come near me, and she reads my number plate.

She looks up, and smiles thinly in my direction. I open the car door as slowly as I can.

And then my world goes black.

The smell of the hospital corridor makes me want to throw up. It is a combination of bleach, latex gloves, pungent food, vomit and strong coffee, which burns at the back of my nose. It is 6.01pm, two hours after I was supposed to be at Charlie's rugby match, and instead I sit on a blue plastic chair, against the wall, waiting to hear what has happened to my son.

As I ran into the school grounds with the police officer, I could see in the distance a team of paramedics wheeling a patient out of the building, and into the ambulance. My son. My beloved, fifteen-year-old son. Unmoving. Unresponsive. Unreal.

"Stop! Stop!" I shouted, over and over again. I waved my arms, I screamed my lungs out, but by the time I reached the top of the driveway, the ambulance doors were closed, the siren was on, and my son was taken away. The vehicle was inches from me. My son inside. Close enough to feel his aura, but too far away to reach in and grab him. Grab him and hold him close to me.

Too far away.

"Don't worry," the policewoman said. "I'll take you to the hospital. Follow me."

Blue lights flashing, sirens on, we followed the ambulance for the full seventeen minutes that it took to get from the school to the hospital. In that time, my eyes did not wander from the back of the vehicle in front, not even for a second.

"Hold on, hold on, please hold on," I whispered all the way there, and when we pulled up outside A&E, the paramedics pulled the stretcher out of the ambulance. I tried to rush over, but the policewoman grabbed my arm.

"Let them do their work," she said. "He is in good hands."

Such a cliché, I thought. Such a bloody cliché. And yet I hoped it was true. His little body, usually so full of energy and love, was as still as a doll. The blue blanket that covered him showed no evidence of what had happened, but according to the policewoman, he had collapsed as they were performing warm-up exercises in the sports hall. That was it. That's all she knew.

The stretcher swung into the hospital and then disappeared into the stark, white corridor.

"You'll have to wait here," the policewoman said. "I will let the receptionist know that you've arrived, and she'll tell the doctors. They'll let you know as soon as there's any news."

I thanked her, and she nodded and bid me goodbye. As she headed through reception and then out into the car park, I realised that I did not even know her name, and I couldn't remember what she looked like. She had been with me at a pivotal part of my life, and I knew nothing about her at all.

In the many minutes since arriving at the hospital, I have tried to get Scott on the phone, but he's nowhere to be found. A litany of texts has been sent to his phone number, his Messenger, his WhatsApp and even his Instagram direct messages, and I go from one app to the other, seeing if he's read any of them. Seeing if he's active.

But there is nothing.

Nothing.

He hasn't even seen one of the messages, never mind read them.

Where the fuck are you?

I type on WhatsApp.

Why haven't you read any of my messages?

All around me, families wait for news of loved ones, while patients wait to be treated for cut hands, mysterious pains, coughs, and head traumas. One old lady comes in with her face smashed up around her eyes.

"I've had a terrible fall," she tells the receptionist. "In all my years, I've never hurt my face like this."

The receptionist assures the woman that because she's hit her head, she'll be seen soon, and takes her to a special room behind the desk. A policeman enters and announces that there will soon be a man coming in who is currently going through opiates and alcohol withdrawal, and then a couple arrive with their young daughter, shaking and holding her covered hand. The little girl isn't crying, but her face is as white as the wall, and her lip trembles as her parents give over her name, address and age.

The funny thing about the A&E section of the hospital is that most of these people had no idea they'd be here today. They got up, made their breakfast, went to work, or school, or out for their groceries, and then something happened which changed the trajectory of their day and sometimes even their lives. Just like me. Making pancakes, listening to Charlie talk passionately about his rugby match that afternoon, and then... and then...

The double doors swing open, and three nurses appear, giggling over some random piece of gossip. I wish I could giggle. I wish I could laugh my head off after hearing that this is all a terrible mistake, and that my son is not currently being worked on by a team of doctors, or surgeons, or both.

I'm so busy looking at the nurses that I don't notice a whitecoat arriving next to my chair.

"Mrs Collins?"

I jump. There in front of me is a forty-something, red-headed doctor, with a clipboard in his arms. His lips are thin, and as much as he tries to smile, they merely crease at the corners.

"Yes, I'm Mrs Collins. Please tell me that my son is okay."

He sits on the empty chair next to me, blinks slowly, and a tiny line forms between his eyes.

And he doesn't need to say anything.

Because I already know that my beautiful Charlie is gone.

Two hours later, and I sit in the shadowy living room of our home, with my son's clean washing folded next to me. It had all been hanging on the line when I got in. Jeans, two rugby jerseys, a pink hoodie, a pair of shorts, and nine socks. Nine socks. Where the tenth one went is anyone's guess. As I unpinned the washing from the line, I held each item up to my nose. Even though they've been washed, they still smell like my son. Talc, soap, cherry sweets, and Lego. That's what my son smells like.

That's what my son smelt like.

Past tense.

Now it will always be past tense.

I grab one of the jerseys from the pile, and hug it tight. As I do so, my phone pings. I haven't told anyone but Scott that Charlie was taken to hospital, but somehow the cogs turn and the rumours begin. I've had friends from all over town message me. My oldest friend Lauren was told by her daughter that something had happened, and she has phoned me several times. She means well, but I haven't been able to bring myself to answer. Let me pretend that he's still here. Just for a little while longer. Just forever.

The message is from Scott.

> What the fuck's going on?! I've been in a meeting all afternoon, and it ran late. Where are you? I'm leaving now. I'll be at the hospital in about thirty minutes.

Thirty minutes? He works less than thirty minutes away from the hospital, but maybe he thinks there will be traffic or something. Either way, it doesn't matter.

> He's not there.

I reply.

> Our son is dead.

CHAPTER TWO

2024

Every day, I miss him.

Every single day I wake up, and for the first three seconds, I'm normal. I'm about to make Charlie's breakfast, get him ready for his day. But then I remember.

He's gone.

And the darkness that enveloped my world ten years ago grabs on tight, and keeps hold until the next morning, when I get those three seconds of lightness again.

Every day, I throw myself into two hours of cardio, weights and then yoga. Lauren says I'm making it up when I tell her that I workout for two hours a day, six days a week, but honestly, when you spend most of your time at home, and get up at a reasonable hour, it's pretty easy to do. Added to that, it's often the only way I can get my mind to stop obsessing over the death of my beloved child.

Of course, the awful thing about being able to quieten my mind for a while is that when I come back into the real world, it's all still there, and then I feel guilty that I haven't been thinking about Charlie for the past couple of hours. So, it's a big, torturous circle really. The only positive thing is that exercise helps me stay fit in body, if not in mind.

I stir my tea, and the spoon hits off the side of the porcelain cup, and makes a tinkling sound. It's comforting in a way. Reminds me of visiting my great-gran during the 1980s, when she'd carefully take the porcelain cups and plates out of her cabinet, and set everything up on the starched white tablecloth, ready for sandwiches, scones and cakes. My great-gran lived about an hour away from us, but you could guarantee, the moment we told her we were visiting, the best of everything would be displayed on her dining-room table.

I miss my great-gran.

I miss those days.

I miss the person I was back then. Isn't it funny how much we change due to circumstances put upon us by things we don't want or understand?

It's raining again, but what's new? It's been a wet, grey summer, there's no doubt about that, but now it's October, and as with everyone else in Britain, I worry about what the latter part of the year has in store for us. My mind drifts off into memories of last summer, when Scott and I stayed in a beautiful, wooden house for two weeks. Just us, for the first time since Charlie died. No stressing over work, no worries about Scott's parents' ongoing health concerns, and no interruptions. Walks around the lake, endless good food, and lots and lots of together time.

Yes, the memory of what happened to Charlie still haunted me every day that we were away, but being close to the water, close to where we spent so much time when he was a kid was comforting to me, and I valued every moment of it. In fact, I ended up dreaming about Charlie several times during that trip, which I took to be a sign that although we couldn't see him, he was still there.

I hear a noise behind me, and before I can turn around, Scott slides his hand underneath my T-shirt, and grabs my waist.

"Morning," he mutters, as he kisses my neck.

"Good morning." I smile.

He gives me a hug, and then turns his attention to the teapot.

"It's just been made," I say, offering my cup as proof. "I wasn't sure if you were coming down yet, or I'd have poured you a cup."

"No worries. I drifted back off, but that bloody dog woke me up. When is anyone ever going to report the little bastard?"

Before Christmas last year, a young family moved into the house next door, and with them came their friendly but oh-so-noisy Dobermann. Ever since then, we've been woken up every morning with it barking in the garden, his owners completely oblivious to the fact that it is waking up the entire neighbourhood.

"Perhaps we should report it," I say. "The council won't tell them it was us who made the call."

Scott pours his tea into a mug with a British bulldog pictured on the side. He takes a swig, and dries his mouth on the sleeve of his dressing gown.

"I'm tempted, but I'm sure one of the new neighbours works at the council. I saw him being picked up in a council van the other day."

I roll my eyes. My husband loves a good moan, but he'll find any excuse not to solve the problem head-on.

"Oh well, we'll have to buy some earplugs, and hope for the best."

Scott laughs.

"I think next door are the ones needing the earplugs, after the noise you were making last night."

I pick up the oven glove and playfully hit his shoulder with it.

"That's so rude! And also, not my fault. I don't recall making a noise before you slid into bed..."

We both giggle like teenagers at the thought of our late-night get-together. It has taken a long time to enjoy the physical part of our relationship again. It seemed so wrong after Charlie's passing. How could we make love, when our poor boy had been taken away? It was impossible to comprehend, especially when I could see his beautiful green eyes and peachy face, in every waking hour. But slowly – very, very slowly – I was able to reconnect with the part of myself that was still married, and now we make love whenever we can, which lately has been quite a lot.

I watch as Scott takes the Weetabix out of the cupboard, and pops two into a bowl.

I love this man.

Our relationship has not been easy these past years, and it has taken me a long time to understand him. In fact, I'm still learning to understand him. Scott cried many times over Charlie in the beginning, but then all of a sudden, he clammed up, threw himself even more into his work, and would only talk about our son when pushed. This has frustrated me over the years, and I've often questioned why he wouldn't want to speak about our memories, but I still love him, regardless. I know that despite the silence, Scott still loves our boy, and recently I have witnessed him crying in Charlie's old bedroom several times. It's upsetting because nobody wants to hear their husband weep, but comforting because it assures me that under his quiet demeanour, he does still care. He does still miss Charlie as much as I do.

I tussle his hair, as I used to do when we were young, and as I did to Charlie when he was here. Scott doesn't have as much hair now as he once had, and it's shorter than it ever was before, but it's still there, still blond, mixed with salt and pepper, and still beautifully styled.

"Oi! I've got an important meeting this morning. I don't want to look like Ken Dodd during it!" He laughs, and then straightens his hair, using the knife as a mirror. Just as Charlie did all those years ago.

After twenty-five years of marriage, I still love my husband with every fibre of my body. How many fifty-four-year-olds can say that? Very few, if my friends are anything to go by.

As early morning heads toward lunchtime, I am aware that I haven't started any work yet. That's the thing about working from home – you're not really obliged to do anything. Well, you are if you want to get paid, but there are times when my brain gets distracted by watching the squirrels stealing nuts outside my window, or the dangly spider that has taken up residence in the corner of my study. But I really do need to get on.

I sigh, stretch my arms over my head, stifle a yawn, and then take a sneaky look at my novels piled up on a shelf next to the door. Memories of my old life. Memories of when I could still consider myself a full-time writer. I can't do that anymore.

Not since Charlie passed.

After that awful day, my life fell into a million shards of turmoil. I got through the funeral in a haze of medication and – I'm sorry to admit – alcohol. I was completely out of it for months, and nothing or no one could make the pain go away. Scott would appear at my bedside with trays of soup or yoghurt, or porridge, and I'd allow myself a spoonful or two, before spending the next ten minutes disposing of the rest in plant pots, the sink and the toilet. Scott would clear the tray and tell me how well I had done, speaking to me like he'd done with Charlie, when he was three years old.

Sometimes my husband would sit on the bed, and cry with me, holding my hand and rubbing my shoulder, while his body would shake in his own despair.

"Please talk to me," he begged. "I've already lost Charlie. I don't want to lose you too."

I didn't reply. I couldn't care less if he lost me. In my mind, the quicker I expired the better. If the world wasn't good enough for my beloved son, then it wasn't good enough for me either. Scott would curl up on the bed, and scroll his phone for something to do, but eventually the light in the corner of my eye would irritate me, and I'd shoo him away with imaginary errands, like buying me a magazine (that I'd never read) or a shampoo (that I'd never use).

I did get out of bed eventually, but the idea of turning on my laptop and writing another novel seemed unhinged to me. The last time I had written anything was when Charlie was in the house, and it seemed fruitless, selfish even, to make up imaginary worlds when my child was no longer in the real one. What a ridiculous job I had. What a bloody stupid, unnecessary job.

It wasn't long before my editor started making gentle email inquiries as to the status of my next novel. I couldn't bring myself to reply, and so he called me and left messages, every day for weeks. I ignored those, too, and six months later, my current two-book contract was cancelled. The news came in the form of a letter, telling me that if I ever decided to write again, they would like to read my manuscript, though made it clear that reading it would in no way constitute a book deal. I knew that I'd let them down, but in that moment, when my world was dark, and painful, and full of pins and needles, I didn't care about my career. I didn't give one tiny shit about it.

Occasionally, Scott would bring me my laptop, and sometimes I'd balance it on the bed, and switch it on, reading emails from excited readers, congratulating me on my latest novel, and asking when the next one would be out.

Never.

Never will it be out.

What was the point of pretending? It was all nonsense. Every part of it.

Soon, Scott returned to work, and the world kept turning, the clocks kept ticking, and I kept mourning.

And then, five years had passed, and I had no idea where they had gone. The only thing I'd written in that time was an article about parental grief. I was proud of it, but it didn't pay my bills or revive my career. Not that I wanted it to.

One day, I switched on my laptop, and after reading my emails, I opened Word. My fingers poised over the keys, I began to type, but found that the only thing I wanted to write about was my life with Charlie. I named characters after him, gave them his hobbies, watched them grow, and then mourned their loss... I persevered, but when the novel was finished, nobody wanted to publish it. I still had a good name in the industry, and most people knew that I'd lost my son, but they didn't particularly want to hear about it. None of the editors ever said that I shouldn't write about my child's death, but they'd drop little hints or comments that the focus on my writing should maybe be more fiction, less working things out.

After three novels failed to sell, I gave up completely, and apart from writing a couple of articles here and there, I haven't written a word since. I haven't even worked on the children's activity books that were my bread and butter, and the celebrity bios have dried up to a bitter, heartbroken crumb. I worked so hard to get my writing career off the ground, and while I would tell Charlie that my dreams came true because of him, they ended because of him too. When my boy left, he took all of my ideas and ambitions with him, and no matter how hard I've tried, they've never come back.

So, I don't write anything anymore.

And I'm not sure I ever will.

For the first five years of mourning, I was in the lucky position of still having a regular income in the way of royalties, and I lived off those quite comfortably. However, with no new books coming onto the market, the money dried up, so for the past few years, I've taken on various jobs to make the ends meet. I've worked part-time in a shoe shop (which lasted two months because I had a breakdown in the middle of the floor, after a woman came in with her little son called Charlie), I've worked afternoons in the library (thanks to Lauren, who has worked there her entire adult life), but was let go because of budget cuts, and I once flirted with the idea of being a meditation teacher, only I couldn't sit still during the course, so I failed.

Now, I've taken a freelance job with Babbage Books, a small, independent – and slightly batty – sci-fi publishing house. My remote job is an organisational assistant, and is a bit of everything, but mainly it means that I oversee the publishing process of each book. The owner, and my rather eccentric boss, is a man called Sam Babbage, who lives in Glasgow with his ginger cat, and who I've never actually met. Instead, we share emails and the odd Zoom call every morning, before I liaise with his team of freelance editors, proofreaders and designers, all scattered around the world.

I've worked at Babbage for two months now, and already I feel as though I've entered *The Twilight Zone*. Sam has a love for crazy ideas and has a full back catalogue, so anyone who asks if they can write a book about any old nonsense will be met with a cheery, "Fabulous! Here's a contract!" Most of the time, the 'author' can hardly string a sentence together, and yet now they're tasked with writing an entire manuscript. My job involves being the wall between these authors, and the editors and designers. Nobody can speak directly to anyone except me. The job is part-time, and that's about all I can manage for now.

I switch on my laptop, and watch as twenty-three emails pop into my inbox. There are seven from Sam giving updates and answering queries, two from Kendra the proofreader, with questions that I have no clue how to answer, and the rest from would-be and trying-to-be authors. There's one from Jacob, an older writer who seems to know what he's doing, but writes books that continually sell a couple of dozen copies. Why Sam keeps publishing them, I have no idea. Maybe he's one of Jacob's readers. Who knows? Today, Jacob wants to know if I can get him onto *The Oprah Winfrey Show* with his new book, *Dinosaurs in Space Part Four*.

I have previously told him that there's no way he'll get on there, since the show doesn't even run anymore. He wouldn't have it though. According to him, if Winfrey can interview Harry and Meghan for a special show, she can interview Jacob too. This guy fancies himself as the sci-fi version of Stephen King or something, and not even the lack of royalties will convince him otherwise.

I fire off a quick email to him, explaining that Oprah's people have unfortunately turned him down, but they'll keep his name on file. It's a lie of course. I wouldn't know how to get in touch with them if my life depended on it, but hopefully it will keep Jacob away from my inbox for at least the rest of the day.

I'm about to reply to Sam's messages, when my phone pings. It's a WhatsApp message from Lauren.

> Hey! Have you remembered that the library is having a charity clothes sale tomorrow evening? If you could sort out some old stuff, that would be terrific. All for a good cause! I'll collect them around 3, if that's okay. They don't need to be in perfect condition, but clean and wearable, please. Thanks so much! See you soon. xx

Ugh. Lauren only told me about the charity sale last night, and didn't mention that she needed the clothes so soon. I look at the *Flintstones* clock on the wall. It's 11.11. I make a wish, and hold a good thought for Charlie – as I always do at this time – and then head to the bedroom to retrieve some stuff that will keep Lauren happy.

I scour my wardrobe for anything I can donate, and find a pair of flared jeans that I bought in 2002, with sparkles and studs all over them. They're about two sizes too small for me now, and even if they weren't, the idea of wearing them makes me laugh. At fifty-four years old, I'm probably too old to wear them, and the only time I ever put them on was when I went to a fancy-dress party as Kiss frontman Gene Simmons. I sniff to make sure they don't smell too much of the back of the wardrobe, and then stick them into a bin liner.

Next, I find an old coat that I haven't worn in years. It is grey-checked, with fake fur running around the outside of the hood. A quick check in the pocket leads me to a receipt that confirms the last time I wore it was to Tesco, on 2 March 2016. I throw the receipt into the bin, and the coat into the bag. Will that be enough to satisfy my demanding friend? Probably not.

For a moment, it passes my mind that maybe I should finally go through Charlie's wardrobe, but the very idea of it brings bile into my throat. I swallow hard to rid myself of the taste, and instead I slide Scott's wardrobe open. Immediately a pair of jogging bottoms and three pairs of jeans plop out onto my feet. He has a habit of folding his casual trousers and sticking them in a pile at the bottom of his wardrobe. This used to drive me crazy when we shared a cupboard, but thankfully now we've progressed to separate areas, so he can do what he wants. I stare at the jogging bottoms. Does he really need these? I doubt it, although I have seen him wear them when he's pottering around in the garage. Best keep them, particularly as Lauren would be sure to turn her nose up at the grease marks on the knees.

I shove the trousers back into the wardrobe, and as I do, my eyes fall upon an old, battered leather jacket, stuffed right at the bottom of the pile. I remember that thing. Scott used to wear it on nights out, but I haven't seen it in years. Maybe even a decade or more, and certainly before Charlie passed. We didn't find any reason to want to go out after he died, and I imagine it was at that point that the jacket was stuck in the bottom of the wardrobe. I pull it out, go to stick it into the bag, and then stop. Best to check the pockets first. Who knows, I might find a tenner in there.

The side pockets house the usual assortment of old change, tissues and a couple of old toffees and from the outside it looks as though there is nothing at all in the top front pocket. Still, I slide my hand inside to make sure, and feel a small card. I pull it out and stare for a couple of seconds, not sure what I'm looking at.

The words *Regency Hotel, Cromer* are printed on the front, along with an artist's impression of the imposing Victorian hotel. On the back is a printed message.

THANK YOU FOR CHOOSING OUR HOTEL. THIS KEY CARD ENTITLES YOU TO A FREE BREAKFAST, SERVED BETWEEN 7AM AND 10AM. Underneath, somebody has written the words *Valid for Mr and Mrs Collins, Room 106*.

Mr and Mrs Collins.

I sit back onto the floor, and stare at the card, as though doing so will reveal the exact meaning behind the words.

I haven't been to Cromer since before Charlie was born.

Or have I?

No. We've both lived in South Norfolk for our entire lives, so heading to the seaside has always been a thing. But it's normally somewhere close, like Great Yarmouth or Caister. Cromer is on the north of the Norfolk coast, so we haven't been there often. Definitely not in the past ten years anyway.

Underneath the breakfast announcement are the words *Checkout 11am, Sunday 20 July, 2014.* 20 July? Almost two months to the day before Charlie died. My face flushes, and there is a flutter in my stomach. How is this a thing? I never went to Cromer in 2014 with – or without – Scott, and yet here is a card that suggests somebody has been with him, and what's more, has used my name.

Mrs Collins. Was it possible that he took his mother away for the weekend, and I've just forgotten? No, that's ridiculous and what's more, impossible. Scott's mother had a small stroke in early 2014 and wasn't really well enough to go anywhere for the rest of the year. And wouldn't I have noticed if Scott went away for the weekend without me? Of course I would, and Charlie would certainly have commented on it.

My thoughts are interrupted by the slamming of the front door.

"Hey you! I've come home to collect my files for the Henderson project. I forgot them this morning."

Scott.

My shaking hands somehow manage to stuff the card in my jeans pocket, and I'm just about to throw the jacket back into the wardrobe when he appears.

"Hey, did you hear me? I'm back to get the files."

I smile slowly, in an attempt to quiet my breath before replying.

"Yes, I heard you. Sorry, I realised you'd left them about five minutes after you'd gone."

"No worries." He looks at the pile of clothes in front of me. "What's this? Having a clear-out?"

"Not exactly. Lauren asked me to get together some clothes for a charity sale at the library, so I'm putting a few things in a bag."

Scott's eyes flit around the items I've already collected, and then up to the leather jacket that is hanging half in, half out of the wardrobe.

"Well, check with me first before giving any of my stuff away. Particularly that jacket. I've got a soft spot for that old thing. I haven't worn it since... since... you know... But I'd still like to keep it."

I nod and he bends to kiss me on the forehead. I have to bite my lip not to show him the card and demand to know what it's all about. I can't. Not yet. Asking him now would only lead to an altercation, or a lie, or maybe – just maybe – a truth that I don't want to address right now.

"You okay?"

He stares at me with his bright blue eyes. The same eyes I stared into when we made love last night. Who else has been staring into those eyes? Who else has been making love to him? Nobody. Nobody at all. It's all a gigantic misunderstanding. Damn my ridiculous over-imagination.

"I'm fine. Just tired." I rub my eyes, and they're sore to the touch.

"Yeah, I'm a bit knackered myself. Maybe get another early night, eh?"

He winks at me, and before I can answer, he's out of the room and down the stairs. I jump up and run to the window, watching his car disappear from the driveway, his hand waving up at me like it does every single time he leaves the house. I watch him go, and then reach back into my pocket for the card.

What the hell is going on?

The Regency Hotel is one of those establishments that often pops up during the local evening news. Maybe there's an actor staying there while they work on an end-of-pier show or perhaps there is a meeting to discuss the development of the new sea defences. It seems to be the Cromer centre of everything, and right now it is the centre of my everything.

Fingers trembling, I open the hotel website on my phone, and study photos of the bar, the restaurant, and finally, the bedrooms. I squint my eyes as I take in every detail of the standard room... The queen-sized bed with blue-and-white duvet, the tiny, yellow wall lights above the bed, and the gigantic bowed window with two purple easy chairs, perfect for people-watching on the pier below.

Did my husband screw another woman in that room?

In any room?

It all seems so far-fetched, especially after everything we've been through, but even so, I need to know.

I press the call hotel button on the website, and my phone springs into action. There's a couple of seconds of silence, and then finally, a voice. I grab the phone with both hands, as the receptionist gives me the greeting that she has likely repeated a thousand times before.

"Good morning, Regency Hotel. My name is Tracy. How can I help?"

I open my mouth to speak, but a strange, gurgling noise escapes instead. I cough, clear my throat and then try again.

"Oh, yes, good morning. I'm not sure if you can help me, but I'm writing a book, and need to know if the hotel keeps records of guests that go back ten years."

"Ten years?"

I can't see Tracy, but I can imagine that at this very moment she's rolling her eyes, her nostrils flared.

"Yes, that's right. In the book, I'm... er, I'm investigating a murder, and need to look through hotel records..."

"Well, there have been no murders in this hotel!" Tracy snaps. "I mean, it's like over a hundred years old, so there may have been one that happened back then, but not since I've been here – and I've been here twenty-five years!"

Tracy talks as though she's the hotel owner, deeply insulted that anyone could imply a murder has taken place in her establishment. I wish I'd picked another excuse as to why I need to know about hotel records. Maybe I should have told her the truth, if not for the fact that the truth is so ridiculous and potentially painful.

"No, no, I'm not writing a non-fiction book," I say. "I'm writing a novel – detective fiction actually..."

Tracy sniffs on the other end of the line.

"I see. So, it's research for a work of fiction."

"Yes, that's it. Research. My detective needs to know who has stayed in the hotel during the time of the murd... um... incident."

There's a pause, while presumably Tracy decides if I'm a nutcase or not.

"Right. Well, I can tell you that there will be no mention of bookings on our computers, because our systems only keep them for five years before they automatically delete. But we do have guest books in our basement storage, which date back for at least fifty years."

Now my interest is piqued. I pull out a notebook, in case Tracy adds anything important.

"And every guest needs to sign those books?"

"Yes," she says. "It's old-fashioned I know, but a major tradition at the Regency. They sign the book when they enter the hotel, and write in their thoughts when they check out. Your detective could look in those to find what he's looking for, but he couldn't do it officially, as that would be against data protection. But if he was sneaky enough, he could get access to them regardless."

I smile, and electricity fizzles in my belly.

"You've been really helpful," I say. "Thank you very much indeed."

"You're welcome. Was there anything else you needed to know?"

I assure Tracy that there's nothing else, and hang up the phone.

So, if my imaginary detective was sneaky enough, he could gain access to the visitors' books... Well, I don't know if my non-existent character is sneaky enough, but I definitely am.

I log on to the Norfolk train website, and book a ticket to Cromer.

"You can't just find a random card and decide that Scott's had an affair, for goodness' sake!"

Lauren sits on my faded fabric sofa, turning the card one way and then the other. Bags of donated clothes lie on the floor, along with the leather jacket which had hidden the card for the past ten years.

"I'm not just deciding that he's had an affair, but don't you agree that it's shifty? At the very least, it is shifty!"

Lauren takes a sip of coffee, swirls it around her mouth and then swallows.

"I can definitely agree that it's a bit weird..."

"Shifty."

"Yes, maybe that too, but there could be a perfectly logical explanation. And if you ask Scott, I'm sure he'll give you one."

I take the card back, and stare at it for the thousandth time today. Taking in the words, begging them to change, begging it all to make sense.

But it doesn't. I sigh.

"Yes, he could have a logical explanation. But he could also lie."

Lauren rolls her eyes.

"I know I've had differences with Scott in the past, but I don't think he's a natural-born liar. He's not like Michael. Michael could lie for Britain without thinking anything about it. Which is why I divorced the bastard. But Scott... No, Scott doesn't lie. Does he? Especially after everything you've been through together."

"I don't know," I say. "Until this morning I'd have probably said no, but now I have no clue. My head is screwed. And did you see the date on the card? Two months almost to the day before Charlie passed away."

Lauren nods.

"Yes, I saw that, and maybe that's what's making you so paranoid about it, what with it being such a terrible year for you all round."

I scratch my temples, and my eyebrows knit together. I have such a headache, and this conversation is making it worse. Lauren is right, 2014 was a terrible year, which then turned into a terrible life. But am I wrong to worry about my husband being unfaithful? I don't think I am.

"I agree on some levels," I say. "However, I think that even if we didn't go through all that we did, I'd still be paranoid about finding what looks like some kind of hotel reservation in my husband's pocket."

"Perhaps paranoid wasn't the best word to use," Lauren says. "But you know what I mean, and I think you should put that card back where you found it, or throw it away or something. The more you stare at it, the worse you'll feel — especially if you're not going to ask Scott what it's all about. What's the point of keeping it?"

I tuck my hair behind my ears, and hope that Lauren will carry on talking, so that I don't have to answer her question.

She doesn't.

"I need to find out what's going on," I say. "Why the hell has Scott kept a card from a random hotel tucked into his jacket for the past ten years? It makes no sense, unless it's connected to something horrendous."

Lauren reaches forward and touches my shoulder.

"Olivia," she says, "he probably doesn't even remember he's got it. Besides, if the worst scenario happened and he did have an affair..." I shoot her a look. "I said if! If he had an affair, it was a decade ago, and there is nothing you can do about it now. Best you forget about it. The past is the past. It's done. It's gone. Forget about it."

Forget about it.

Lauren's words vibrate in my ears.

Forget about it?

I know that no matter what happens, forgetting about anything that happened ten years ago is not something that I can do. I know this because a year after Charlie passed away, I began to obsess about things that happened a good two decades before that... Actually, saying that I obsessed about things is not correct. It was one thing, singular. One deeply terrible, painful thing.

1993. The year Scott left me for another woman.

<h1 style="text-align:center">CHAPTER THREE</h1>

Scott and I were childhood sweethearts in a way. We didn't meet in school or anything like that, but we did get together when we were teenagers. It was 1988, I was eighteen and he was a year older. He was working as a glass collector and barman in the local trendy (but ever-so-slightly run-down) pub, The Gamebird, and I was working as a secretary, trying to save enough money to go after my dreams of attending drama school and becoming an actress.

To this day, I remember what Scott was wearing when I first clapped eyes on him – crisp, white shirt, with a skinny grey tie to match his skinny grey trousers. He was blond, wore one gold earring, and his hair was thick and spiked up at the top, but with a tendency to flop toward the sides. I thought straight away that he looked like one of the Bros guys, but when I told him so, he pretended to drop the glasses he was carrying.

"Ugh! Give me a break," he squawked, and his hand darted up to his hair. "I am nothing like them. If I'm like anyone, it's Simon Le Bon, circa 1984."

We both laughed. Him, because he honestly believed that to

be true, and me because I used to have a crush on Simon Le Bon, and I could see no resemblance at all.

"I'm Scott, by the way."

He smiled, revealing a set of perfect teeth on the top, and slightly crooked on the bottom.

"I'm Olivia," I replied.

He looked around to make sure that the landlord wasn't watching him, and then sat next to me, placing his collected glasses onto the table.

"You come here often?" he asked.

"Bloody hell, now it's my turn to cringe! I'm here with my friend, Lauren. She's at the bar. We come here ever so often. Other times we go to Page Three or The Knights' Lodge."

"Page Three? You must be desperate. It's a knocking shop in there."

I raised my eyebrows.

"Oh really, and you'd know that, how?"

"I've heard the rumours."

We laughed again, and then Lauren returned from the bar, clutching our martinis. She gave Scott a disgruntled look, and I knew what she was thinking. She was meant to be staying at my house after the pub, and if he dared say he'd walk me home, she'd have to play gooseberry. That had happened once before, and I'd never heard the end of it.

"It was good to meet you, Scott," I said, as Lauren slid into the booth next to me.

He reached for the glasses, told me that he hoped to see me in there over the coming weekend, and then disappeared into the crowd.

"I bet you never see him again," Lauren quipped.

But she was wrong.

From that night on, Scott and I were inseparable. He lived with his parents in a small village about twenty minutes from where I lived with mine, but that didn't stop us connecting. Luckily there was a good bus service, and on those nights when we were too late getting to the bus stop, it gave us a good excuse to stay over. It was a wonderful time. The whole summer was full of day trips to the seaside, evenings in the pub garden, and sex. Lots and lots of sex.

We also talked about absolutely everything. I confided in him about my acting dreams, telling him that as soon as I'd saved enough money, I was going to audition for drama school. In turn, he told me about his dreams of working in PR or marketing, just as one of his favourite uncles had done, some years before. The determined way he spoke about it all convinced me that he was as ambitious as me, and it made me feel good to know that we were both striving to do something with our lives; that he would understand how important my dream was, and how much I needed it to happen. But then, as summer faded into early autumn and the leaves began to die, Scott announced that he didn't want me to go to drama school.

"We've only just met," he said, his eyes downcast. "If you go away, we'll never see each other again."

"I'll be home at weekends," I said. "Besides, I haven't got quite enough money to go there yet, so it will be another year before I even audition, never mind start."

"That will make things even worse," he said. "We'll be even more in love by then."

"Don't be silly." I rubbed his cheek, and felt his stubble beneath my fingers. "We'll find a way of making it work. I promise."

And I one hundred per cent believed that it could work. I even wrote down plans in my journals, which would enable us to see each other as often as possible. I'd present them to Scott, so proud that I'd been able to work things out, but it seemed to make things worse. One day I showed him a RADA course prospectus, but instead of finding any interest in there, he merely nodded and placed it on my bedside table. I went downstairs to make us a cup of tea, but by the time I returned to my bedroom, the brochure's edges were bumped and creased, and I was sure they hadn't looked that way before.

I had always wanted to be an actress, but over time, the subject became such a prickly one that in the name of love, I was willing to forget about going away to drama school, and opted to find something closer instead.

"I can maybe do local courses, and get my qualifications that way," I told Scott, though I knew that finding a decent class would be almost impossible.

"You could," he replied, "or what about joining amateur dramatics, then you can do your acting stuff, without ever having to give up your day job."

I hated that he referred to my dream as 'acting stuff' but I agreed because I was a teenager, in love with this floppy-haired bartender, and didn't want to do anything to spoil our new relationship. I convinced myself that I could find a decent local class, and maybe go to drama school when I was older and more settled, but deep down I worried that I was about to give up my dream. At that moment, however, it seemed like the only way forward.

The decision made my parents happy. They had never been into the whole acting thing, so when I dropped my plans they no longer had to worry about me becoming a drug-addicted Hollywood star, or booze-addled failed has-been. Yes, it is safe to say that they were ecstatic that I gave up that dream, and it all made sense to me at the time too. I convinced myself that while I had always been interested in acting, I wasn't sure how I could possibly support myself living away from home and studying at drama school. Yes, the decision not to go was something of a relief. A definite relief.

Wasn't it?

Looking for something else to pour my heart into, I decided that I'd like to be a writer. It would be easier to break into that business, I thought, and besides, I wouldn't need to leave home – and Scott – in order to pursue it. Scott seemed to like this idea, and encouraged me to write unpaid articles for the local free newspaper, on the off-chance that they may publish them. They didn't, but I carried on writing, regardless. My boyfriend then passed his driving test, and took an apprenticeship in a local marketing firm, which meant he could give up the pub job, and we could be together every evening. It was bliss. It was perfect.

It was too good to be true.

Just before Christmas 1988, we were sat on my bed, and Scott burst into laughter.

"What's up with you?" I asked.

"Nothing really. It's just that… It's just that I have this really weird feeling that we'll get married soon."

"Married? Slow down, we're still teenagers!"

"Okay," he laughed, "maybe not married yet, but engaged. A long engagement. What do you think?"

I giggled, and my insides turned into knots. I knew there was no way I was ready to get married, or even move in together, but engaged? Engaged with a beautiful ring on my left hand? I could maybe see that. I could see that in every kiss, every smile. I could see that in everything!

"Okay," I said. "Let's do it."

We were ecstatic, but our parents were mortified that we were moving too fast. However, I was so blinded by love that even if I lived to be a hundred years old, I would never want to marry anyone else. We were officially engaged on New Year's Day 1989, and both exchanged rings during a trip to Great Yarmouth. My ring was a round ruby, with tiny diamonds around it, and Scott's was a band with our initials engraved on the top. However, while the rings were a sign that we would one day walk up the aisle, we were still very young, so until we were ready, we'd stay as we were, living with our parents, working, and saving up for our future.

And we were happy! In spite of the postponed acting dreams, we were the happiest couple I knew. Well, that is until four years later when everything imploded.

It was 1993. By that time, Scott was working his way up the marketing ladder, and his job was the most important thing in his life. I didn't mind, because he was really terrific at it, and could come up with ideas faster than anyone else in the office. His enthusiasm got him more than one promotion, and several pay rises. He was on a roll, and I was so proud of him.

While my fiancé was engrossed in making it big, I was trying hard to build up my writing career. I was offered a weekly movie-related column in my local newspaper, and while it only paid pennies, I was so thrilled to have it. I would scribble any spare moment I had, which was difficult when I still had my day job, too, but always in the back of my mind was the thought that one day this could all lead to something big. Maybe I could even earn enough to put myself through drama school, sometime in the future...

Although it's hard for me to admit, looking back, I realise that yes, I maybe did neglect Scott during that time. Not because I didn't love him, and not because I didn't want to spend time with him, but because this was the first paid writing job I had ever had, and I wanted to make it a success. I thought that ultimately, I was building something for our future, just as he was with his marketing career.

Except, it didn't quite work out like that.

Scott would come to my house, and I would already be sitting at my primitive computer, writing down my thoughts on movies such as *Grease*, *Some Like It Hot*, and *Gone with the*

Wind. I'd give him a quick hello, and then turn back to my work, while he sat on my bed and watched stupid shows on television. We'd share the odd piece of conversation or news, and I'd read my column to him while we had a cup of tea, and by 10pm he'd be on his way. A quick peck on the lips and out he'd go, and I'd get back to researching my next column.

In my twenty-three-year-old brain, this was a perfectly fine way to behave. I was trying to build a career, and Scott was surely happy about that. After all, it wasn't my fault that I had to factor everything in around a day job. My fiancé was able to go after his dream career through the day, which left the evenings and most weekends free. I couldn't do that, and so my ego told me that he would be perfectly content just to be in my presence every evening, and that our engagement rings were a sign that we would always be okay, no matter what.

I was wrong.

In fact, I had never been more wrong in my life.

Months of almost no conversation followed, and then one day Scott began talking about the receptionist at work. Gabby Haine her name was. He started telling me 'funny' or 'amusing' things that she'd said, and he'd laugh about them while I tried to work out what was so hilarious. Then he began sharing more personal stuff about Gabby, like how she and her boyfriend were using a mix of diaphragms and spermicide gel as birth control. I asked why the hell she would ever share that with him, and he shrugged and said they were friends, and that's the sort of stuff they spoke about...

As the name Gabby Haine became part of my everyday existence, my mind woke up to the realisation that Scott may like this woman a little too much. From then on, I made more of an effort to give him attention. I would work on my column as soon as I got home from the day job, and then I'd talk to Scott from the moment he arrived, until the moment he left.

Unfortunately, nothing I did worked. His visits grew shorter and shorter, and while I was now fully committed to making the relationship work, he was checking out. I knew that fact before he said a single word about it.

I remember when he was working overtime one Saturday morning, and I thought I'd surprise him by taking him out to lunch. By this time, I'd passed my driving test, and bought an old Ford Fiesta, so I drove all the way to the office block and waited outside, until finally he came out with a woman. Gabby, I presumed.

She had straight, red hair, hanging down her back, a long, thick fringe, and looked slightly younger than me. She was wearing a denim skirt, denim jacket, pink sparkly shirt and white stilettos. Her large, square handbag was across her body, and had a picture of a multicoloured cow face on the front. Scott saw me first, his smile faded, and then he said something to Gabby, and she stared right at me. Even from twenty feet away I could see her scowl. She had a large, bulbous nose. That's not an insult; it's merely an observation. After they had said goodbye, Scott got into the car.

"Gabby was wondering why you're here," he said.

"What the fuck has it got to do with her?" I snapped, and he shrugged. Nothing more was said, but that whole week I thought about the woman with the long red hair, who had questioned why I'd met my own fiancé after work. I decided right then that she was someone I needed to keep an eye on.

One summer weekend, I suggested that Scott and I go on a picnic. We hadn't been anywhere in ages, because Scott had gone past the point of caring enough to spend much time with me at all. I was surprised when he agreed to go. In fact, I was ridiculously happy, and thought maybe it would signify a turnaround in our relationship.

It did, but not in the way I expected.

It was a sunny July day when I pulled up outside his parents' house in my old banger of a car, loaded up with sandwiches, scones, cakes, quiche, Coca-Cola and anything else I could fit into my picnic basket. I was so excited to go out on our adventure, and as we drove toward the local forest, Buddy Holly sung out from my tape deck, and I spoke animatedly about the afternoon ahead.

"Maybe we can go for a walk around the woods," I mused. "Or sit under a tree in the shade, and enjoy ourselves." I nudged him provocatively, but he stayed silent. He wasn't happy, I knew he wasn't happy, but it wasn't until we'd arrived at the woods that I discovered how miserable he was.

As we sat at a wooden picnic table, flicking flies and wasps away from our lunch, a young family played nearby. The children were occupied with a frisbee and laughing uncontrollably, while their parents held hands over their picnic blanket, and nibbled at their sandwiches.

"I can't wait until we get married and have kids," I said, twirling my engagement ring around my finger. Scott's shoulders hunched, and he avoided eye contact. "Did you hear me? I said, I can't wait until we get married and..."

"I heard you."

His words were stilted, as though his will to live had left his soul.

"Are you okay?" I asked the question, but I didn't really want to know the answer.

"I don't want to be with you anymore," he said. "I think we should finish."

Just like that. A sentence so deep that it tore my heart into a thousand shreds, but at the same time, so short in its simplicity. I pressed my fist to my mouth, and prayed that this was all some kind of fever dream. A cold chill expanded into my core, and even though it was summer, my whole body froze. I looked over at the family again, all of them oblivious to what was going on thirty feet away from them.

"Please don't do this to me," I begged. My voice shook, and I tried to stare into Scott's eyes, but he turned his head away. "Please don't finish with me. Not here. Not now."

He shook his head.

"I'm sorry, but I need to get this off my chest. It's been driving me mental... I've met someone else, and I want to be with her."

My body buckled over the table, and I could hardly catch my breath.

Gabby Haine.

I knew it would be Gabby Haine before he'd said the words.

Over the next few minutes, Scott explained how for the past six months, he and Gabby had spent their lunchtimes together, and at first it had been purely friendship. However, the more time he'd spent with her, the more he had become attached to this woman, and now he wanted to be with her.

"Have you slept with her?" I asked. My skin tingled in anticipation of an answer I did not want to hear.

"Not really."

"Not really?! What the fuck does that mean?"

"We fooled around a bit," he said. "In the back of her car during one lunchbreak. But I didn't have sex with her. I didn't want to do that to you."

I covered my face with my hands, embarrassed for Scott to see me. I didn't want him to see my shattered hopes and dreams, tearing me apart.

"Olivia? Are you okay? Olivia!"

He shook my arm, and I whipped him away.

"How dare you!" I snarled, and the family next to us stopped for a moment, as a silence descended the woods. "How dare you fool around with someone else, when we were still together!"

And then a dreadful, all-encompassing thought passed into my brain. For the past couple of months, our sex life had been the most active it had ever been. Despite us not getting along, Scott had been overly interested in sleeping with me.

"That's why you've wanted sex so often, isn't it?"

His brow furrowed, and his blond hair stuck to his sweat-soaked forehead.

"What do you mean?"

"You were emotionally into her, so you had sex with me to relieve yourself, didn't you? Didn't you?"

"You can't control who you fall in love with," Scott said. He had neither confirmed nor denied my realisation, and I struggled to stop myself from throwing up my sandwich.

"You're in love with this woman?"

Scott hung his head, and avoided all eye contact.

"I think I am, yes. I'm so sorry, Olivia. I never wanted to hurt you."

Minutes before this conversation, I had been ravenous for our lunch, but now I could quite happily vomit under the nearest tree. He tried to grab my hands, to say sorry I presume, but I shrugged him off and instead dumped all of the leftover food into a nearby bin. He folded up the tablecloth and tucked it under his arm.

"Aren't you going to say anything?" he asked.

"There's nothing to say. You've made up your mind."

Scott went to take the picnic basket from my hands, but I ignored him, marched to my car, and dumped it into the boot.

"What about this?" He held out the picnic blanket, and I snatched it from him so hard that he recoiled. I hoped it had given him fabric burns. He surely deserved them. I closed the boot with a bang, and then silently drove Gabby Haine's new boyfriend home, as Buddy Holly sang 'Heartbeat' in the background. I dropped him outside his parents' house, wished him well and then stared into my side mirror, hoping that he would watch as I drove away.

He didn't.

He was gone.

He had been gone emotionally for many months, but now he'd gone physically too.

And I was utterly, utterly broken. More broken than I ever expected to be in the whole of my life.

As days turned into weeks, I would go to work every morning, walk around in a haze for most of the day, and then sit in darkness in my bedroom in the evening. As luck would have it, my column was cancelled due to lack of budget, so I couldn't even write that anymore, but I did fill a journal with notes, criticisms of myself, and general breakdowns. I was confused and conflicted because I had enjoyed researching and writing my column, and it had been a real boost to find something that I was good at. It had felt so beautiful to have a dream. It was what I was supposed to do with my life.

And now it was all gone. The column, the dream, and most of all, the fiancé.

I could just about deal with my heartbreak during the day, but at night I would cry myself to sleep, and then dream about Scott, replaying our final conversation in lavish, colourful detail. As if that wasn't bad enough, whenever I closed my eyes, I could see them together. Gabby Haine with her red hair spread out across her back, while my fiancé got his thrills underneath her. They were always naked. Always naked. I didn't want to obsess about these images, but it was unavoidable. Were they doing it at that very moment? The idea made me sick, but as far as my mind was concerned, there was no switching off. I had to feel the pain. I had to see the pain. I had to be the pain.

One evening after work I went into town, officially to go to the bank, but really it was to try and see Scott. He would always park in the multi-storey car park, and walk through the dark tunnel into the main centre. When we were together, I would sometimes wait for him after work, on the corner opposite the tunnel, so that I could have a hug before I went home. Now that we weren't together anymore, I figured I could 'accidentally' bump into him in our place, and he'd throw his arms around me and love me like he had before.

But as I stood there, waiting and playing with the zip on my handbag, a familiar couple rounded the corner. It was Scott, and he was laughing and holding hands with Gabby Haine.

Holding hands.

I backed up, as close to the wall as I possibly could get. I prayed that they wouldn't see me, but I needn't have worried. They were too engrossed in each other to see anyone else at all. So, I stood in the shadows, mascara running, and hair hanging over my face like a wretched Victorian woman, and I watched them walk all the way up to the newsagent on the corner. We used to go in there to buy chocolate, and magazines, and sometimes books. And now he was going in there with her.

His new love.

I drove home, hands gripping the steering wheel, and praying that the squeezing sensation in my chest would not lead me to collapse. When I walked into the house, my mum told me off because that night's dinner – beef biryani – had gone cold, and she'd had to throw it away. I couldn't have eaten it anyway. I couldn't stand a single mouthful.

Lauren came over that evening and rubbed my back and told me that perhaps it was all for the best.

"You'll meet someone else," she said. "And maybe finally go to drama school... Or maybe you'll get back together in a couple of years. When you've both grown up a bit... although to be honest, I'd much rather you did the former."

I hung on to the idea that we could get back together because I couldn't face being with anyone else. I felt that way the whole time we were apart. Even when a colleague told me that the guy in the next office was secretly in love with me; even when an old friend was tipped off by Lauren that I was suddenly single, and gave me a call. I didn't want either of them. I didn't want anyone but Scott. Even when my cousin insisted that I go on a date with her neighbour's interested son, it was awkward and strange. When he leant in to kiss me, I didn't stop him, but the taste of his lips was bitter, and full of my own self-loathing.

By the end of the month apart, I'd lost almost a stone in weight, and my chest was in a constant state of panic. Would I ever be happy again? I had no idea.

But then... Scott came back.

He actually came back.

It was a Sunday afternoon, and we had just finished dinner. I was on my way upstairs to listen to some customary sad music – Cher being my favourite crying companion – when the doorbell rang. I held my breath, sure that it was probably someone collecting for charity, but hoping so much that it would be Scott. I had spent many hours sitting on the floor of my parents' bedroom, staring out of the window, and begging his red Ford Sierra to cruise around the corner. As far as I knew, however, he'd never been near our house.

Until that day.

I stood at the top of the stairs, and watched as my dad opened the door to reveal Scott, clutching a huge bouquet of pink, red and white carnations. Funeral flowers, my gran would have said...

"Hello, is Olivia in, please?" he asked.

My dad took one look at him and slammed the door in his face.

"Dad!" I screamed. "Dad! How could you do that?"

"I hope you're kidding," he grunted. "That lad is coming nowhere near you, ever again!"

In retrospect I know that Dad was protecting my interests, and our family, but my mind was frazzled, and I insisted I be able to talk to Scott. There was no sense in this, other than despite what he had done, I still loved him, and my heart still leapt when I heard his voice on the doorstep. My twenty-three-year-old self had mourned him every day of those four weeks, and I could do it no more. My parents wouldn't let him into the house, so instead we sat in his car, and he explained how he'd made a mammoth mistake, and didn't want to lose me. Apparently, going out with Gabby Haine wasn't quite what he thought it would be, and he missed me.

"She's not you," Scott said. "And it's you I need."

Heat radiated through my chest, and the weight of the past months lifted from my shoulders. Those were the words I desperately wanted to hear, but even so, my head begged me to proceed with caution.

"But what about not being able to control who you fall in love with? What about that?"

Scott laughed, and rubbed his eyes. His trademark blond hair flopped onto his forehead, and it took all my strength not to brush it away for him.

"I didn't love her," he said. "I have no idea why I thought that way, never mind said it."

We talked for hours, about anything and everything, and by the end of it, I knew that I had to take him back. Mistake or not, I forgave him, because he was my person. My mum and dad were rightly furious that we were reconciled, but Scott assured them that it was over with Gabby, and that the whole episode had proved to him how much he loved me. My mum gave him the silent treatment for weeks, and while my dad would talk, the conversation was cold. My parents had no idea if they could really trust him again, and they were worried about their little girl. I didn't appreciate that at the time, but now I do.

Now I appreciate everything.

What would have happened if I had said no to getting back together? I would never have found out, because in truth, there was no chance of me ever doing that. I was bent, I was broken, but so ecstatic that we were reunited that I agreed when Scott told me he never wanted to discuss 'his biggest regret' ever again. All the days he'd spent with her in the months leading up to our break, the times he'd slept with her in the same bed that we'd previously slept in, and the conversations they'd likely had about what a boring fiancée I had been... Scott wanted every part of it to be forgotten, and I was happy to go along with the charade. I was a young woman, still madly in love with the man who had broken my heart, and willing to try and ignore every mistake he'd ever made.

They say that time heals all wounds, but I think that's nonsense. I never completely healed to be honest, but the subject was over as far as Scott was concerned, so any questions I may have had never received any answers. After a time, though, I knew that if we were going to move forward, then I really did need to let go, at least as far as I could. I had to learn to trust again, and while they still worked together, Scott assured me that they were now just workmates. Not even friends, and certainly not lovers.

I was wary, but strangely I also felt safer in our relationship than I had in the past. This was mainly because I knew that if he hadn't really loved me, he would never have come back. If he hadn't wanted me or Gabby, he'd have said goodbye to her and moved on with someone else, but he didn't. He'd come back. He'd chosen me. After everything, he'd chosen me.

Several months later we decided to move in together, and to prove once and for all how committed we were, we chose to buy a house, instead of renting. A twenty-five-year mortgage was surely a sign that we were serious, and I was happy to donate all of the money I'd saved for a possible future drama school place. It wasn't much, but it was emotionally significant. The terraced Victorian house was tiny, but perfect for our needs, and we were content there, building a life together. Scott continued building his career, and I still worked my day job, but wrote whenever my fiancé was busy playing games on his computer, or out at the pub with his mates.

Five years after that, we had our beautiful, coveted baby, Charlie, and then a few months later we got married. We did things a bit topsy-turvy I know, but it was all perfect. Everything happened when it was meant to. We were a happy little family for those first years, and if the Gabby incident ever popped into my mind, I'd dismiss it as ancient history, and try to remain in the present...

But the terrifying thing about the mind is that nothing is ever really gone. Anything can bring it back. We'd drive past his old place of work and I'd stare into the blue-rimmed windows, trying to catch a glimpse of the past. Did they screw each other in there? I had no idea, and yet I thought that maybe they had. I'd remember the day I picked him up, and Gabby had stared right at me, or the time Scott told me about her preferred method of birth control, and it would hurt me all over again.

One day when Charlie was five, Scott suggested a family picnic in the same woods where he had finished with me for Gabby. I couldn't do it. I couldn't walk through those trees, knowing that my pain was still imprinted in the leaves, the bark, and the roots. Scott thought I was being ridiculous – he barely even remembered finishing with me in there – but he had never been in that same position of pain. He could never know what I'd been through. What I still went through.

And so I never fully forgot about it, and there were times when Gabby Haine would pop into my mind for no reason. When social media burst onto the scene I spent a while trying to find her profile on Facebook, and then Instagram. Not because I was obsessed with her at that point, but because I was curious to know what she looked like now. I never did find her though. She must have changed her name, or blocked me, or died.

Even now, I often wish that she has died.

A terrible, painful, tragic death.

Life went on, Scott's career continued on an upward trajectory, my writing career took off, and we moved out of our tiny house, and into a four-bedroom new-build. Our little family was tight, and bonded, and joyful. While Scott's indiscretion occasionally entered my mind, I was too busy with my career, school activities and sports to notice. But then our wonderful little boy passed away, and my mind broke into a thousand jigsaw pieces, all of them trying and failing to fit together again.

And one day, while washing the dishes in an attempt to keep myself busy, I turned on the radio for a bit of company. There was a movie quiz, and one of the questions asked was what year the Sharon Stone film *Sliver* was released. The female contestant screamed.

"1993! 1993! I remember because it was at the cinema when I got married, and that was in 1993!"

"Correct!" the presenter said, and then for a bonus prize, they asked about other world events from that year.

The very mention of 1993 was like a punch to my stomach, and before I could do anything about it, the whole Gabby Haine incident clattered into my mind. I shook it off, but that evening when I went to bed, she danced her way through my brain and then my dreams. As Scott snored beside me, all the pain, all the rage that I had felt twenty-one years before, punched at my head like a prizefighter, and there was nothing I could do to stop it.

In the days ahead, I began dissecting every moment of that long-gone year. I tried to figure out why Scott did it, and what it had all meant. Yes, it had been two decades since the incident, and I had just lost my child, but obsessing over that heartache was all I could do. It was all I wanted to do, and I had no way of stopping it. Scott would try to put his arm around me, or kiss me on the lips, and I'd bat him off. I didn't want him to touch me, or speak to me, and definitely not make love to me.

He was still hurting from losing Charlie, and he cried every single day, but I refused to let myself give him any kind of comfort. I wanted him to hurt. I wanted to punish him, first because it had taken him so long to come to the hospital when it had happened, and secondly because of how much he'd hurt me all those years ago.

I never spoke to him or any of our family and friends about the games my mind played on me. As far as they were concerned, I was upset because I missed my son. That was true of course, but the Gabby Haine stuff pushed its way through my mourning and screamed into my ears, every single day. Gabby was the first thing I thought about when I opened my eyes, and the last thing I thought about as I went to sleep. In between, I would spend my days lying on Charlie's bed, willing him to come back, and then feeling guilty when Gabby appeared in my mind as I did so. He never knew anything about the things that had happened before he was born. He'd have no doubt thought it was ridiculous if I had told him.

"It's ancient history, Mum," he'd have said, and he would have been right.

But the thing is, what's ancient history to a youngster is not always ancient to someone my age. I thoroughly believe that the older you get, the more relevant the past becomes. Tucked away in your subconscious, waiting for the opportunity to raise its head once again. Call it nostalgia, call it memories, but it's there. It's all still there.

Sitting in Charlie's bedroom, I would pick up tiny toy soldiers that he'd had since he was a kid, turning them over in my hand, knowing that the last time anyone had touched them was when my son was alive. Sometimes I'd slide my hand under the bed to try and find a piece of paper, a pebble, a note, or any other thing that would show me that he was still there, but apart from a couple of old tissues, I never found anything profound.

And through it all, at the back of my mind every day was the Gabby Haine incident.

And that truly terrified me.

About six months into my obsession, I confessed my thoughts to Lauren, and she persuaded me to go to therapy. Scott wanted to come with me, but I said no. How could I explain to him that while I was mourning our son, I was also gripped by something he'd done twenty-one years before? He'd have thought I was crazy. I probably was, but when I explained the situation to the therapist, she narrowed her eyes and twirled her pen between her fingers.

"I've seen this happen before," she said.

I was stunned.

"You have?"

"Yes, many times. You see, your mind has gone through one of the worst traumas you could ever go through, but the way it is dealing with that, is to turn attention to another trauma, another pain that happened many years ago. It wants to deal with that, because it can't bear to deal with the real problem, which is the loss of your son."

That explanation was something I hadn't comprehended

before, but it made sense, and gave me more comfort than I ever could have imagined. I continued going to see her for the next ten weeks, and after many hours of therapy and self-help, I managed to get through the tunnel that led to Gabby Haine, and back into the deep well of despair caused by Charlie's passing. I wrote down everything I thought about the woman who stole my fiancé, and then I burnt it in the drum of an old washing machine in the back garden. It felt like a release.

But now.

Now, she is back on my mind, three decades after I first heard the name, Gabby Haine. She is the reason I know that Scott was – and is – capable of falling for somebody else. And she is the reason why I cannot just brush another possible affair under the carpet, because that's all I've ever been allowed to do with the first one.

And the pain still kills me.

But I am not the naïve twenty-three-year-old that I once was. And if my husband of twenty-five years has had an affair, then that is something he will discover.

CHAPTER FOUR

The front door slams, and I hear Scott's keys being dropped into the bowl at the bottom of the stairs.

"Hey, sweetie! How's my girl today?"

His girl.

It takes every fibre of my being not to scream and shout and demand to know what he was doing on the 19th and 20th of July 2014, two months before our darling boy passed away. Tonight's pasta bubbles on the stove, and the hotel card is still in my jeans pocket. I run my finger over the rigid edges. Who knew a piece of cardboard could hold so much pain? How am I going to eat dinner this evening? I'm in no mood to do anything, especially eat. And now this has kicked off my suppressed memories of Gabby Haine too. Why, oh why did she have to come back into my mind?

Because there's a chance that my husband has been at it again, of course.

I stir the pasta bows, and boiling water sloshes out of the pan and hisses onto the stove. As I reach for a piece of kitchen towel, Scott comes up behind me, threads his arm under mine, and turns down the gas. He laughs.

"Good evening! I wonder how many times I've told you not to boil the pasta? It needs to be simmered. Always simmered."

The bubbles disperse as the heat retreats from under the saucepan. I force a smile, but I stay quiet. Scott has been telling me for over two decades that I'm making pasta wrong, but I don't care. Charlie loved my soft, boiled pasta, and Scott has eaten every bit I've ever made him, so I must be doing something right.

Or maybe not.

It's hard to believe I'm doing anything right, after today's discovery.

"What a day I've had," he says. "Three meetings, with three different clients, but it was all good. Everyone seemed pleased with the results."

I couldn't care less about what Scott did at work, but I nod and smile, and he doesn't seem to notice.

"How was your day?" he asks. "Not as busy as mine, I hope. Did you get much done?"

I turn off the gas and throw the pasta into our vintage metal colander – a wedding present from my grandmother, all those years ago. A great cloud of steam whooshes up from the sink, as I shake off the water.

"Grab me the pesto..." I throw the pasta back into the pot, and Scott pours a jar of pesto over the top.

"Cheese?" he asks.

"Yes please."

We sit at the table and eat for several seconds in silence, until Scott realises that I didn't answer his question.

"So?"

"So, what?"

Scott laughs, rolls his eyes and swallows before answering.

"I asked if you'd got much done today? Either with your writing, or the Babbage work stuff."

I look him dead in the eyes. In that moment I want to scream out all of my pain. I want to remind him that no, I didn't get any writing done, because I haven't written anything worthwhile in a decade. I want to tell him that the Babbage work is still piled up and ignored on my laptop. I want to grab the hotel card from my pocket, and grate it into his pasta. I want to lean over the bowls and grab him by the throat.

But I don't.

Instead, I smile, and try to stop the broken pieces of myself from bursting out and scattering all over the floor.

"I got a little done," I lie. "I did about two hours of Babbage stuff. I'll have to catch up with that later, as I didn't quite do my hours."

"I'm sure Sam won't even notice," Scott says, and he's right. There have been times when I've taken a sneaky day off for shopping, or a doctor's appointment or whatever, and Sam has never questioned it. If he messages me while I'm out, I reply via my phone, and as long as the work is all done by Friday then he doesn't care. Or at least if he does, he never says anything.

Should I tell Scott that I've booked a train ticket for a day out in Cromer? No, it's probably best that I keep everything about the Regency Hotel to myself. I don't even know if I'll find anything while I'm there, but I don't want to provoke my husband into thinking that I might have discovered something, or worse, that I want him to go to Cromer with me.

No, I can't say anything yet. Not until I know for sure what's going on.

"It's supposed to be up in the twenties on Saturday," Scott informs me. "Do you fancy a picnic? We could go to Great Yarmouth or somewhere. Make a day of it."

A picnic.

A picnic like the one we had when he finished with me for Gabby Haine...

We've had many picnics in the years since then, of course, but the very mention of picnics after today's discovery rattles my insides.

"Eating outdoors in October? I'm not sure I'm that brave."

I force a laugh, but it comes out awkward and stilted. If I don't watch out, Scott will know that there's something wrong.

"Well, all this global warming has made the temperatures rise, it would seem. So, are you up for it? It could be fun, before winter sets in."

I shake my head.

"I'm sorry," I say. "I'm not in the mood for a picnic."

And that's the truth.

The next morning starts with a series of emails from Sam, asking me to check the status of a novel that he commissioned eight months ago, but still hasn't been sent in. I don't have to check on it, because I know exactly what's going on. The person writing the book – I can't bring myself to use the word 'author' – messaged me three months ago to say that he wouldn't be able to write it after all, since writing was way harder than he could ever have imagined.

No shit.

I fire off a quick email to Sam, reminding him of this development – which I had told him about at the time – and then I grab my handbag. My boss doesn't know I'm taking the day off, but so long as I have my phone with me, he'll never know. I can always do some work on the train or if I stop into a café, but for now, the Regency Hotel is my only concern.

I check the time, grab my coat, and head for the station.

The train into Cromer is packed with late-season holidaymakers, all clutching huge holdalls, or worse still, suitcases. Luckily for me, I have a reserved seat, and I fight my way through the throng, and finally sit down. I've only just done that when my phone pings. It's Lauren.

> Hey! What are you up to? I've got the day off if you want to meet for coffee.

My chest lurches. When Scott asked what I was doing this morning, I lied and told him that I was meeting one of Sam's batty authors, who happened to be in Norfolk, researching his latest novel. Now I'll have to say the same thing to Lauren, firstly in case she happens to bump into Scott, and secondly because after the way she dismissed my discovery of the card, she likely wouldn't approve of me researching it further.

I press reply.

> I wish I could, but I'm meeting an author today. Yawn! Will catch up with you this evening if you like. Scott is going to visit the in-laws, so he'll be gone till late.

> Great. Also, thanks for the charity clothes. What with all the excitement yesterday, I completely forgot to tell you how grateful I am.

Excitement? I'm glad that my best friend thinks it was excitement. She always has enjoyed a bit of scandal, as long as it doesn't involve her. As for the charity clothes, if she hadn't asked for them in the first place, I wouldn't be on this journey to Cromer. I'd be in my quiet little office, sending emails to the Babbage authors, and having a nice cup of tea.

I send her a thumbs up, and then I switch off my phone. I'll come clean to her later on, when I hopefully have some news, but the last thing I need at the moment is a thousand questions, and a lot of judgement. Unfortunately, that is definitely what I'd get if I confided in my best friend at this moment.

"You're meeting an author?"

The voice startles me. I turn to the seat next to mine, and see an older lady wearing a purple beret with a blue feather sewn to the top. She's staring and pointing at my phone.

"Erm..."

"Sorry love," she says. "I couldn't help but see your message. I wasn't trying to pry, honest."

I smile sweetly, and tell her that it's no problem at all, and that everyone does the same on the train. It's a lie of course, since I've never done that – or at least I don't believe I have – but I'm so anxious about my trip to Cromer that even if one person believes that I'm going to meet an author, that's fine with me. If enough people believe it, then maybe I will too.

The Regency Hotel stands proudly in the heart of Cromer, yards from the bustling town centre, and the colourful pier. I've seen it so many times in photographs, postcards and on the television, that it always seems strange seeing the Victorian building in the flesh. I can't help but run my fingers along the red bricks as I make my way toward the entrance – a large, imposing doorway, with smooth tiles at the door, and a thick burgundy carpet that sweeps the corridor. I follow it until I finally reach a rounded space, with lifts and a grand staircase on one side, the glass-walled restaurant and reception desk on the other. I pause for a moment, trying to find my bearings, and the woman behind the counter looks up and smiles.

"Good morning. Can I help you?"

In all my versions of how entering the hotel might go, I hadn't figured on the reception being so small and quiet. I thought that there would be all kinds of people mulling around, giving me a chance to slip to the basement archives without any trouble. I had even studied their website to see if it looked as though the staircase led down to the basement as well as up to the rooms, and was thrilled to see that it did. I planned on moving behind the crowds of holidaymakers, and heading there undetected, but with nobody but me in the foyer, there is no hope of that.

"Good morning." I move toward the desk and clock the woman's name tag. Geraldine. Good, because if it had been Tracy from the phone call, that might have caused a problem. She smiles again.

"What can I do for you?"

"I'm supposed to be meeting my friend in the restaurant," I say. "Is it through there?"

I point toward the door, even though it's entirely obvious that it is indeed the restaurant. The tables, chairs and sign give that away pretty easily.

"Yes, just through there," Geraldine says.

"Thank you."

I quickly run to the loo, and then I wander into the restaurant, take a seat and order a cup of tea. I am dry from the train, and besides that, tea has always had a soothing effect on my nerves. The waiter brings it over in a white porcelain teapot, with an accompanying pastel-green cup and saucer, and tiny milk jug. I look at his face, expecting to see some kind of recognition that all is not what it seems, but luckily, it's just my imagination running wild again, and he seems to notice nothing but a middle-aged woman, warming herself up after a walk to the beach.

The tea is hot against my tongue, and before I know what's

happening, the top of my mouth is burnt. I swallow quickly and add more milk to the liquid. However, before I can take another sip, I hear a bustling sound from reception. A large group of what looks like coach-trippers has appeared at the counter, and Geraldine is on her feet, dishing out key cards and pointing them toward the visitors' book.

Now's my chance.

I throw a tenner onto the table, grab my handbag and head out into the reception. The chatter and bustle of the visitors ensures that nobody can hear or see me, but it also means that I can't get to the stairs, because there are dozens of suitcases and people in the way. In a panic, I slip quickly into the lift, and close the doors behind me. My hands shake, which is ridiculous because I've never felt that way before when entering a lift. I take a breath and scan the control panel. From top to bottom it goes 3rd floor, 2nd floor, 1st floor, ground floor and then B for basement. Next to that button is a small, printed sign that says *Staff Only*.

I press it anyway.

If anyone sees me there, I took a wrong turn on my way to the bathroom... Yes, I couldn't see a toilet in the restaurant and figured it must be on another floor. It sounds like complete bullshit, but it's the only thing I've got to go with.

The lift lurches into action and within seconds the doors slide open and I'm met with a long corridor, with half a dozen closed doors coming off it. It looks like something from a Victorian sanatorium, except for the open fire door at the end. As soon as I see it, I'm both concerned and relieved. Concerned that there may be a crowd of hotel staff waiting to come in at any moment, and relieved that if anyone does in fact catch me here, I can be out of the door and up the steps before they can stop me.

Despite the tea, I still feel thirsty, and there is an unpleasant taste in my mouth. I've never done anything like this before, and I'm terrified. My whole life I've been the good girl, who never goes against the rules. I was the one who would sit on the pavement while my friends nicked sweets from the newsagent, or I'd be the one just pretending to swig out of the bottles of cider they somehow pilfered from the local pub. Being naughty was never something I did... Perhaps that's why my husband cheated on me...

I dismiss the thought and take a deep breath. This trip is not about blaming myself for anything. It's about finding out the truth, so that I can step into the future with a clean head.

Maybe.

Tracy the receptionist told me that the visitors' books were kept in the basement, but she didn't say exactly which of the six offices housed them. She wasn't that loose-lipped, which is disappointing. I take one step forward, my flat pumps silent on the black-and-white polished tiles, but unfortunately, my phone goes off in my pocket. Shit, I forgot to put it onto silent. I grab for it. Scott is calling, but he's the last person I want to talk to right now. What would I possibly say to him? "Oh, I'm currently creeping down a hotel basement hallway, to prove to myself that you're a dirty cheater." No, best not. I decline the call, and shove the phone back into my pocket, but not before there is movement at the fire door.

I stand rigid, but since I'm in the middle of the hallway, there's no escape from the young waiter staring at me from the door. He's wearing a white buttoned-down shirt, with the sleeves rolled up, a pair of black trousers, ruffled black hair and has a cigarette hanging out of his mouth. Add a flat cap and he'd look like someone from *Peaky Blinders*.

"Are you okay?" he shouts from the other end of the corridor, and I nod aimlessly, my first reaction being to lie.

"I seem to have taken a wrong turn," I say. "I was looking for the toilet."

He laughs, stubs the cigarette out under his black shoe, and then ambles along the corridor toward me.

"The public toilets are upstairs in reception. The only ones down here are for the staff. Unless those were the ones you were looking for?"

I shake my head, and the man smiles.

"There's no money here, y' know. Most of our transactions are digital nowadays, and the rest goes into the safe, so if that's what you're here for..."

Blood rushes to the top of my head.

"I'm not a thief! I'm honestly looking for the toilet."

"Funny though," he says, "because I saw you heading into the toilet upstairs just minutes ago, so either you have a very short memory – and a weak bladder – or you're not looking for the loo at all."

I grip the strap of my handbag so hard my knuckles turn white. My mum always said that I was a terrible liar, and I guess she was right. I'm about to run out of the fire door, when I realise that this cocky staff member could help in my quest for the visitors' books, so I come clean.

"Okay, you're right, I'm not looking for the toilet."

His eyes narrow, and a tiny line appears on the top of his nose.

"So, if you're not looking for money – or the loo – then what are you looking for? Because there's nothing interesting here. Believe me, I've looked."

He winks and laughs. This guy fancies himself as something special.

"The truth is, I'm looking for the old visitors' books."

"The what?" He screws his face into a knot, as though he's never heard of such things.

"The receptionist told me that every guest signs the visitors' book when they come into the hotel. Is that not true?"

"I'm not sure if everyone signs it." He shrugs, and looks behind him at one of the many closed doors. "But there are visitors' books on the reception desk, and a whole load of old ones in the archive."

"Great. Can I see them?"

He scratches his neck, and looks over my shoulder – presumably to check if there are any other staff members around.

"I could point you in the right direction, but I'd need to know why."

"Family research." I smile, inwardly begging him to believe me.

"Family research?"

"Yes. I'm a genealogist. I research my family tree and stuff. I'm hoping that I might be able to find my mum and dad in one of the books. They came here on their honeymoon."

He looks behind him, and then back at the lift area.

"I don't know. If you get caught in there, I'll get the blame. I could lose my job."

"I promise you won't," I say. "If anyone comes down, I'll tell them that it was all my own doing. I won't mention you at all."

He lightly grabs my arm and hurries me toward a white door with a panel of wired glass at the top. There is a large 3 printed next to the door handle.

"They're all in there," he says, "but I don't know what kind of order they're in. Nobody ever goes into that room, except to throw the books onto a shelf at the start of every year."

"Thank you. What's your name, by the way?"

"Joseph. Yours?"

"I'm Olivia."

"Nice to meet you. Just don't get caught down here. Not everyone is as unbothered as I am."

"Thanks, Joseph. I promise I'll be quick."

He holds his hands up, eyes wide.

"Be as long as you like," he says. "I'm off my break now, so what you do has nothing to do with me."

Joseph was right. The books are in no order at all. In fact, you could say that they're a complete catastrophe. The one closest to the door is 1981, while the next one along is 1962. 1956 is filed next to 1997, and 1948 is just along from 2004. Luckily the dates are all embossed on the spines, and so it doesn't take me too long to go through them. Keeping one eye on the glass panel in the door, I run my fingers along each one, until finally...

There it is.

2014.

My hands sweat as I retrieve the volume, and dust catches in my throat, forcing me to cough into my elbow in an attempt to silence the sound. I lay the book on a cluttered wooden desk and open it to a random page. The word 'July' stares at me in tall, gold letters, and it feels like a death threat. I scrape my hand through my hair, and my muscles twitch at the base of my neck. How can I do this? I've come all the way to Cromer to see if I can find the name of the woman my husband has probably had an affair with, and now I'm not sure that I have the strength to do it.

This might change everything.

One way or the other.

Every fibre in my heart screams at me to put the book away, to go home and get on with my life and my marriage. It's been ten years after all. A decade of holidays, Christmases, shopping trips, Sunday drives, and nights curled up on the sofa, watching the latest Netflix drama. Ten years of marriage, of sex, of laughter, of loss, of heartbreak, of tears, but most of all, love.

Do I really want to destroy what we've got? What we've worked so hard for?

No, I don't.

I turn the page.

CHAPTER FIVE

I'm not an expert at hotel statistics, but the 19th of July 2014 seems to have been a busy day at the Regency Hotel, with ninety-seven incoming guests, including two coach parties, one from Wales and the other from Kent. My finger slides down the page, trying to find my husband's name, but at the same time hoping that I don't. Finally, after searching through five pages, I see it.

Scott Collins.

My vision blurs, and my eyelids feel as though they are about to close involuntarily, but I force myself to read on.

Scott has listed his address as Stanchurch – our hometown – but leaves out the important details, such as street name and house number. His signature is his usual clumsy outline, and in Notes he has written the nondescript, *Wonderful stay. Food delicious.* That's it. That's all he wrote.

I'm not sure what I expected it to say, I mean, he was never going to write something like, *Food delicious. Affair exciting.* But somehow, I did expect it to say something more substantial. Something I could figure stuff out from.

My eyes flick to the next line. The words 'Mrs Debbie

Collins' stand out at me, and my mouth fills with saliva. Mrs Debbie Collins? Who the hell is she? Because she definitely isn't me, that's for sure.

Debbie has left her address blank, and once again hasn't added any other details. Her Notes section consists of the equally uninspiring, *Great trip. Nice to get away.* Get away from what? From Mr Collins' wife?

A pain flashes across my forehead. What is going on? What does this all mean?

I have absolutely no idea.

I take a photo of the page, and then bang the book shut. I need to get out of here. If this is the building where Scott and Debbie conducted their affair, then I have no interest in being here. I take a look down the hall to make sure it is all clear, and then I head out of the fire door, up the steps and back out onto the street.

My train home is not for another two hours, and the day is taking a turn for the worse, with drizzle – 'wet rain' as my mum calls it – soaking my jacket and my trousers. As I plod up the cold October streets, my mind whirs, and I know that I need to find somewhere to shelter. It seems as though everywhere is closed, and when I finally find a tiny café nestled in one of the quiet streets, I could cry.

"Good afternoon," says the small brunette behind the counter. "Take a seat anywhere, and I'll be right over. Here's a menu."

She hands me a large sheet of laminated card, and within seconds I'm huddled over it at a small round table at the window. There are only two other people in the café, and one of the waitresses is mopping the floor, ready to go home. I don't want to be one of those people who keeps the staff later than they need to be, but I'm desperate for a cuppa. Still, before I order, I study the closing time on the bottom of the menu. 6pm, it says. It's not even close to that, so I order tea, two crumpets and a cookie, and then turn on my phone. Straight away I'm met with the photo I took of the entry in the visitors' book.

Debbie.

Debbie Collins.

Only that's not her real surname, is it? Or if it is, it's a huge coincidence. Maybe it's a fake first name, too, but it's the only thing I've got to go on at the moment, so I'll have to hope that it's true. My tea arrives, and I nibble a crumpet, but can't take my eyes off the phone. In fact, I'm so busy staring at it that I don't notice a shadow appear at the window, until it eventually knocks and I jump. It takes my eyes a couple of seconds to readjust, but when they do I see Joseph standing outside with a cigarette in his upturned mouth. I wave, he stubs out the cigarette on the windowsill, and then comes into the café.

"Hi, Trudy," he says. "Coffee please. A large one."

"No problem, love. Plonk yourself down and I'll bring it straight over. Cake?"

"No, no cake today. Got to watch my figure."

They both laugh as Joseph pats his stomach. Got to watch his figure? He speaks like a wide boy from the 1980s. In a fictional world, he'd be a sidekick of Del Boy and Rodney.

He slides up to my table, and motions to the chair.

"Do you mind if I sit here?" he asks.

I look around at the virtually empty café.

"No, help yourself."

"Thanks. I know there's plenty of other seats, but I'm interested to know if you found what you were looking for this afternoon."

He sits next to me, and takes off his cap. His black hair is damp with drizzle or sweat or both, and he runs his hand through it before finally relaxing into the chair.

"So?" he asks.

"So what?"

"Did you find what you were looking for? Didn't you say you were a gynaecologist?"

I laugh and tea comes close to running out of my nose.

"Not quite. I said I was a genealogist."

"Same difference," he says and then we both laugh. Trudy pops a large mug of coffee in front of him, and he rubs his hands together. "Lovely. Just what I need."

"Will you be paying separately?" Trudy asks.

"No, no, I'll get these," Joseph replies, and I throw my hands in the air.

"No! I'll get them. I owe you one after your help earlier."

Trudy nods, then ambles back off to the counter, where a man with a spaniel is asking if he can bring it inside from the cold. She assures him that he can, and they head off to a free table in the back corner. I take a sip of my tea and offer Joseph a crumpet. He screws up his face, shakes his head and then accepts it.

"I'm trying to cut down, but if you're offering, I don't want to cause offence."

We sit in silence for a moment, me nibbling on my jammy crumpet, and him stuffing half of it into his mouth as though he hasn't eaten in a month.

"I did find something," I say at last.

"You did? Great!" He grabs a napkin and dabs at his mouth.

"Yeah, but it wasn't much though. I was a little disappointed."

"Those things only have a couple of details in them," he says. "I've no idea why they keep them going, except for nostalgia or something. So, what did you find?"

Talking to this twenty-something lad with the cheeky-chap exterior is somewhat comforting. Maybe it's because he's around the age that Charlie would have been, had he lived. I often look at young men and imagine what my boy would be doing now, if he'd gotten the chance to stay here a while longer. I'll never know, but somehow, I find solace in talking to people his age... The age he'd be now, rather than the age he was then. And now I find myself wanting to open up to Joseph. Not in a weird kind of way, but as a kind young stranger who I'll never see again.

"To be honest, I'm not here to do family research."

"Figured as much," he says, and looks me square in the eye. "Why?"

"It's not exactly something that happens very often in the basement of the Regency. Besides, you had that shady look about you." My eyes open wide, and Joseph laughs. "Don't worry, that's not an insult. It's just that I was a bit shady myself when I was a teenager, so I know a guilty look when I see it."

I take another bite of crumpet, and some of the butter escapes at the side of my mouth. I lick it off before I reply.

"Oh yeah? How were you shady? If you don't mind me asking."

"Maybe shady is a bit of an exaggeration," he says. "It was a bit of shoplifting here and there. A bit of breaking and entering into empty houses and stuff... The usual kind of teenage behaviour, really, and it didn't last long, but I'm particularly proud of how good I was at getting in and out of houses without anyone knowing I'd been there."

He laughs, and I think back to my beautiful Charlie, and how – at the age of fifteen – he would never have thought to steal, or break into a house. He was quite content with playing his rugby, collecting his Transformers and watching television. The pain of losing him envelops me once again, and now, talking with this stranger in a café I do not frequent, I am vulnerable. I miss my boy.

"Don't tell me, you're a private detective, aren't you? You're looking for a philandering husband."

His voice makes me jump.

"No, I'm not a detective," I say, "but you're correct about the philandering husband."

His eyebrows raise, and he takes a swig of coffee.

"I knew it. Your own?"

I nod, and tears escape from my already tired eyes. Joseph passes me a napkin.

"Thank you." I dab at my face. What the hell am I doing here, investigating my husband and pouring my heart out to a stranger?

"I'm not being funny," he says, "but it seems crazy to me when people your age have affairs. I feel like that kind of stuff should be over by the time you're in your fifties. Maybe even your forties, come to think of it."

I shoot him a look, but then realise that compared to him, I'm ancient. Besides that, he's right. I used to worry through my twenties and thirties that another Gabby Haine (or even Gabby herself) would come into our lives, but since I've become middle-aged, the anxiety has dispelled somewhat. Having an affair seems like a younger person's game, but then maybe I'm naïve. Maybe we all are.

"To be honest, I have no concrete evidence so far. But if Scott – my husband – has had an affair, then he had it ten years ago."

Joseph whistles.

"Ten years ago? Jesus, I was fourteen, ten years ago. It's a lifetime!"

"For you it is, yes. For me, ten years ago isn't that long. You'll learn that as you get older." I fight off the urge to tell Joseph that ten years ago my son passed away, at just a year older than him. Not because I'm uncomfortable mentioning him, but because I know that if I start talking about Charlie, I'll end up falling to pieces, and I can't do that here.

"So, he checked into the Regency, did he? That's why you wanted access to the books, to see who he was with?"

Joseph's voice brings me out of my daydream, and back into the cosy café. The windows are steaming up, but I can still hear the rain on the other side, heavier now, and thrashing against the glass.

"Yep," I say. "That's why I wanted access to the books. Except I didn't find out much. All I saw was my husband's name, and the woman's first name. But even then, I'm not sure that she'd have used her real one. I do know that she borrowed my surname to make it look as though they were married."

Joseph shakes his head and screws up his nose.

"My mum cheated on my dad when us kids were tiny. We never knew anything about it until years later, when Dad finally broke down and announced his discovery to the entire table at their twenty-fifth wedding anniversary dinner. I was a teenager at the time, and was absolutely mortified!"

"It's our twenty-fifth anniversary coming up." I sigh. I should be excited to celebrate something so grand, but in all seriousness, I couldn't care less.

Joseph's phone pings.

"Shit," he says, "my girlfriend's car has broken down. I'll have to go."

"No problem. It was nice to speak with you. Thanks for helping me out today."

He throws a fiver onto the table, and I try to give it back.

"This is my treat," I say, and he shakes his head.

"Tip for Trudy," he replies. "As for today, you're welcome. Look, do you have a mobile? Maybe I could have a root around to see if there are any other records anywhere. I could get in touch with you if so."

"That would be terrific." I hand him my business card. He stares at it, and his eyebrows raise.

"You're a writer?"

I shake my head, and wave the comment away.

"I used to be... I'm not anymore, but my phone number is the same."

He nods, we say goodbye and then I'm on my own again. I look at my watch. It will soon be time to go home. Home to the man who is suddenly a stranger to me.

And I'd rather be going anywhere else in the world.

CHAPTER SIX

"Surprise!!" A chorus of voices greets me as soon as I walk into our dark house, and I'm dumbfounded. The lights flicker on and it takes a couple of seconds for my eyes to adjust to the brightness. I have no idea what's going on, but in front of me is Scott, my parents, Lauren, her daughter, and a smattering of various neighbours, friends and family members. They're all wearing blue-and-red pointed party hats, and some blow into whistles or wave balloons. I am bewildered and have no idea what I'm doing, so I don't do anything at all.

"Say something then," my dad grunts from behind Lauren.

"I... I... I don't know what to say. What's going on?"

Scott laughs, steps forward, hugs me and then takes my coat.

"Surprise," he whispers into my ear. "And happy silver wedding anniversary, baby."

"Silver wedding anniversary?"

My mind goes to a picture of my train ticket. No, it's not our anniversary. Our anniversary is the 10th of October. Today is only the 8th. Scott laughs.

"I know, we're two days early," he says, "but it's hard to get everyone together in the same room, and I've got back-to-back meetings on the actual day, so we're celebrating now. To be honest, I was beginning to worry that you wouldn't get back here on time."

"I got held up." I manage to get the words out, but I'm conscious of saying too much, or revealing where I've really been today.

"The author couldn't stop talking about himself, eh?" Scott smiles the same way he did when we met all those years ago. I miss those days.

"The author?"

"The one you saw today?"

Blood rushes to my head. I had temporarily forgotten that I used the author meeting as an excuse to disappear for the day. I nod, and rub my temples.

"Sorry, I'm just bloody knackered," I say, and my husband laughs again.

Our guests quietly wait for me to say something substantial, but instead I grin, and blurt out an awkward, "Thank you for coming." All I wanted to do tonight was have a shower and then see Lauren while Scott was out. Why on earth are we having a party on a Tuesday? Who has a party on a Tuesday? My husband, evidently.

"I thought you were visiting your parents," I say, as I look around the room. "Did they come to the party? I can't see them."

Scott shakes his head.

"No, I hoped they would, but Mum has a cold and doesn't want to leave the house. You know what she's like."

I throw my handbag over the coat hook, and then everyone gathers around me, wishing us both a happy anniversary, and handing over cards, and flowers, and gifts. My mum cries and tells me how beautiful I was as a bride, and Lauren laughs and asks if I remember how her mother boycotted our wedding day because I wouldn't let the bridesmaids (of which Lauren was one) wear peach. I nod, and smile, and once again thank everyone for coming, for bringing their gifts and their kind thoughts. I put on a party hat, let off a banger, and plaster a huge grin onto my face. I whoop at the gifts, and aww at the chocolate cake, and pretend that my tears are ones of happiness.

But inside.

Inside, away from the noise of family and friends, I am wailing.

My husband kisses my cheek, and squeezes my bottom when nobody is looking. I laugh and accept his advances, and clutch onto him as though I'll drown if I let go. But all I can think about is that if I ever find out the truth of what he was up to with this Debbie woman, it would kill me.

And it might kill him too.

The guests flit from room to room, eating the buffet food, catching up with those they haven't seen for a while, and telling jokes. It seems as though everyone wants to talk to me about what we were doing twenty-five years ago. The flowers, the cars, the eccentric vicar, the aunt who refused to come to the church unless we paid for her taxi... Nothing is off-limits where such special memories are concerned.

"Do you remember when Uncle Alan got so drunk he threw up all over the neighbour's car?" asks my mum. "We were so embarrassed!"

"It wasn't the neighbour," adds my dad. "It was a taxi, and the driver demanded money to clean it up. When Alan pulled some out of his sporran, he accidentally flashed his crown jewels!"

"That's enough, Ken," my mum scolds. "Nobody wants to know about Alan's crown jewels, thank you very much!"

"Oh, come on, Carol. It's a great story."

My tipsy dad rolls his eyes, and elbows me.

"I don't care what your mum says. I thought it was funny!"

He puts his arm around my shoulder, and I laugh, because that memory has always been up there when it comes to silly things that happened at our wedding. However, while my face may be smiling, in reality I can hardly stand all the dissecting that is happening right now. Until recently, our wedding was the best day of my life, but now it's tainted. Now, I don't know if my husband even loved me enough to marry me.

Why did he marry me?

That's another question to add to my list today.

"Dad, I've got to pop to the loo. I'll be back in a minute."

I unravel myself from his grasp, and he kisses me on the ear. I then fight my way through the guests, and head upstairs, not to the toilet, but to Charlie's room. My safe haven. The place where I can sit in peace and remember a time when I was happy. A time when I was a mother, a time when I was wanted and needed. A time when I believed that my husband was faithful.

I switch on the light, and I'm shocked to see Scott sitting on the bed, quietly crying while holding one of our son's Transformers. He squints at the sudden bright light, and then looks up at me.

"Are you okay?" I ask. "I didn't notice that you'd left the party."

Funny, no matter how much this man has hurt me, I still want to know if he's okay.

"I had to get away," he says. "Uncle John started talking about Charlie's christening, and how the vicar soaked the whole front row with the holy water."

I sit next to him, and put my hand on his thigh.

"It's all right," I say. "It's okay for people to speak about Charlie. It's okay for you to speak about him too. In fact, it would be welcomed."

Scott shakes his head.

"It's too hard," he says. "If I don't talk about him, then I can pretend that the worst hasn't happened. I can pretend that he's still playing somewhere."

"I understand that," I say, "but at the same time, they say that the moment people stop speaking your name, you die again. And I don't want my child to die again. I want his memory to be with me – with us – forever."

Scott fiddles with the Transformer, flicking it from a truck into a robot. I've seen Charlie do that so many times that I could probably even manage it myself.

"I don't like talking about his death," he says. "I can't cope with it."

"I don't want to talk about his death either! But I do want to talk about his life, and I'll continue to talk about it, because that way he is still alive in some way. Besides... if there is a heaven up there, I'd like Charlie to look down and be happy that we're still celebrating his life. I wouldn't want him to think that we don't even remember he existed."

Scott takes a huge sob, holds the Transformer to his face, and cries more than I've ever seen or heard him cry before. I am heartbroken that he may have strayed ten years ago, but in this moment he is still my husband, and he needs me. He actually needs me.

"I love you," he says.

"I love you too."

I throw my arms around him, and hold him so tight I fear he may be crushed. We sit on the bed and cry together for the first time in years. Suddenly, the idea of finding out what he was up to at the Regency Hotel a decade ago seems pointless. Ridiculous even. What Scott did – or did not do – has no bearing on our relationship now.

I let my head fall back, and the lightness of spirit washes over me. I am grateful for this moment, because if Scott can be this vulnerable with me, then maybe something is cracking open for him, and he can heal.

And maybe I can heal too.

When we finally rejoin the party, we're greeted by a flood of people laughing and predicting that we have been upstairs having an early anniversary celebration.

"It was nothing like that," I say, as I squeeze Scott's hand, and hope that nobody notices our red eyes, and sniffly noses. If they do, they're polite enough not to say anything, and before long, we are both talking to the guests as though we've never been away. Eventually though, most of the food has been eaten, the gifts opened, and the party finally disperses. As Lauren heads out of the front door, she pulls me to one side.

"How did it go today?" she asks.

I'm startled. Does she suspect that I was snooping into the past? Do I look that guilty or uncomfortable?

"Today?"

"With the author. You said you had an author coming into town."

"Oh, the author." I breathe a sigh of relief. "Yes, it was okay. Completely nutty, but I've come to expect that from Sam's authors."

"Great." Lauren looks back into the kitchen to make sure we're not being overheard, but Scott has gone out into the garden for a cigarette. "Did you speak to Scott last night? You know, about the card thing."

I shake my head.

"No, no I didn't, and to be honest, I probably won't. I've thought about it and decided that you were right. No good can come from trawling into the past."

I kind of believe what I'm saying. Yes, I did go off to Cromer to investigate the possible affair, but after my conversation with Scott earlier, I'm not sure that I want to do anything that will sabotage our relationship. Lord knows we've worked hard enough for it.

"I agree," Lauren says. "To be honest, I don't think he would do that to you anyway. I think the Gabby Haine situation was enough for him. He learnt his lesson thirty years ago!"

She kisses my cheek and then heads out of the door. *Gabby Haine.* There's that name again. I roll it around my tongue...

Gabby Haine

Gabby Haine

Gabby Haine

And then I wonder...

The name Debbie is similar to the name Gabby. I mean, it shares some of the same letters, and kind of sounds the same. Is it possible that I read the name wrong? No, surely not. It definitely said Debbie.

Didn't it?

In spite of my recent declaration to not bring up the past, I can't help but pull out my phone and study the photograph once again. It's a mistake, I know it's a mistake, but I can't help myself. I can never help myself.

I squint at the letters in front of me. Yes, it does seem as though the entry in the visitors' book says Debbie, but what if I'm reading it wrong? What if I'm so involved that I can't read properly? Or what if Gabby Haine wrote Debbie to disguise her identity? After all, the woman did borrow my surname. Would it be too far-fetched to think that she could have slightly changed her first name too?

I know how ridiculous it sounds, and how unlikely it is that the woman was Gabby. But stranger things have happened, haven't they? I mean, it was always unlikely that my son would die of a heart attack aged just fifteen, but that happened, didn't it? So why not this?

My mind races, searching for answers to questions that aren't fully formed. It has been three long decades since Scott and Gabby hooked up, and so much has happened since then. But what if they reconnected somehow? What if they ran into each other and the love Scott thought he had for her back in 1993 suddenly became something real, something deeper than what he'd experienced back in the day?

What if?

What if that happened?

Or what if I'm totally losing my mind?

At this point, I really don't know.

***

By 11pm, everyone has gone and we've tidied the rubbish away, and put the uneaten food into the fridge.

"Did you enjoy the party, my love?" Scott stares deep into my eyes, his mouth turned up at the corners, so proud of himself.

"I did enjoy it, thank you."

"And are you impressed that I can keep a secret from you?"

My stomach turns.

"Actually, I am," I say.

"Good."

"As long as that's the only secret you've kept from me."

The words leave my lips before I can stop them, and Scott's eyebrows furrow.

"Of course it's the only secret I've kept from you. Well, that and other surprises, like Christmas presents and the like. That's it. I'm an open book, as you know."

He smiles, and as I look into his eyes, I try to see something that will tell me the truth about his ability to keep secrets. Long-lost, long-forgotten secrets. Surely if he has done something in the past, there will be a flick of the eyelashes, or a sudden look to the left, or the right, or wherever people are supposed to look to when they're hiding something. But there is nothing at all. He seems happy that he managed to pull off a little get-together, without me knowing anything about it, and I'm happy to go along with the charade. If indeed there is one.

Scott yawns.

"I'm off to bed," he says. "I've got a meeting tomorrow with the big boss. You want to come upstairs with me? We could continue the celebrations?"

"I'll be up shortly," I say. "I just want to read for a while, first."

"You and your late-night reading." He kisses the top of my head. "Okay, my little bookworm. I'll see you later. I'm glad you had a lovely party."

I pull my novel out from the side of the chair, and open the page.

"I did. I'll read a few chapters, then I'll come up. I've come to a really exciting bit."

Scott leans over and studies the cover. It's a story about the fight to save an end-of-the-pier theatre, and the cover shows a photo of a beach, a pier, and the water lapping underneath.

"That looks like Cromer," he says. "I bet it was based on that."

My head jerks back, and adrenaline tingles through my body at the sound of the word.

"Cromer? I can't remember, I haven't been there in years. Have you?"

I don't know why I ask that question, but I can't help hoping that he doesn't answer. Scott shuffles from one foot to the other, screws up his face, and then looks to the ceiling.

"Not recently, no. I think the last time I was there was with you, before Charlie was born." He shuffles again, and then clicks his fingers. "Yes! That was the last time. Remember we had fish and chips on the seafront, and a gull swooped down and grabbed a chip right out of your fingers. You were furious!"

I laugh at the memory. Yes, that was an infuriating day, but also a happy one.

"Yes, that's the last time I was there too. But are you sure you haven't been back since?"

His eyes flick to me, and then away again. I'm aware that I'm the only person I'll hurt if he answers truthfully, but I can't help myself.

"No," he says. "I definitely haven't been since then. I've never felt the need, to be honest."

Why am I torturing myself by having this conversation? I'm not sure, but I need to push it further. I need to see how he'll react.

"Maybe we should go back one of these days, to see if the gulls are as aggressive as they once were. Maybe an anniversary trip... Maybe this weekend?"

He swallows hard.

"Let's wait until next summer," he says. "The British seaside isn't the most pleasant at this time of year."

"True."

He must have forgotten the conversation we had where he

asked if I'd like to go to Great Yarmouth this weekend. Unseasonally warm weather he said...

He kisses my hand, and then pats my head, before disappearing upstairs. I wait until he's gone and then slam the book shut. I can't possibly read tonight. Not after he has blatantly lied to me. I sit back and digest the fact that hours after we both sat on Charlie's bed, consoling each other over the death of our beloved child, my husband stood next to me and lied. He must think I'm stupid.

I probably am.

I throw the book onto the sofa. I might not be in the mood for reading anymore, but I won't be going to bed early, either. Scott can lie there all night because I've got better things to do than have sex with my possibly/probably adulterous husband.

Things like obsessing over Gabby Haine, for instance.

While I am fully aware that it has been a lifetime since I last saw or heard of anything concrete where she is concerned, just like ten years ago, my mind will not give me peace. While it is unlikely, I still can't help but wonder if she is the woman at the heart of the hotel card controversy, and that idea rots my insides. Has Scott been pining for her all these years, and finally gave into his feelings in 2014? Has my whole life with Scott been a lie? Has he been in touch with her all this time? My head aches with the thought of it, and the pain torments the twenty-three-year-old girl who lives deep inside of me.

I message Lauren.

> You know how you mentioned Gabby Haine earlier? Well, do you think she might be the woman Scott met up with in 2014? Or am I being crazy?

A reply comes straight back, accompanied by a shocked emoji.

> Yes, you're being crazy. What a ridiculous
> thought. Why would you think that?

Because they apparently fell in love in 1993.
Why couldn't they reconnect now?

A row of laughing emojis appears on my screen, and then:

> Why would they? They broke up for a reason –
> mainly because he loved you. Besides that, do
> you really believe she has spent even one
> moment thinking about Scott over the past
> thirty-odd years? Or you for that matter? No,
> she's out there living her own life, probably
> married with a couple of kids. Maybe even a
> couple of husbands! There's no way they would
> have reconnected. No way at all.

Are you sure though? Until I found that card, I
thought there was no way he'd ever cheat on
me again, but now everything has changed.

> First of all, he didn't technically cheat on you
> with her. By his own admission, he slept with
> her after he'd finished with you. It was a 'We
> were on a break' situation.

Lauren loves a good *Friends* reference, but this time it makes my eyes sting. Yes, we might have been 'on a break' when he went all the way, but he was still invested in her, and they fooled around, whatever that may mean.

Big whoop.

I reply.

He still did something with her, and he
emotionally cheated too. What about that?

I can imagine Lauren's eyes rolling from behind the phone screen, and she's typing for at least five minutes before her next message arrives.

> All I know is that it was years ago, and you've been happily together ever since. You've got a house, you had a beautiful son, and you even had a leg-bonking, yappy dog for twelve years. You were/are completely invested in your life together! Besides that, you're both middle-aged now. You're completely different people. And so is she, if she's even still alive. You never know, do you? Besides, I'd tell you if I thought that Scott was still in touch with her, but I don't, so I'll say this – the past is gone, done. Just get rid of that bloody hotel card, sweep Gabby Haine under the carpet like you did all those years ago, and forget about it. No good can come from things that no longer serve you. Keep moving forward. And go to bed!

Should I mention Scott's recent lie about not being in Cromer since before Charlie was born? No, it's too late to get into a deep discussion about it. Also, I know that I'll never get support for my obsession from Lauren. We've known each other since we were eleven years old, and over the years she has continuously reminded me that I am the most dramatic of us both. Basically, she will listen to my crap, comment on my crap, but she has no real time for it. She's a meditation, self-help guru-type, always buying spiritual philosophy books and banging on about living in the present moment. Yes, she may mention her ex-husband Michael's indiscretions sometimes, but she doesn't appear to dwell on them – at least not around me. She's grounded and in full contact with the sensible part of her brain.

Not like me.

Not like me at all.

An hour later, I am slumped at my desk, nursing a cold cup of tea. It's the early hours of the morning, and I should be in bed, but the urge to search for Gabby Haine on Facebook is too much. I know I shouldn't do it, not after what I went through the last time my obsession crept in. I temporarily destroyed myself, and vowed never to do it again, but I tell myself that if I find her on Facebook, I will see how much she's aged, what terrible things have happened in her life, and finally put the past to rest. While she likely isn't the woman who Scott went to a hotel with in 2014, she still burns her venom into my heart. Finding her will cure all that. Finding her will cure me. At least cure me of that particular torture.

I log on to Facebook and enter her full name as I knew it to be.

Gabby Haine.

Nothing.

I try only her first name, only her surname, and even her last-known town address, but nothing. Again! Damn it. But she must have a Facebook account. Everyone has a Facebook account, don't they? Even Scott has one, though he tells me he hates the platform and is only on it to keep in touch with his hiking pals. I'm not his friend on there. In fact, I didn't even know he had an account until years after he'd created one, because he was always so vocal about his hate for social media. I only happened to find out that he had one because I was friended by someone we both used to know from the pub, and I scrolled through his friends list in search of anyone else from the past. I had no idea I'd find my husband on there, but I did.

Scott Collins. The words stood out as though written in diamonds, and the profile pic was a pair of hiking shoes. I asked if it was him, and he denied it, but once he knew that there was no way out, he was forced to admit it, and then accused me of stalking him online. I was astounded, and had a bit of a meltdown because after all his outbursts about how awful the platform was, my very first thought was that he was only on there so that he could talk to other women. He laughed at my suspicions, and said that my paranoia was the reason he hadn't told me about his account in the first place.

"You're always thinking I'm speaking to other women, or being with other women," he shouted. "I'm sick of it."

I was furious, but I couldn't deny the accusation, because he was telling the truth. I have always been paranoid, but that is purely because of what happened to us in 1993. Time is not always a healer, as I have discovered.

I give my head a shake. No use fretting about Scott's failure to tell me that he was on Facebook. It was years ago when that happened. Gosh, it must be at least ten years ago...

Ten years.

Ten years.

The same amount of time since he apparently visited a hotel with his 'wife' just months before our beloved Charlie passed away.

My mind scrambles as I try and confirm that it has actually been ten years since I discovered his Facebook page. Yes, Charlie was still with us, and was about to turn fifteen. I remember because he was in a school play the morning after we'd fought about the Facebook account, and we'd both had to pretend that we were perfectly all right with each other. In reality, I wanted to strangle Scott right there, in the middle of the school hall. He never did send me a friend request, and to be honest, I wouldn't have accepted it anyway.

I try to work out in my head when my discovery must have been. Was it before or after his trip to the Regency Hotel? It must have been before, because it was still term-time. Yes, the play was likely an end-of-year thing, so finding his account must have happened in early to mid-July, days before his trip to Cromer. Oh God, did Scott make the Facebook page so that he could keep in touch with his side chick? And is she Gabby Haine? I need to know.

I search for Scott in the hope that he'll have his friends on show, but no, he's locked his account. All that's there is the age-old profile photo. *No posts available*, it says below it.

Damn.

Trying to find Gabby has always been a non-starter, and tonight is no different. I rub my eyes, painful from crying and the stress that comes with worrying if your partner has been unfaithful. And then I remember.

I remember my Ancestry account.

About fifteen years ago, my mum and I went through a phase of working on our family tree. I subscribed to Ancestry so that we could find our distant ancestors, and for a time we'd spend every weekday morning gathering records and putting together our tree. Then we hit a dead end, as is often the case, and we gave it a break. Permanently as it turned out. I ended up cancelling my subscription, because I couldn't justify the cost when it wasn't being used, but I still held on to my account details, in the event that we might reignite our interest again. I reach for my little blue book of passwords, find the details and log in.

Immediately, I'm met not only with my family tree, but a slew of messages from people asking if they're related to me, or requesting to access our research. I ignore them all. If they've waited over a decade to get a reply from me, then it's likely they've forgotten all about me by now.

I tap on the search bar and type in Gabby Haine, along with her year of birth – 1972 – because I know that she was two years younger than me.

And there it is. Gabby's birth record.

And more importantly, her marital record.

Since I haven't paid my subscription in many years, I can only see the basic information, but even from this small snippet, I can fathom that her married name is (or at least was in 2001) Clarkson. Gabby Clarkson, married to Robert Clarkson.

Finally, after all these years, I have a married name. Why on earth did I not think about checking Ancestry before? Never mind, at least I have it now. I write it in my notebook, and my hands shake as I open Facebook again, typing in Gabby's new name as though my life depended on it.

Nothing.

That's not completely correct. There are several – more than several – Gabby Clarksons, but they all live overseas, or look different, or... or...

They're just not her.

Dammit.

My eyes sting, and I look at the clock. It's 1.37am, and I'm knackered. It's been a long, stressful day and I need to get some rest. Scott will hopefully be asleep by now, so I won't have to talk to him, or do anything else with him, so I pop the notebook back in my desk drawer, power-off my phone, and head to bed.

I can continue my search, tomorrow.

CHAPTER SEVEN

There's a crazy man currently signed to Babbage Books, who has absolutely no concept of what it means to be an author. I could ask myself how on earth he got the contract, but the answer, of course, would be Sam. Sam, the man who loves a great idea. Bernard Potter might not be a writer, but he did (according to Sam) have a terrific idea – a romantic ghost story, set on Mars. No surprise that my boss signed him immediately, but this man has never been published before, and because he was signed on the spot, he now thinks he's the new James Patterson.

I'm supposed to give his manuscript the once-over and then pass it along to an editor. However, Bernard's 'book' is only twenty thousand words long, littered with spelling mistakes, and written in what can only be described as something resembling a shopping list. Has this man ever read a book before? I'm doubtful at this point.

I'm in the middle of firing off a polite email, when the house phone rings. Nobody ever rings that line, except maybe PPI people or scammers pretending they're calling from the Microsoft IT department, so I stay still and press pause on my

CD player, to see if Scott gets it. He works from home several times a week, and today happens to be one of those days. My CD player spits and stalls and then Ella Fitzgerald's voice continues to float out, as though I didn't ask her to stop singing in the first place. I need a new player, but as Lauren says, "who even uses them nowadays?" Perhaps I should invest in an MP3 player, or even create a Spotify account, but the thought of my music being out on a cloud somewhere, instead of safely tucked away on my shelf fills me with horror. I turn the player off at the plug, and Ella's voice grinds to a halt, as Scott appears at my study door, his face grey.

"That was my dad. My Mum had another stroke and has been taken to hospital. I'm going to go through there."

A tingling, dizzy sensation buzzes around my chest, and I throw my hands up to my face. I have never been particularly fond of Scott's permanently miserable mother, but I wouldn't wish another stroke on her. I wouldn't wish anything on her at all.

"Oh shit. Is she going to be okay?"

"I'm not sure yet. Dad said she was determined to walk into the ambulance, but the paramedics made her sit in the chair. That's got to be a good sign, right? That she wanted to be independent?"

"Of course. Of course."

I cross the room and hug Scott tightly. His shallow breaths sync with my own, and despite my discovery of a possible affair, I feel nothing but compassion for him. We hug for a moment, and then he kisses the top of my head.

"I'll be back as fast as I can. I'll probably be out for the rest of the day. I've left my laptop on though, just in case I'm back early, and I've got my mobile, so if there are any work calls, they can still get me."

He plays with the buttons on his shirt cuffs, his fingers white at the tips.

"Don't worry about coming back. Stay as long as you need to. Everyone will understand."

He nods, gives me one final kiss, grabs his car keys and then disappears out of the front door.

An hour later and I've finished my Babbage Books work, a good ninety minutes before I'm meant to. I lean back in my chair and gaze out of the window. Outside, next door's cat plays with the leaves on the bush that resides in the flower bed opposite our front door. When we moved in, the bush was tiny, but now it has taken over at least three feet of space, and needs to be pruned. When Charlie was little, he used to wind Christmas lights around that bush, so that he could see them from the window. It's a tradition I haven't been able to continue. It seems so pointless since he went away.

I move, and my shadow catches the eye of the cat. He takes a break from swatting the leaves, and we both stare at each other in silence. He's confused. Are we friends? Will I open the front door and let him in for a treat and a comfy nap on the sofa? Or will I shoo him away as I usually do?

In the end, I watch him, aware of the fact that the last time I saw him playing outside, my life was quieter. I was living a middle-aged life with my husband, playing Scrabble in the evenings, or watching crazy programmes like *Married at First Sight*, or *The Great British Bake Off*. I was looking forward to our twenty-fifth wedding anniversary, and the rest of our life together.

But that has all been twisted, thanks to the discovery of the hotel card, and it won't ever be the same again. My thoughts are interrupted by a jangly tune coming from the box room where Scott normally does his work. I know this tune. It's the same one that pops up when one of his colleagues is trying to video-call him.

I wander into the room and stare at the screen. It's Matthew, one of the apprentices that Scott has taken under his wing. Should I answer it? Should I tell him that my husband has been called away urgently, and can I help instead? But then I remember that as much as I know about Scott's workplace, thanks to overhearing him when he works from home, I don't work there myself, and certainly couldn't answer anything that Matthew – or anyone else – has to ask.

I turn to walk away, but then curiosity gets the better of me. Maybe Scott's Facebook page is open on his laptop. Maybe I could find Gabby Haine – or Gabby Clarkson as she is now – on his list of friends. More importantly, maybe I can find the elusive Debbie. Maybe I can find both. I wait for the apprentice to stop calling, and as soon as he does, I click onto Scott's homepage and there, as hoped, is the icon for Facebook.

I hold my breath.

Should I click on it?

Am I prepared for what I might find?

Yes. Yes, I think I am.

The familiar screen appears before me, and with it a pile of posts from Scott's friends. There is an update from a hiker in Canada, complaining about the weather, then there is one from a *Star Wars* fan group selling a toy Yoda, and then yet another from a metal-detecting forum, advertising a new detector. Metal-detecting? Since when was Scott ever into metal-detecting? It doesn't matter. His taste in that kind of hobby is not something I'm interested in. I scroll for a few more seconds, but nothing takes my interest, so instead I click onto Scott's profile and go to his friends list.

There are twenty-four.

Twenty-four? Scott wasn't kidding when he told me that he doesn't use the platform to make friends. I have around six hundred, and I thought that was a relatively small amount. By rights, Gabby Haine Clarkson should be close to the top of the list, but I scroll past C, G, and then H. Nothing. She's not on there. I check out the letter D, too, on the off-chance that Debbie is listed, but once again, I come up with nothing.

So, if there was something going on, either with Gabby or this mysterious Debbie, it either isn't anymore, or she's not on his Facebook friends list. Fair enough. But just because they're not there, doesn't mean that there's not going to be anything else that could help me. I grab my phone and send him a message.

> Hey you. I hope everything is okay. How's your mum?

A message comes back two and a half minutes later.

> Not good. She's stable but the doctor said that the next 24 hours are crucial. Would you mind if I stay over here this evening? I don't want to leave my dad, and I want to be here just in case.

> Of course I don't mind. I'll be absolutely fine.

I pop the phone onto the desk, and get back to Scott's friends list. It's only going to take me a couple of hours to go through the profiles of twenty-four people, but knowing I have the entire night is certainly a bonus. I pop to my study to grab my notebook, run to the kitchen to stick the kettle on, and then settle down.

Scott has some of the most boring friends I've ever seen. There's Trevor, a bloke from Minnesota, who collects hiking boots and posts video reviews on his Facebook page. Not that he hikes in them. Oh no, he merely walks up and down the hall, then reports back to anyone crazy enough to watch him.

I scrub Trevor off my list. He's definitely not the person I'm looking for.

Next there's Paul. Paul owns a parrot called Stanley, who can say cheeky words such as 'bugger', 'crap' and 'boobies'. Nope, Paul's not fruitful to my research, but his parrot is pretty cute, I'll give him that.

Sarah McIntire is interesting. She lives in Cromer, and looks to be about forty years old. Younger than me, still pretty, and according to her profile, works as a dance teacher. How does she know Scott? The fact that she's from Cromer makes me want to know more about her. I tap on the part of her profile that says how she has interacted with Scott, and I'm met with the revelation that she has been a friend for ten years. Unfortunately, the only other interactions appear to be standard Happy Birthday posts, with attached memes of cakes, or gifts, or dancing frogs and the like.

Suspicion running through my blood, I poke further into her profile, and discover that for the past fifteen years she has been running a vintage car group. My husband has always been into vintage cars, often restoring them in the garage in the evenings and days off. I click through to the page and sure enough, there he is in the list of members, and his posts are random photos and mentions of cars he likes and hopes to own one day. Her replies are all polite and matter-of-fact. If Sarah is the woman Scott went to the Regency with, then they've kept it well-hidden.

I cross her off my list.

I work my way through most of Scott's friends, scouring their pages, their friends and family, their likes, and wants, reviews, and complaints. I'm looking for anything, any little thing that could tie them to my husband in a romantic or sordid way, but so far there's nothing. Absolutely nothing. In conclusion, Scott has the most boring Facebook life in the world. I mean, I'm not overly active on there myself, but even I have some photos and other details of who I am as a person. The only thing to be found with Scott is that he likes hiking (he goes every Sunday, whatever the weather), is interested in vintage cars, likes *Star Wars*, dislikes most reality television, and reads approximately two books every decade. There is no trace of anyone called Debbie, and Gabby Haine is either in disguise, has fallen off the face of the earth, or has been maimed in a diabolical accident.

I hope it's the latter.

I rub my head. It's aching from staring at the screen for hours, and when I look up, I'm surprised to see that darkness has now descended. I had been so invested in the Facebook page that I hadn't even noticed. God, I'm obsessed. Totally, utterly obsessed. Again.

I decide to check out the few remaining people another time, leave the box room as I found it, and hide the notebook in my study, ready for another day.

I wake up to the sound of my mobile ringing. I had kept it on in case there was an update about Scott's mum, but as I grab it from the bedside cabinet, I'm shocked to discover that it's 10am. I'm late logging on to my workspace. Shit.

The number is not one I recognise, but I accept the call anyway, worried that Scott's phone could have gone flat and he's now calling from another number.

"Hello?"

My voice is groggy from going to bed too late, and my lips are dry and brittle at the edges.

"Hello. Is this Olivia?"

"Yes, speaking."

"Oh hi, it's Joseph from the Regency Hotel. How are you?"

Joseph? It takes me a moment to recognise that this is the young lad who showed me where the archive room was. When I do realise who I'm talking to, I swallow hard.

"I'm okay, thanks. How are you?"

I rub my eyes and manage to pull myself up from the pillow.

"I'm good," he says. "Listen, you know the guy you were looking for the other day?"

"You mean my husband?"

"Yeah, yeah, your husband."

I grip the phone tight, and pinch my thigh. What is Joseph about to say?

"What about him? Did you find something? Did you find more records from ten years ago?"

There's a silence on the other end of the phone, then the line goes muffled and I can hear far-away voices.

"Joseph? Are you still there?"

"Yeah," he says. "I just had to talk to a guest. No, no, I haven't found anything from ten years ago, but... Well, this could be something or nothing, but I thought you should know..."

"Know what?"

My tongue sticks to the top of my mouth. I'm not sure I want to hear the answer, but I have to.

"There's a couple in the restaurant right now, and they're having breakfast."

"Okay?"

"Well, didn't you say that your husband's name is Scott, cos this guy just signed the bill and his name is Scott Collins."

My mouth falls open, and the muscles in my shoulders go weak.

"Well... well... it must be a coincidence, surely. My husband is visiting his parents at the moment. His mum had a stroke and..."

"Yeah, I figured it was probably a different couple altogether, but I thought I'd check, because it's a little weird, isn't it?"

Joseph is right, it is a little weird. In fact, it's more than a little weird. It's completely bizarre. My head pounds right at the point where my nose meets my forehead, and my hands shake as I pull the duvet around me.

"Are they still there?" I ask.

There's a moment's silence.

"Yes. I can see them from here. They're right next to the door."

"Can you take a photo?"

I can hear Joseph take a breath before he replies.

"No way," he says. "We're not allowed to take photos of the guests without their permission. I'll lose my job."

"Please! I need to know if it's my Scott! Pretend you're checking your hair in the phone or something, and snap a photo. Please, I'm begging you."

He lets out a long, deep sigh.

"Okay, hang on."

I can hear rustling, a click and then the line goes dead.

"Joseph? Joseph, are you still there?"

I stare at the screen, but the call has been disconnected. Shit. I throw the phone onto the bed, then grab it again, heart set on pressing the redial button. As I struggle to open the phone app with my shaking hands, there is a ping. It's a WhatsApp message from Joseph.

I place the phone on the bedside cabinet in front of me, and watch as the clock ticks through the next five minutes. I get up, sit down, cross my arms, swallow over and over again, chew my lips and rock forward and back. I want to look at the photo, but can I actually look at it? It can't be him, can it? Not really.

As my stomach rolls, I lift the phone, open the photo and enlarge it as much as I can.

And there is Scott.

My Scott.

And he's holding hands across the table with a woman I've never seen before in my life.

I drop the phone onto the floor, and retch. Scott is in a hotel with a strange woman.

And today is our twenty-fifth wedding anniversary.

"This is unbelievable! Who the hell is this?"

Lauren perches on the edge of my sofa, and attempts to enlarge the photo further than I already have.

"Don't bother trying to make it bigger. That's the best it can go without getting pixelated."

She places the phone onto the coffee table, and we both sit back as though we've touched an explosive device. In a way we have.

"Just unbelievable," she says. "What are you going to do?"

"I have no idea. But it is him, isn't it? I'm not being neurotic and seeing stuff, right?"

Lauren shakes her head, and then picks up the phone again.

"You're not seeing stuff. It's definitely him. But who the hell is the woman?"

"I have no idea. It isn't Gabby Haine though, I know that much."

I blink hard. I am relieved that it isn't her. If it had been, that would have confirmed all the fears I've had and I couldn't handle that, even more than I can't handle this.

I can't handle any of it.

I slide over toward Lauren, and we both study the photo. The shot is not the best, given how far away it was taken, but some things are clear. First, this woman has long blonde hair, hanging loose to her waist. She is of slim build, and looks to be around the same height as Scott. She's wearing a red dress with short sleeves – not in keeping with today's cold October weather, and she's smiling.

"I know we can't see her whole face, but she looks pretty plain to me," I say.

Lauren nods.

"They say that about side chicks though, don't they? Always a level down from the wife. Easier, not better…"

I open my mouth to reply, but then the phone rings and we both jump.

"It's Scott," Lauren whispers, and hands it to me. I stare at the phone for a minute, and then something deep inside forces me to press the accept call button. I put it on speaker, and place the handset on the table between us.

"Hello?"

"Hey, sweetie, it's me."

Lauren and I exchange glances. What is he going to say? My throat rattles, and I fear I'll have an anxiety attack at any second. My friend reaches forward and grabs my hand, and we get through it together.

"Hi," I say through gritted teeth.

"Happy anniversary! I'm so sorry I can't be there. Good job we celebrated the other night, isn't it?"

I ignore his good wishes. Why should I wish him a happy anniversary when he's probably sat on a hotel bed with his mistress?

"How are you? How are things with your mum?"

I ask the questions with as much interest as I can muster, but it's not easy. I hear him sigh.

"Better than expected," he says. Lauren and I glare at each other. "Mum's stroke wasn't as bad as they thought it was, thank God. They kept her in overnight, but they think she'll be out later today."

"I'm glad to hear it," I say, though at this moment I don't even know if my mother-in-law has had a stroke. Was it all one sick story so that he could get a night in Cromer with his lover? If so, who does that? Only the vilest person on earth would pretend their family members were ill, so that they could embark on an affair. And yet some people must do it. Some people are seriously that evil.

"You sound really far away," Scott says. "Do you have me on speaker?"

Lauren throws her hand to her mouth. I'm sure that the last thing she wants is to be drawn into this. She waggles her finger at me, a signal not to tell him that she's here.

"Yes, I have you on speaker," I reply. "I was in the middle of my Babbage work, so I have you on my desk."

"Not for the first time!" He laughs. I look over at Lauren, and she pretends to stick her finger down her throat. I ignore his attempt at a joke. Who would even do that if their mother was ill?

"Did you stay at your dad's overnight?"

There's a pause on the other end of the line, as though he's conjuring up what he's previously rehearsed in his mind.

"Yes, I did. He was really upset, so I camped down in my old bedroom. It was weird to say the least."

Lauren shakes her head wildly and scratches her forehead. I bite my lip and try not to say something I'll regret later. If I'm going to get an answer to all the questions hurtling around my body, then I need to be calm, and not give Scott any reason to presume that I'm onto him.

"That was probably a good idea," I say. "I bet your dad was frantic."

"Yes, he was. You know how much he loves my mum."

"Well, they've been together for a long time. He's bound to be worried."

"Yeah," he says. "Anyway, I hate to hang up on you, but I told the boss I'd keep the line free, in case of any work calls."

Of course he did. Not even an affair can stop the work calls.

"Will you be home later?" I ask.

Another pause.

"Yes, I hope so. It'll be late, because I want to make sure that mum is settled in before I leave, but I definitely should be there before you go to bed. I'll give you your anniversary gift then."

"Okay, I'll see you then."

"Love you," he says.

"Bye."

I press the call end button, and sit back in my armchair.

"Wow," Lauren says.

"Wow," I reply. "So, now we know the real reason why he threw the anniversary party two days before our big day. He knew he wasn't going to be here for the actual date. Who does that? Who cheats on their wife on their silver wedding anniversary?"

Lauren tilts her head to the side, and rubs her nose.

"I guess some people must do, but I didn't think Scott was one of them."

"Neither did I," I say, and then I burst into tears. Lauren huddles ever closer to me, and puts her arm around my shoulder.

"Just let it out," she says. "Let it all out."

She hugs me for a while, and then leans over to retrieve a tissue.

"Thank you," I say, as I dab at my nose. "How could he do this to me? How could he do it to us? I thought we had a good marriage!"

"You did! You did have a good marriage. You maybe still do. It's maybe all a huge mistake and he'll explain everything when he gets home."

I throw the tissue onto the coffee table.

"Do you really believe that?"

"No, not really."

We both sit back on the sofa, and digest what has happened. Twenty-five years ago, we were at our wedding. We were exchanging rings, and making toasts, and saying vows that I have never broken. If someone had told me then that this would happen, I'd have slapped them and called them a liar. But now the pain burns into my bones, and I'm not sure how I'm going to get through if all of this is true.

"What are you going to do now?" Lauren asks.

"I think I'm going to have to visit his parents, because we can safely say that he's not with them, and they might know what's going on."

"You're going to visit them now?"

Lauren sits up straight, and stares at the clock on the mantelpiece.

"Yes," I say. "As soon as I've tidied myself up."

"Then I'm coming with you."

I wash my face in the kitchen sink, but avoid my reflection in the little mirror on the windowsill. The fear of infidelity singes a hole through our entire marriage. Yes, I'd had some doubts and worries over the years, but who doesn't? At this point, I believed we had settled into a quiet, middle-aged existence. But now? Now I am fighting to control my breathing, in the fear that I'm about to have a panic attack. During the past ten years, I've had several attacks, all related to memories of when Charlie died. But every time I've experienced them, my husband has been beside me to rub my arm and tell me to breathe through my nose and out through my mouth.

Not this time though.

Nor ever again.

CHAPTER EIGHT

Ever since Charlie passed away, I haven't really been comfortable driving. Lauren says that it's probably a menopause thing, since she's the same way, especially if the journey requires dual carriageways or motorways. I'm not so sure if it's the same with me though, since before Charlie passed I used to drive everywhere with him and never thought a thing about it.

To be honest, my problem is that I can still remember pulling up at the school, and hearing the awful news that I'd lost my son. It's an association thing, so that now I don't drive anywhere without pondering that day, that minute, that moment. It's something I've struggled with for a decade, and so I frequently take the train, or the bus, and if anyone dares ask why, I pretend that petrol is too expensive, or the roads are too icy, or there are too many idiot drivers.

But today...

Today, things are different.

Scott's parents still live in the same home he grew up in, in a tiny village about twenty minutes away from where we live now, and driving on my own to see them is something I've never done before. But in spite of the fact that I need to drive through dodgy, hardly-surfaced country lanes, on a rainy autumn day, I can't get in my car fast enough.

"Hold on a minute," Lauren shouts, as she runs toward my Honda Civic. I stay silent. While I'm grateful of my friend's presence, if she hadn't arrived at the door by the time my key slotted into the ignition, I'd have gone without her.

She buckles her seatbelt, leans over and gives me a hug.

"I'm so sorry," she says.

"So am I... Are you ready?"

She tugs on her seatbelt.

"Yes, I'm ready."

I slam the car into reverse, and bolt off the driveway.

The rain thrashes onto my car, and as the sun disappears over the hill, I just about manage to avoid the countless potholes at the side of the road. Several times Lauren gasps as I whip the car round the holes, and we have a near-miss with a vehicle coming the other way.

"Look out!" she shouts at the top of her voice. My mum is a huge back-seat driver, but she's nothing compared to Lauren.

By the time we pull up outside Scott's parents' house, we're both exhausted. I can't remember the last time I was here. I'm embarrassed to admit it, but it was before lockdown. While that was a terrible time for most of us, it also provided ample excuse to keep away from people you don't like, which in my case was my in-laws.

It's not that they're bad people, it's just that they haven't ever gelled with me, and vice versa. When I met Scott, and went full-on into a deep relationship, they were shocked, especially as I was Scott's first serious girlfriend, and we were both still teenagers. They were concerned when we got engaged so quickly, and then when we broke up over the Gabby Haine fiasco, I was told by Scott's loose-lipped cousin, Cynthia, that they seemed to be okay with it.

According to her, all they said when he broke the news of my departure was, "It's maybe for the best" and they accepted Gabby into their family with hardly a question asked. In fact, Cynthia told me that despite the fact that they'd only been dating for a matter of days, Gabby went out with them all when it was Scott's dad's birthday. Scott has never told me this, but I've always known that Gabby had a foot firmly under the family table for the long four weeks that he was officially with her.

The same table that still sits in their dining room today.

Well, at least it did, before I stopped visiting them.

I'm not surprised that Scott's parents weren't bothered about him dumping me, because I have never felt any kind of connection to them, and have always felt his mother to be more than a little judgy. First, she would comment on my clothes, then when we moved in together, she'd criticise my lack of housework knowledge. When we had Charlie, the judgement carried over to how I dressed him, how many times I took him to baby gym, or baby dance, or whatever the hot class was at that time. It used to drive me nuts, especially when Scott would stay silent during any criticism she dished out.

"Gosh, it's been a long time since I've been up this way," Lauren says. "I can't remember the last time. Maybe when I was going out with that Mark bloke. Remember him? He wore Nirvana T-shirts, but was really a One Direction fan."

I know that my friend is making small talk to alleviate the awkwardness of this visit, but I have no time for it. I grab my brolly and run from the car to the front door. Lauren catches me up seconds later with her wax jacket hood pulled right over her head. Together we huddle under the small porch area, though that and my brolly does little to stop the horizontal rain coming over us. The red paint on the door is chipped and cracked, and the surrounding wood is rotten at the bottom. I don't even know the last time the house was painted inside, never mind out, but it looks as though it won't last for much longer if they don't get it sorted. I make a mental note to tell Scott to help them fix it, but then I remember why I'm here, and that the chances of my husband and I ever conversing about his parents' front door are negligible.

I press the doorbell and I can hear the ring from somewhere deep inside. When nobody appears after a minute, I press it again, and knock, but still there is no sign of life.

"There's nobody here," Lauren says.

A moment of relief sets in for me. Has this all been a huge misunderstanding? Maybe the man in the Regency Hotel is not my husband after all. Don't they say that everyone has a doppelganger? Well, maybe I've found Scott's! Perhaps it's all true and he did stay in his childhood bedroom last night, and now he and his dad are at the hospital, waiting for his mother to receive news that she can leave.

My first reaction is to laugh.

"What's so funny?" Lauren asks.

"Nothing really. Except that I've been so stupid. Of course, Scott wasn't lying to me. He'd never lie about something so important. He must be at the hospital. There's no other explanation."

Lauren nods her head, but her eyebrows are knitted together. I suspect that she doesn't believe my theory. Instead, she tries to peer in through the frosted glass window next to the door.

"You might be right," she says, but the words are stilted. "There's definitely no sign of life in there. Besides, only a weirdo or a sicko would make up a stroke story."

She might be agreeing in a supportive way, but at this moment my heart believes that Scott is genuinely with his ill mother, while giving support to his lonely, concerned father. I am so relieved.

I lean my head against the door, and start to cry. Tears fall and converge with the rain on the door. Both streams combine into one, while I cry, and cry, and cry.

Relief!

Dear, sweet, relief!

Lauren rubs my back as though I were a young child.

"Come on," she says. "Let's get out of here. I'll buy us a cuppa."

"Olivia?"

We both gasp, and I pull my head up from the door, patting at my cheeks with my gloved hand. It's Audrey, the lady who has lived next door to Scott's parents for the past fifty years – at least. I sniff, and laugh, and get myself back together.

"Audrey! I haven't seen you for years. How are you?"

She frowns, and her mouth turns up at one side.

"I'm doing well, dear. Thank you for asking... But are you okay? You seem upset."

I laugh again and shake my head.

"No, I'm just a bit cold and wet." I motion toward the front door. "When there was no answer, I figured I'd end up standing on the doorstep, getting wetter by the minute!"

"Yes," Lauren says. "She was frightened she'd end up a drowned rat – like me!" She rubs the sleeves of her coat, and beads of rain flick onto the ground.

"What do you mean there was no answer?" Audrey asks.

The older lady approaches me with her head tilted to one side, looking from me to Lauren and back again. She doesn't know if this is a trap, a scam or both. I lower my umbrella and adjust my eyes. I haven't seen Audrey in many years, and I'm sad to see that the passing of time hasn't been particularly kind. Her eyes are sunken into her skull, and her sparse hair is pressed against her head. Wrinkles have gathered around her lips and neck, and her skin is the colour of paste.

"Scott said that he and his dad were going to collect his mum from the hospital this evening," I tell her. "But since they're not here, I'm presuming they've been called in earlier."

Audrey frowns and rolls her lips into her mouth.

"Hospital? I'm not sure what you're talking about, my love."

Lauren looks at me out of the corner of her eye. She's assuming that Audrey is losing her memory, because that is what's happening to her own mother, and it has made her suspicious of just about everyone who says anything remotely strange.

"The Hosp-It-All," she says loudly. "Olivia's mother-in-law is in the hospital."

She draws a square in the air, as though she's taking part in some kind of mime game.

Audrey moves closer, sniffs and lowers her voice to a whisper.

"I know what a hospital is, dear. Have you girls been... have you both been... drinking? You look as though you might have been."

She rubs my arm, and then backs off again, scared to be out in the rain, or perhaps terrified to be so close to the woman who is weeping on her neighbour's doorstep.

"No, I haven't been drinking. I'm driving." I point toward my car, and she nods.

"I'm glad to hear that," she says. "And you?"

She stares at Lauren, who grimaces and waves her hands in the air.

"I'm completely sober," she says. "There's been no drinking around here. Except if it's you who's doing it."

Audrey's face clouds over. She's had enough of us.

"No, I have not been drinking, but you can understand my confusion."

"Which is?" Lauren folds her arms, and stares straight into Audrey's eyes.

"That there's no way Scott could be at the hospital with his parents," Audrey says. "You've either been drinking, or you've caught a chill from all this rain."

I move from one foot to the other, unable to stop fidgeting. Lauren's eyes are all over me.

"What do you mean?" I ask.

"Darling," Audrey says. "Scott's parents both passed away during Covid."

Shivers travel down my torso. What is this woman talking about? She really is losing her memory.

"Audrey, Scott's parents live here – right next door to you!"

She puts her fingers to her mouth, ignoring my statement.

"Now when was it?" she says. "I think it must have been toward the end of 2020. Yes, it was, because my Ray had just got the Christmas tree out of the garage when we heard the news that Barbara had gone. Timothy wasn't far behind her, died during Christmas week if I remember rightly. Surely, you must have known."

I run my hand down my neck, and steady myself on the front door.

"We should go," Lauren whispers. "I think maybe Audrey has lost it."

Thankfully the sound of the rain stops Audrey from hearing Lauren's words, and while I know that there's a possibility that the old lady may have a few memory problems, I'm inclined to believe every word she's saying. She seems so sure, and why would she lie? How could she make up such a specific story? But then again, how could they be dead? How could I not have known? My mind whirls. Am I going insane? Am I losing all sense of reality? Maybe I am.

"It's baffling to me that you didn't know. Did you know?" Audrey stares at me through narrowed eyes.

"No, I... Maybe I... Maybe I forgot."

Audrey nods her head.

"You've been through a lot in the past ten years," she says. "You're bound to feel a bit up and down sometimes."

"How did they die?" Lauren's eyes burrow into Audrey, as though they're in a courtroom.

"Oh," she says. "It wasn't the Covid that got them, which was a surprise to most of us on the street. No, it was sepsis for Barbara, and I think that Timothy had a stroke shortly afterwards. I'm a bit shaky on all the details, but if you ask me, I believe he died of a broken heart. They'd been together so long; he didn't know what to do with himself. Scott sold the house not long after, but the next couple didn't like the village and moved out about six months ago. It's sat empty ever since."

Through the mist in my eyes, I look up at the house, and everything I have ever done in there comes flying back to me. I first slept with Scott in his bedroom. I cried when he told me he loved me and wanted to get engaged. I cried even more when I dropped him here after he'd admitted he was in love with Gabby Haine. We celebrated Christmas afternoons here in the early days, and I carried my baby son over this very doorstep to meet his grandparents, a week after he was born.

"This must be a terrible shock for you," Audrey says through the rain. "I know you two had separated, but I thought that Scott would have had the decency to tell you that they'd passed. It's awful that he didn't. What on earth was he thinking?"

Separated.

Separated?

Scott had told his parents' neighbours (and maybe even his parents for all I know) that we had separated.

"Oh God!"

Lauren and I gasp at exactly the same time, then the weight of my body feels too much for my legs, and liquid pours into my mouth. My friend throws out her arms to catch me, but before she can, I stumble to the bushes and throw up everything I've eaten in the past five hours. Which thankfully isn't much.

"Oh goodness!" Audrey shouts. "Wait there, my dear. I'll get you a drink of water."

She turns toward her house, but I wave her away.

"I'm sorry," I say. "I have to go."

"But, Olivia…"

I leave Audrey chuntering away to herself as I sprint to my car. Lauren jumps in after me, and without looking behind, I drive off down the rainy, slippery road, and quietly pray that there is a huge juggernaut heading straight toward me.

Lauren wants to stay with me, but I can't bear the thought of going over and over the details with her. I drop her off with the promise that I'll be in touch with anything I find, and then back home, I have a cup of tea, sit in the quiet, darkened living room, and think about four years ago.

Audrey said that Barbara and Timothy passed away toward the end of 2020. It is easy to remember that time because of everything that was going on. The lockdowns, the ban on Christmas parties (for everyone except those in power, allegedly), the tears, the fears, and the strangeness of it all. Scott worked at home, and apart from necessary outings, and his Sunday countryside hiking trips (which Scott assured me were legal, but I have no idea if that's true), we spent every day together, including Christmas. We played games, we bought presents online, and we FaceTimed my parents during the holiday season. Scott told me that the last thing his parents would understand was video-calling, so we never did speak to them that way. Instead, he spent hours on the telephone every evening, making sure they were okay.

At least that's who he said he was calling during 2020, but he certainly wasn't speaking to them into 2021, since according to Audrey, they were gone by then. I'm not a fool. I now suspect that he was talking to his lover, but I didn't have a clue at the time. I was too busy wondering how to get through the long, dark days of lockdown.

And now I have questions, and I need to know the answers.

I turn on my laptop and head straight to the newspaper archive. I had originally subscribed to that website so that I could use it for book ideas and research, but when my writing dried up, I never cancelled my subscription. Today, I'm glad about that.

I search for Barbara and Timothy Collins, and then narrow the search to November and December 2020. No announcements come up in any of the local newspapers. Not a single word is said about two people who had lived in the area for their entire lives. Nothing. I'm so confused. Maybe Audrey is the one who got it all wrong. Maybe Lauren is right, the old lady has developed dementia, or is simply getting forgetful.

Besides, wouldn't I have noticed if Scott had been dealing with a death in the family? Even if he couldn't go there because of the lockdown, it was his parents for heaven's sake, and yet I have no recollection of any kind of horror, or worry, or despair, and wouldn't there have been all of those things if his parents had passed? True, my husband was never what you'd call a mother's boy, but surely, you'd have to be a psychopath not to react to the death of even one parent, never mind two! Yes, Scott is most certainly a liar, but a psychopath? That is a bit of a stretch.

The whole thing is ridiculous. Poor Audrey. She must be suffocating under the weight of old age. But to make sure, I come out of the newspaper archive and then open Google. I close my eyes when I press the search button, praying that there are no hits, but then my chin hits the floor when the very first item that comes up is a PDF of my in-laws' village newsletter, announcing their death.

Announcing their death.

Sadly, we have lost two of our own during the past couple of weeks. Timothy and Barbara Collins, valued and treasured members of our community, have passed away. The couple had lived in the village for all of their married life, and raised their beloved son, Scott in the same house. Some of you may remember that in 2018, we all celebrated the couple's 50th wedding anniversary in the village hall. It was a wonderful night of dancing, singing, and champagne. The couple will be missed by all who knew them. Sadly, we are unable to go to their joint funeral because of Covid restrictions, but we encourage everyone who loved them to light a candle and hold a good thought for the Collins family.

I can't believe what I've just read. Audrey was correct, the couple did die. But how can that be? How could I not know? A fluttering feeling escalates around my solar plexus, round my back and up into my head. Is this all my fault? Did I enable Scott's deception because I was never interested in keeping in touch with his parents? Did I give in too easily on the few occasions when I thought I should contact them, but Scott advised against it, leading me to believe that they hated me more than I realised? I have no idea, but I do know that lockdown made it a lot easier for my husband to sweep their deaths under the carpet, and pretend it had never happened. And that is unbelievable.

Underneath the article is a photograph of Timothy and Barbara, arm-in-arm at their golden wedding celebration. They are both smiling into the camera, seemingly no cares in the world. And yet two years later they were both gone.

I sit back in my chair and rub my temples. I remember that party. It was one of the last times I ever saw the couple. Despite our differences, I made a concerted effort to do my very best for them, because it was their big day. Scott didn't have a clue what to buy, but I trawled every antique shop to find what I thought would be the perfect gift – a beautiful vase with a thick, golden trim at the top and bottom. It was expensive, but I had to get it, particularly as I knew if I left the purchase up to Scott, they'd likely get an Amazon voucher or a cheesy framed photo of the family. I was right, they did seem to like it, and I even received a hug from them both when they opened it. However, during the handful of times I visited them after that, it was nowhere to be seen. When I eventually asked what had happened to it, Barbara giggled awkwardly and admitted that it had fallen off the windowsill and shattered.

But did it fall?

Or was it pushed?

I never got to find out.

But that's all irrelevant now. The vase is gone, Timothy and Barbara have gone, and all that is left is an overgrown garden, a chipped, peeling front door, a newsletter with their smiling faces staring out at me, and their DNA alive and well in Scott.

Scott, the psychopath.

Scott, the man I married exactly twenty-five years ago, but no longer know.

Scott, who might as well be dead too, because frankly, why is he here at this point?

I send the obituary to Lauren, and then immediately receive a WhatsApp message. I presume it's from her, but it's from Scott. Once again, bile rises in my throat as I read his words.

> Hey honey, Mum is much better. She's been discharged, and I've delivered her home. Now I'm coming home myself. Bloody knackered! See you soon. Xx

The insanity of it all makes me burst into laughter. How could this be real? How could this possibly make sense to anyone but Scott? And why? Why would it need to make any sense?

What else has he been up to?

Except for checking into the Regency with his latest side chick, of course.

CHAPTER NINE

"You need to get out of there before that bastard comes back. Come over here. Bring a bag. You can stay the night." Lauren's phone calls are always straight to the point, but while I appreciate the offer, I need to stay here. I want – no, need – to see what Scott will say, what contrived tale he'll come up with about his mum's visit to the hospital.

I blow out a long stream of air, say goodbye to Lauren, and lean my head onto the desk. What kind of man does this? What kind of fully-functioning human pretends that his parents are still alive, when they're clearly gone?

What a sick, sick thing to do.

I can't get my head around it.

But then a different thought occurs to me. Over the past ten years there have been many times when he visited his parents, or they needed him to spend the afternoon repairing the shed, or helping to clean out the fish pond. Granted, for six of those years the requests could have been true, but for the latter four? No. There were no fence panels to erect, no door knockers to install, no stereos to fix. No anything.

Except, of course, a nice excuse to get out of the house and into the arms of God knows who. And that brings me to his hiking Sundays. Every single weekend my husband heads off with his boots in a bag, and drives out into the countryside for his regular ramble. It doesn't matter if it is raining, snowing, icy or blazing hot, Scott will head to the hills, because he loves the hobby so much. I'm not interested in it, so never go with him, but when he comes back, he's always full of tales of what he saw and where he went. But now a thought occurs to me. In all the years that Scott has been hiking, I don't think I've ever seen a photograph of the sheep he sees, or the interesting clouds that pass above him. Added to that, I never go near the bag where he keeps his hiking boots, because I know they will be covered in mud, and I'd end up cleaning them. Or would I?

I sprint to the understairs cupboard, and search in the back for his hiking bag. I reach in, praying to be met by a pair of the grubbiest boots you could ever find, but when I pull them out, they are pristine. They have been walked in, yes, but hiked through muddy fields? Absolutely not. Either Scott cleans them off before he gets home, or this is another one of his lies.

I know which one I believe.

A couple of hours later, I've moved to the kitchen, but my mind is no clearer. My mouth is as dry as cotton, and I realise that I haven't had anything to drink for hours, so I boil the kettle for a cup of tea. As it is bubbling and chuntering toward boiling point, I hear Scott's key in the lock.

I freeze.

"Hey! I'm home!"

His keys rattle into the little saucer that stays on the shelf beside the door, and then I hear his shoes being thrown into the cupboard. In all these years, he's never once put them in there tidily, but I should be glad he's taken them off. He doesn't always.

"Hello? Are you home?"

My hands shake as I grab an extra mug out of the cupboard, and throw a teabag into it. I wish it was arsenic. I wish it was something that could do him serious harm.

"Oh, you are in! I thought you'd gone out." I have my back to Scott as he comes into the kitchen. I'm overly fussing with the tea, when he slides his arms around my waist. Cold shivers scatter around my back and up into my ribcage. I want him nowhere near me, and I certainly don't want his hands around my body.

"Happy anniversary," he says. "I'm so sorry I couldn't be with you this morning."

I want to tell him to get off me. I want to plunge the bread knife into his throat. I want to grab the kettle and throw boiling water in his face.

But I don't.

I have no idea why.

Instead, I smile, and turn round and hug him back. My arms are like stone, and I clutch at him as though I'm on a cliff face, hanging on for dear life. I'm grieving, but not for Barbara and Timothy. I'm grieving for myself. I'm grieving for Scott. I'm grieving for us, and for the life that I believed was real.

"Happy anniversary," I say through tears. "I did shout hello when you came in, but you mustn't have heard me over the kettle."

I can hardly look at him, but I know his eyes burrow into mine.

"Are you okay? Why are you crying?"

I wave off his concern with a giggle.

"I'm fine. I just... I just missed you today, that's all."

"I missed you too. Being at the hospital was not how I wanted to celebrate our anniversary. Good job we had the party early, isn't it?"

A good job indeed. Good timing too. Not at all suspicious...

"I'm glad that you're home," I lie, as I hand him a cup of tea.

"Thanks. Glad to be home," he says, as he reaches into the biscuit barrel. "God, I need this cuppa. Have you any idea how awful the tea is in hospital? It barely passes as tea, to be honest."

I want to slap him. Yes, I remember how awful it is, because I sat drinking it while the emergency doctors and nurses tried to save our son. It was too late, of course, he had technically gone long before, but still, at least they tried. At least they were there.

Unlike Scott.

Funny, I always believed him when he told me he was in a meeting that day. Although I was pissed off for a long time that he couldn't even gaze at his phone during that afternoon, I never doubted where Scott was. I doubt him now though. I doubt every single thing that has ever happened in our marriage.

And that realisation shatters me.

The hours after Scott arrives home pass in a blur. There are so many lies. So many stories that he must have concocted on his way back from Cromer. There is talk about the tests his mother had to go through, the tears from his father, even the kind of snacks available in the vending machine. It takes every bit of my strength not to explode and tell him that I know what he's been up to.

But that's also the reason why I can't explode, because I don't know everything. Until then, I need to stay quiet. Yes, I could shout and scream and tell him that I know his parents are deceased, and that he spent last night with another woman in Cromer, but the logical side of myself stops me. I know that if I do all of that stuff, he'll deny it – or at least he'll deny what he can get away with – and I'll end up more confused than I am already. No, jumping in will not help me now. I need to bide my time, gather as much information as I can, and then hit him with it.

Literally.

While Scott catches up with work emails, I sit on my bed and stare at the photograph on my phone. The blonde petite woman with the wide smile. The hands as they hold each other. My husband, laughing in the company of somebody who isn't me, on our twenty-fifth wedding anniversary.

And it destroys me.

It absolutely destroys me.

This woman is much younger than me. She must be in her thirties, maybe mid-thirties at the most, but possibly younger. I'm fifty-four. I have wrinkles under my eyes, and my hair is thinner than it once was. The skin on my neck is crepe and I no longer wear low-cut dresses, because as much as I work out, my breasts are not what (or where) they once were. They definitely won't be like those modelled by the woman in the photo.

And I hate my body for that.

I hate myself for that.

Every inch of myself.

I force myself to stare at the photo, at every little detail of it. The back of my head throbs, and I cover my mouth with my pillow to try and soften the sounds of my crying. I dry-heave, I choke, and I let out a silent scream that can be heard by nobody but my demons.

My son is gone.

My marriage is wrecked.

I am wrecked.

I'll never be the same again.

By the time Scott slides into bed beside me, I'm under the covers, pretending to be asleep. In reality, my eyes are open wide, and I spend the next hour watching the outline of my husband as he breathes next to me. The night before, he was lying next to somebody else, and I despise the feeling, and I hate him in equal measure. It kills me that I can't speak to him about it. I can't yell, and scream and do all of the things that I want to do, because I can't deal with the lies in this moment. I can't let him have an exit from the conversation, the tales, and ultimately our marriage.

So instead, I get out of bed, drag myself to the bathroom, and vomit into the toilet.

The next day my eyes are on fire. I get up early, throw on my robe and then head to the kitchen. Scott is crunching cornflakes into a bowl. He's had this habit since the time we met – he'll fill the bowl halfway with cornflakes, pour in the milk, and then crunch it all into a soggy mixture. The very sight of it makes me want to heave again.

"Good morning," he says. "How's the headache?"

"Still going strong."

"Are there any paracetamol in the cupboard?" Scott doesn't wait for an answer. Instead, he reaches around me, opens the door, and brings out an unopened box. "There you go. Don't have them on an empty stomach though."

I take the box, but I have no intention of taking a tablet. The masochist inside wants me to feel the pain. Every part of it.

Scott looks at his watch, and takes a breath.

"Right, I need to get to work. I'm working from home though, so we can go out for lunch if you like?"

No, no, we cannot go out for lunch, you cheating, lying, manipulative bastard.

The words stick in my mind, as he kisses my forehead, grabs his bowl and heads up to the spare room. I wipe his kiss off. Who wants an adulterer's kiss on their forehead? Nobody.

Breakfast is not an option for me today, so instead I make some tea with lemon, and then I head to my desk to do some Babbage work. Given that I didn't sleep at all last night, work is the last thing I want to do, but I am so behind in my correspondence that I know questions will be asked if I don't.

I rub my eyes, take a big gulp of tea and open my first email. It's from Sam.

```
Hey Olivia, I didn't hear anything from
you yesterday. Are you okay? If you
could get me the Dave Holmes manuscript
as soon as you can, I'd be grateful. Oh,
and also, I need to know the status of
Geoff's photos for his next book. It
goes to press in two weeks. Thanks.
```

I groan. Geoff is another non-author who has attempted to write a non-fiction A-Z book of every alien mentioned or featured in every Hollywood movie from the silents to the present day. The book is a good seven hundred A4 pages, and I can guarantee that it will sell five copies – to himself. However, Sam is passionate about the project and wants it out as soon as possible. Why, I have no idea.

Underneath Sam's email there is one from Geoff himself, entitled *Pics*. I am hesitant to open it, because Geoff is an argumentative soul who doesn't seem to understand the smallest query or suggestion. Last week I told him that the photos needed to be three hundred DPI at least, and he assured me they were. Unfortunately, when I received them, not only were the pictures a tiny seventy-eight DPI, but Geoff hadn't scanned them. Instead, he had taped the pics onto his bathroom wall, and had taken photos of them at a weird angle, showing not only the tape, but his blue-and-white bathroom tiles, complete with etchings of anchors and fish.

It had taken three days of coaching to get Geoff to understand why we need high-resolution photos for the book, and now here they are… one hundred DPI, which Geoff assures me is the highest they can possibly go. I can't give it another moment of my time, even if I wanted to. I've had enough of Geoff, and his attitude, and his bathroom, so instead of getting into another discussion, I press the forward button, and send them off to Sam, with the assurance that it's this quality or nothing. Whether the photos get into the book is anyone's guess, but I'm past caring. I'm past caring about everything.

As I gaze out of the window and contemplate turning off my computer, I can hear Scott in the next room, taking a Teams call. Moments later, he arrives at my door.

"Where would you like to go for lunch?" he asks.

"I can't. I think I might be coming down with something. I'd hate you to catch it… Especially since I'm sure you'll be spending a lot of time with your parents this week."

I want to see him squirm.

"My parents? Yes, yes, I suppose I will. Well, it's a shame about lunch, but let me know if you change your mind."

He blows me a kiss and heads off into his office, seemingly without a care in the world. I remain at my desk, wondering what is wrong with me, and why my husband has found comfort in another woman just days ago, another one ten years ago, and then the one that started it all – Gabby Haine.

I pull out my notebook, and stare at her married name. Gabby Clarkson. I click on Facebook and search again, but there's no one who looks remotely like her. I play with the pen, and draw doodles all over my notebook. How can it be that I have never been able to find this woman on social media, no matter what her name is? And then a thought occurs to me. I might not be able to find her, but maybe her husband will be a totally different matter. I type his name into the search bar, and the first Robert Clarkson who comes up, lives in the nearby town of Salt. Salt is a fairly large town in Norfolk, which is surrounded by a large, imposing forest. We've been through there many, many times, and in fact I took Charlie there once for a rugby tournament.

I click on Robert Clarkson's profile, and the first thing I see is his bio – *Spending the years rebuilding my life after a painful divorce. I'll never again let my ex-wife torture me the way she did when we were together.* Crikey, that's dramatic, even for my standards. I can't stand people who pin things like that on their Facebook page, but in this instance I'm quite intrigued, especially if it turns out that the ex in question is Gabby.

His friends list is locked, but he does have a photograph of himself that has a load of likes and comments. I scan all of them, and my eyes pop when I see the name Veronica Haine. Could she be related to Gabby? I click on her page to find out, and there on her friends list, after decades of searching, is a thumbnail photo of someone who looks familiar. Gabby Lawrence, it says her name is.

I can't click onto her profile quick enough, and when I do, there she is. Her long, red hair has been cut to her shoulders, and is a much lighter shade with lots of pink highlights, giving it a strawberry-blonde look. But she's undeniably the same woman. Same bulbous nose, same thin-lipped mouth, same everything, but the wrinkles are new of course, and she's heavier than when Scott dated her. But then again aren't we all? When I visualise her in the 1990s, I see her wearing skinny jeans, and glittery tops, but now she's wearing a blue flowery dress that reminds me of the sort of thing my mum would wear, and a thin, pink headband. Her bio is as cringy as her ex's.

I am who I always have been. I will always be me. Every inch of me, is me.

Cringe, and barely makes sense, but in spite of that, I've found her. After all these years, I've found Gabby Haine. I can't believe it, and my shoulders and forearms tingle from the shock.

I crane my neck to make sure that Scott isn't coming, and then I scroll her page, taking in each and every post. While most of it is private (including her friends list), there are a few snippets of her life available. For instance, her favourite television programmes include the TV show *This Morning, The Apprentice* and *Game of Thrones*. A strange combination, but who am I to judge? She has a cat called Bambi, but no sign of any children. Her favourite place to go on holiday is Malta, and her drink of choice is vodka and Coke. There is a large photo of a basket of pink wool, with the caption, *Beautiful. Could literally curl up and go to sleep on this stuff.*

What?

There are quite a few other public profile photos that have garnered comments and likes from her friends. I search through each one, making sure that my husband hasn't had any kind of interaction with her. He hasn't – at least publicly – and for that I am grateful.

There isn't a great deal of in-depth information to be gained from her Facebook page, but in addition to already knowing that she divorced Robert Clarkson – and seems to have broken his heart – I gather that another marriage, presumably to the Mr Lawrence who gave her a new surname, has also ended. She doesn't address the situation with a public post, but a comment on one of her profile photos from someone called Carla Smith, confirms it.

Sorry to hear about your separation. You look fabulous though, hun. Doesn't know what he's missing!

Gabby has liked the comment, and replied.

Thanks babe. It's a long road. Not sure if I'll ever be happy again, but I'm getting there.

Bless you. Take it day by day, he doesn't deserve you, Carla has written, and Gabby has liked it.

My head is dizzy. So, it looks like her husband left her, and she has been hurt by the whole thing. What a shame, but welcome to karma, Gabby. How does it feel? I hope it's the worst pain you've ever experienced in the whole of your life.

So, that's that. I've found Gabby Haine. At last, after three decades of wondering what the hell happened to her. I can't believe I've finally done it. Especially today, when I'm struggling to work out what on earth has happened to my life.

The funny thing is, she looks like a normal, everyday, basic – somewhat vanilla – woman. I guess over the years my vision of her has become so exaggerated that in my head she might as well be an actor on the big screen. Everything about her is bigger in my mind. I don't mean bigger in weight, just in persona, or in aura, or something. Like, she could be one hundred feet tall and I wouldn't be at all surprised. But instead, her Facebook page shows her as a middle-aged woman, twice divorced, with wrinkles and odd clothes choices, like the rest of us. She's a human being, and that's always been a strange thing for me to comprehend.

I hear a noise from the other room, and click out of Facebook and back into Word. I can hear Scott going into the bathroom, but when he's finished, he doesn't come into my study like he normally does. Instead, he goes straight back to his desk, and two minutes later I hear him on a work call.

The autumn sun is bright in my study this morning, and casts a blinding shadow across my laptop. Before I do any more research, I pull the curtains behind me, and as I do, my computer beeps. It is an email from Sam. I presume that it's going to be a complaint about Geoff's photos, but I'm wrong.

Hi Olivia. Listen, this is a bit of an odd one, but this morning I've received an anonymous email from our website. There's no name, and no contact details, so I would normally delete, but this message is a little weird. I'm not sure how to explain it to you, so I've taken a screenshot of it and attached it to this email. Don't know what else to say about it, so hopefully you can shed some light? Thanks. Sam.

An anonymous email from the website? I have no idea why that has anything to do with me. I don't do any work on the website, nor am I part of the customer services team. Intrigued, I click on the photo, and up comes the message:

Dear Babbage Books, I am writing to make you aware that one of your employees is bad-mouthing your company on Facebook. Her name is Olivia Collins. I wouldn't normally send a message like this, but thought you should know that someone who is supposed to be a devoted member of your team is actually anything but.

I stare at the message, and every muscle in my face contracts. What the hell is this? I am completely confused and have no idea what this person is talking about, nor how they even know I'm working at Babbage Books. And furthermore, when and where did I slag off the company? I never mention them, apart from when I'm posting new books on the official company Facebook page, and that's done from a second account. I don't ever share the posts under my main account, because quite frankly I'm not proud of the books Babbage publishes, it's as simple as that.

My eyes burn, reading and rereading the message. Who would do this? And why? It makes absolutely no sense to me. No sense at all.

"Oh, you look serious. Everything okay?"

Scott stands in the doorway of my study, one elbow on the door frame, and his head tilted to one side. God, doesn't he have a job to do? He's the last person I'm going to share this weird information with, so I nod, and smile as broadly as I can. The muscles in my jaw ache. Everything aches.

"Just some more crap from Sam."

"The usual then." He laughs.

"Yep, the usual."

"You want a cuppa? I'm about to put the kettle on."

"That would be great. Thanks."

"No problem," he says. "You sure you're okay? You look a bit agitated."

Oh, fuck off, I scream in my head. *Leave me the fuck alone.*

But instead of saying that, I rub the back of my neck, and groan.

"I've got a bit of neck ache. Probably another effect of this virus."

"Well, if you don't feel better soon, get yourself off the

laptop and into bed. No use wearing yourself out. I'll bring you some more paracetamol with your tea."

Accepting a cup of tea from my cheating husband is the last thing I want to do, but if I had turned him down, there would have been ten minutes of questions concerning my welfare, and whether I'm hydrated enough. It's better to say yes and send him on his way. Besides, after the shock of the anonymous email, coupled with finally finding Gabby on Facebook, my mouth is dry, and I could do with a drink.

I am one hundred per cent sure that the message to Sam is completely made up, unless I have been posting rude shit about the company without my knowledge. I shake my head. No, that's a ridiculous thought. I'm stressed and I am heartbroken, but I'm not a nutcase. Not in that way, anyway. But how did this person know that I work at Babbage? And what was the incentive for making up lies about me?

I lean my head against my hands. I'm warm, and clammy, and my skin is in desperate need of some moisturiser. Maybe I really am coming down with something. I wouldn't be surprised, after the past week. It's bizarre that just five days ago I was completely unaware of anything wrong with my life. Apart from not having Charlie anymore, of course. In that regard, there will always be something that is wrong with my life. Always.

But the rest of it was okay.

I reply to Sam's email.

```
Hi Sam. I'm completely at a loss as to
why you received this bizarre message. I
can assure you that I haven't said a
word about the company to anyone online
at all. I have lived too much of a life
to not know that criticising your
workplace online is a slippery (and
```

crazy) slope. I don't know what this
person's intentions were when they wrote
the message, and how they would know I
worked for you. The only people who know
that are friends and family, all of whom
would never make up such nonsense. Not
in a million years. I hope this helps,
and can only apologise for the strange
inconvenience this may have caused.

I send the message, and two minutes later I receive a reply.

Thanks for this. Don't worry about it.
It could be a disgruntled author, or
someone who has seen your name on the
website and thought they'd play a game.
I haven't seen the comments myself — did
a quick search but couldn't see anything
— so the whole thing could be
fabricated. Either way, let's forget it
and get on with the day. Thanks. Sam.

The idea that it could have been an angry author is a possibility, though I have to say that in spite of my frustration with most of them, I'm always kind, and helpful and not at all rude. I'm certainly not rude enough to warrant a terrible email written to the bloody owner of the company! And what does Sam mean, they could have seen my name on the website? Since when? Last time I looked on the site, there were no contact details listed at all, but I do know that Sam has recently hired an IT guy to work on some new features...

Oh God.

I bring up the site, and sure enough, at the top-left corner is a new list of links... About Us... Our Books... Publish with Us... and Our Team. Our Team? I open the page and in front of me is a photo of Sam, wearing an alien T-shirt, and holding a pile of Babbage books. Underneath is a short bio, telling the tale of how his love for sci-fi and books combined and developed into the formation of the company.

I scroll, and I'm greeted with photos of the editors, the proofreader, and the secretary. Finally, at the bottom of it all, there is a black-and-white photo of me, sitting at my desk. I immediately recognise it as an author photograph that was taken to accompany my last published book. Whether or not Sam cleared copyright for it is a mystery, and not my concern. Under the photo is a bio that Sam must have put together himself:

Olivia Collins is our latest team member, and the person who deals with all of our authors and their books. She has had various books published in the past, and lives in Norfolk, England.

As far as I'm aware, this website listing is the only place I'm mentioned as an employee (or hired help) for Babbage Books, but how would someone find me unless they were on the page?

It isn't until I come off the website that I realise.

Google.

I search for my own name and up comes many listings for the books I've written, but there, about six entries down, is a link to the Babbage Books website, and in particular, the page with my name and photograph all over it.

Shit.

But who would hate me enough to contact my boss with a load of crap about stuff I had allegedly said? Who would make up such lies to hurt me? It makes zero sense.

Unless...

Unless it is the woman who was spotted with Scott at the Regency. The other woman. The side chick. The whore who is currently screwing my husband. There is a distinct possibility that she is the one behind this, and although I have no way of knowing for sure, I do know that if and when I find out, I won't take it quietly. Sleeping with my husband is bad enough, but going after my job? That is diabolical. In fact, it's positively evil.

CHAPTER TEN

"Where's Scott tonight then?" Lauren sits opposite me in the living room as we both nurse large mugs of tea. I had no intention of inviting her over, but she bombarded me with so many messages throughout the day that I felt obliged to. More for her mental health than mine.

"He's at a work do. His company are up for some award or other."

Lauren shakes her head.

"Were you invited?"

"Yes, but I told him I wasn't going. I couldn't face it. For all I know, his mistress might be there. After all, it wouldn't be the first time he was involved with someone he met through work."

"True."

My friend takes another look at the email I printed out from Sam. Her eyes flit over each and every word, and then she nods.

"You're right about this email," she says. "This looks like the work of someone who knows you. Or at least someone who knows of you. There's a vague possibility that it could be a crazed author, but if it is from the latest Regency woman, that worries me. She could be trying to destroy you, to make way for her."

Bile rises in my throat, but since I've barely eaten anything all day, it goes no further.

"Don't worry about that," I say. "After the Gabby Haine incident, I've always said that I'll never fight for Scott again. If someone else wants to wash his underpants, and put the toilet seat down after he's been in there, then they'll be welcome to it."

Lauren nods, and we sit in silence for a moment. She suspects that I'm lying, but she is wrong. I told Scott when I took him back in 1993 that if he ever did anything to hurt me in the future, he'd never see me again, and I've always taken that stance. Yes, we have had ridiculous arguments in the past, and times when I wondered if we'd ever get through, but I dismiss that as normal, everyday couple problems. As long as there was no other woman involved, I was always prepared to hold on and work for my marriage. Even when Charlie died, and we went through the bleakest time of our entire lives. Even then I held on – we both held on – but now that there have been lies, and deceit, and the stench of not one but two extra-marital affairs, I will hold on no longer.

Or at least I'll hold on only until I'm ready to leave.

"Oh, talking of Gabby Haine... Look what I found this morning." I open Facebook, click on Gabby's profile and hand the phone to Lauren. She stares at the page for a moment, lifts her glasses to see better, and then chuckles.

"Bloody hell! It's her, isn't it? You've found her at last. Crikey, how did you do it?"

"It's a long story, but let's just say it took a bit of investigating."

"Wow, there's a bit of Miss Marple in you."

Lauren scrolls through Gabby's page, her eyes wide. She has only ever seen Gabby a couple of times, and that was after Scott had left me for her. Lauren told me at the time that while she hadn't spoken to the woman in question, she had been sure to give her the dirtiest look she could muster.

"Be careful not to accidentally like anything," I say. "The last thing I want is for Gabby to know that I've found her."

"I'm being careful," Lauren says. "Wow, apart from the hair, she hasn't changed much, has she? She's giving off Live, Love, Laugh vibes with that bio though."

She hands me the phone.

"Don't you want to look at the rest of her posts? I couldn't stop looking when I found them."

Lauren laughs.

"You're okay. I'm intrigued that you've found her, but I think the flowery profile pic and bizarre bio are enough for today. Besides, we've got more important things to talk about. Like what the fuck your husband has been up to in recent years, not over thirty years ago."

"True." I know where Lauren's coming from, but at the same time I thought she'd be more interested. I mean, it's all kind of related, isn't it? The lies, the stories, the obsessions. It all runs into each other.

Or maybe it only runs into each other in my fragile head.

"I wish you had come over last night." Lauren's voice interrupts my thoughts. "All of this could have been over by now."

I shake my head.

"I can't do that. I need to know exactly what's going on. I need to do some research both for myself and for any divorce proceedings down the road."

She shoots forward in her chair.

"Divorce? Do you think you'll actually divorce? I never thought it would get that far."

If words were knives, Lauren's would go straight through my heart.

"You're suggesting I don't? You of all people? Didn't you divorce Michael as soon as you found out that he was cheating? How is this any different? In fact, this could be worse, since it's not just this indiscretion we're talking about, is it?"

"What do you mean?"

"Scott could have cheated ten years ago too. Don't let the discovery of this Regency Hotel woman make you forget the other one from a decade ago."

She takes a sip of tea, and then lets out a sigh.

"Yes, that's true. Gosh, they should name a room after him, he's given them so much business."

"That's not funny."

Lauren laughs, and rubs her forehead.

"I'm sorry, I know it's not funny. I'm trying to make things a little lighter, though God knows it's hard... But about Michael, I suspected that he was cheating on me for years before I left, but I never said anything about it because I hoped that I was wrong."

"You weren't though, and that's my point. You got the information you needed and then you left. Now I have to do the same."

The words throttle me. I know that I have to leave. I know that I cannot stay with someone who – it appears – has been cheating on me repeatedly over the years, and even kept the news of his parents' death from me, so he could carry on cheating. It's sick. He's sick, and I'd be sick too if I let that behaviour carry on.

"But anyway," Lauren says. "This isn't about Michael and me. This is about you, and your relationship has always been stronger than mine."

"I'm not sure about that."

"It's true," Lauren says. "And maybe I'm hesitant about you leaving because it's all so unbelievable. I mean, after everything you've been through together, I thought that you and Scott would be happy forever. Call me naïve, but even when we were outside the house, and that neighbour woman was going on about how Scott's parents are dead, I still thought she must be getting mixed up. Even today, a part of me thought that it must all be a huge mistake. But that obituary... I can't... I just can't understand or deny even a bit of it."

I drain the rest of my tea. It makes me gag, but I force myself because I know that in order to get through this, I still need to drink. Food I can cut down on – and heaven knows I don't have an appetite anyway – but drinking is another thing altogether. The last thing I want is to end up dehydrated.

"How do you think I feel?" I ask. "I have to sit here and listen to Scott prattle on about how ill his mum is, all the time knowing that they have both passed. Not only that, but I must be the thickest person on earth for not suspecting he could do this to me."

Lauren waves me away.

"I'm not being funny, but presuming that your husband would not hide the death of his parents is not being thick. It's being normal! How the hell is anyone supposed to figure that shit out? It makes no sense at all. And I know it took me a few years to forgive him for the way he treated you back in the 1990s, but since then I've come to think that he's maybe, possibly one of the good guys."

"And now?"

"And now I think he must be a whack-job. Or a narcissist. Or both."

I play with the buttons on my blouse. They're smooth and round, and remind me of when I was little, and my mum would dress me in the mornings. Back then I was loved and cared for, and lucky. I'm not so lucky anymore.

"What kind of wife doesn't know that her husband's parents have died?" I ask. "I should have gone to visit them regularly. I should have taken the slightest bit of interest in their lives. If I had, Scott would never have been able to keep their death from me. I feel like an utter fool."

"You need to stop obsessing about it," Lauren says. "Very few people like their in-laws, and yours weren't the most likeable of people. It takes nerve to cut ties with family members you don't like. It's not your fault your husband is an undercover nutcase."

"Do you think she's prettier than me?"

"Who? Your mother-in-law?"

"No! Scott's other woman. The latest Regency woman."

Lauren's nose wrinkles, and the rest of her face crumples.

"Oh please! Of course she isn't. They never are! Look at the skank Michael cheated with. She looked like a crackhead who'd been dragged through a sewer. But you shouldn't even be asking yourself this question. Pretty or not, this is Scott's fault, not yours. You are perfect as you are, and don't you forget it!"

She wags her finger at me, and then picks at the side of her nails. A habit she's had since school, and one that I've realised gets worse when she is stressed.

"Stop picking your nails."

Lauren shakes her hands.

"Can't help it. It's my coping mechanism." She reaches forward, touches my knee, and I burst into tears. "Oh, girl, just let it out. Let it all out, and then leave. Leave, leave, leave."

I nod, and assure my friend that the moment I have enough evidence filed away, I will. But I can't do anything until that point, whether I want to or not.

When Scott gets in, it's 10.30pm. He gives me a rundown of the wonderful night he's had, and shows me a photo on his phone of the team receiving an award. I pretend to be admiring the celebrations, but really I'm scouring the picture for anyone who looks as though she might be screwing my husband. After a couple of seconds, he takes his phone back, and I can't help but wonder if that's because he's scared of receiving a notification from his mistress, while I've got his phone.

"I'm going to make a cup of tea," he says. "And then do you fancy an early night?"

I stifle a laugh, not because it's funny, but because of the idiocy of having the nerve to still sleep with your partner when you've got someone else on the go. I know this happens to many people – including men – but it still baffles me.

"Not tonight," I say. "I'll have a cup of tea though."

He nods and heads into the kitchen, while I contemplate the logistics of ever sleeping with him again. In truth, the whole subject gives me chills. When Scott left me for Gabby Haine, I had to get an STD test, just in case 'fooling around' meant that he had slept with her before we broke up. I couldn't get a quick appointment at my GP, so I went to a private clinic, where the woman asked me a hundred invasive questions, and then subjected me to even more invasive examinations. As I lay on that cold, plastic bed, with a tiny blanket over my stomach, and my knickers and trousers on a nearby chair, tears streamed over my face and into my hair. The nurse comforted me, and told me that she knew exactly what I was going through. I didn't ask her how though. My own pain was enough. I couldn't take on somebody else's too. That test was the most humiliating thing I had ever gone through, and not one part of it was my fault.

And now I realise that in spite of being married for twenty-five years, I'll have to repeat that test, repeat those questions, and know once again that none of it is my doing. So, no, Scott, no, I do not want an early night with you. Not tonight, not this week, not ever.

But thank you for asking.

It is 11.36pm, Scott has long since gone to bed, and I suddenly remember that I still have his friends list that I printed from Facebook. None of the so-called friends were of any use to me while trying to find the elusive Debbie, but it now occurs to me that they could perhaps help in my quest to find the woman he was with at the Regency the other night.

I had hidden my research away in the bottom drawer of my desk, and now I quietly slide it open and retrieve the folder. It's not what you'd call substantial, but contains the friends printout, the ten-year-old Regency card, and the notes of everything I've found out about Gabby Haine. Not that she's the person I need to concentrate on at the moment, but the fact that I've discovered her Facebook is huge, and you never know what I might find out in the future. But for tonight I put my notes on her aside.

The list of names stares up at me, most scrubbed off because they were irrelevant to my investigation into Debbie. The hikers, the fossil hunters, the random people he knew when he was a teenager, they're all gone. I can dismiss all of those in my new research, too, because I'm presuming that they have no link to the latest woman either. Even the questionable women I looked at last time can be scored off because none of them look remotely like the woman I'm looking for tonight. However, there are five other accounts that I hadn't deleted previously because I was unable to dismiss them straight away. All but one have objects or animals as their profile pics, and not much additional information, but I begin going through every one, trying to find something – anything – that could lead me to the latest Regency woman.

First, I click on Joanne Miller. Her profile pic is a garden, showing a lilac rose with a ladybird balanced on the petals. I didn't see anything of use last time I looked her up and this time it is even worse, since I am now viewing her under my own – non-friend – page, rather than Scott's. Her profile is locked like some kind of secret service agent, and her friends list is private, so there's not much else for me to look at with her. I'm pretty sure she's not the woman in the Regency Hotel, however, as looking closer, the background of her profile photo looks to be of a wooden American house. I come out and go into the next one on the list: Matilda Green.

I didn't dismiss Matilda's account last time, because once again she didn't have a profile pic, and also there were some rather interesting pictures of her in a bathing suit, which Scott had liked. Not that there's anything wrong with that, I guess, except when you suspect that your husband has had an affair with her. Then you have a problem. Trouble is that once again, I can't see anything further on her profile because now I'm viewing her as a stranger, rather than a friend. I lay my head onto my hands. Damn, this is hopeless, and it's so late that I could fall asleep right here at my desk.

I look through the next two profiles with as much luck, and then finally, I search for Suzanne Abbott, the last woman on my list. Strangely, her actual page doesn't come up at first. Instead, a list of posts related to women with her name are scattered on the screen in front of me. I begin to scroll, and my mouth falls open when I get to the fourth entry. There is a photograph from 2022, showing an older lady hugging a younger, blonde woman.

The same blonde woman from the photo Joseph sent to me.

The same blonde woman who was holding hands with my husband just a day ago.

My fingers shake so much that I can hardly enlarge the photo, but with blood ringing in my ears, I manage to do it. The blonde woman is tagged in the photo as Suzanne Abbott, and according to the description, it was taken at a party for 'Aunty Margaret', who seems to be the older woman with her. There are three comments:

Sarah MacMillan: *Aww, beautiful pic. Hope you're both keeping well. Haven't seen you in ages!*

Suzanne Abbott: *Thanks, Sarah. We had a great time. Hope you're doing well, hun.*

I don't know who the 'we' is that Suzanne is referring to. Her husband? Or is it my husband?

It can't be.

And yet, it very well might be.

I click on her name, and it takes me to Suzanne's actual Facebook page. There is a short bio – *Here to be happy. Here to love. Here to be me.* Ugh, she's another Gabby Haine type, with her stupid Live, Love, Laugh bio vibe. I scroll and click through to the About Suzanne page, and discover that she was born in 1990. Numbers flit around in my mind, and I realise that makes her thirty-four. I go onto her most recent photo, and examine every inch of her face. Call it good genes, good make-up or good filters, but either way, the photo makes her look a good five years younger than she is. How can she look so young? Well, maybe it's because she's a solid twenty years younger than me.

I say it out loud, with feeling.

"She's twenty years younger than me. Twenty years! Two decades!"

Before I can stop myself, I burst into tears. Strong, violent tears. I have always been seconds away from crying at any given point, but recently it's been even worse. I cannot stop the water from pouring out of my eyes, and as my chest heaves, I grab the bin underneath my desk, and throw up the packet of crisps I had forced myself to eat earlier. Then I head to the living room so that Scott doesn't hear my hysteria.

This woman. This blonde, petite young woman. Is she sleeping with my husband, or was it a total coincidence and huge misunderstanding that she was at the Regency with him a day ago? Surely, it's all a coincidence. Surely it is!

And yet... And yet I know that there are no coincidences. Not really, and not in this instance. My jaw shakes, and I hug my stomach, willing myself to remain calm. But no matter how many times I try to tell myself that it's okay, I can't stop weeping, because I know that it's not all okay, and perhaps it never has been.

I lift my head and silently scream into the empty room. Our living room that was once full of a child's laughter, of Uno, of *Balamory* DVDs and The Wiggles CDs. This room where Scott and I played music and danced after Charlie had gone to bed. Where we made love sometimes, and laughed often. This room which is now empty of everything except distress, and deceit, and lies. So many lies.

Hands shaking, I pick up the phone and message Lauren. I could try and ring her, but I know there's no way I'd ever get the words out. Not tonight.

> Meet me for breakfast tomorrow morning. I think I've found the latest woman.

A reply comes back straight away.

> The woman from the Regency? Tell me now!

> No, I'll let you know tomorrow.

Wow. Can't wait!

I send her a love heart and then turn off my phone.

———

Lauren's favourite café is called the Beany Bean, which is exactly halfway between her house and mine. It wasn't always my favourite, but the distance had something going for it, so I quickly got used to it. It's Saturday, and while I don't normally do any Babbage Books work at the weekend, I'm aware that I'm so behind that I'll have to do some catching up when I get home.

It's at times like this that I miss my writing career even more than I normally do. I used to frequently write on a Saturday, but spending time with my characters never felt like work, and I loved getting a few hours in. Now I can't think of anything worse than opening my laptop on my day off, but I don't have any choice today. I park up and wait for Lauren, and when she appears, we briefly hug and then walk silently into the building. No words asked. No words given. All will be revealed when we sit down.

Unfortunately, it's 9.30am, and the café is full of parents and children, making the most of a lazy day.

"Ugh, we might be unlucky here," Lauren says.

I nod, but my head automatically goes back to my darling son, and how I was once one of those parents. I used to love taking him into coffee shops when he was little. He'd sit with his tiny cup of hot (warm) chocolate, and a gingerbread man, and I'd drink my tea and laugh as I wiped the cream off his top lip. Those were the days. I always knew I'd miss them when he grew up, but I never knew that he never would grow up, and I would lose those days anyway.

"Hey, ladies!" Betty, the owner of Beany Bean, waves to us

from behind the busy counter. "There are some tables in the back room if you can't get one in here. Just go through."

"Thank you," I say, and we push our way through the prams and buggies gathered at the door and into the quiet, carpeted room at the back. It's not normally open at this time of the day, but Betty has seen us regularly since she opened five years ago, and is willing to make an exception.

"No problem," she shouts. "Grab a menu and I'll be through to take your order in a minute."

In comparison to the bedlam of the front room, the back area is a haven. There's nobody in there, except an older gentleman reading his newspaper, and he nods and smiles as we take a seat next to the window. His little Yorkshire terrier sniffs the air and then retreats underneath the table, disappointed that we're not holding any treats.

"So," Lauren says. "What's going on?"

Thirty minutes later, and my heart has been poured all over the table. It spirals around the coffee, uneaten cake, the printouts and the notes I've made about Suzanne Abbott. Lauren sits back in her chair, stares at my phone for the hundredth time, and then picks up the printed photo of the woman at the Regency.

"It's the same woman, isn't it? The same woman who was in the photo. I'm not going insane, am I? It's her!"

Lauren nods.

"Yes, it's definitely her. I know the photo isn't the best quality, but there's no mistaking her. She's even wearing the same boots, or at least it looks like it."

I pick up the photo and then my phone, and examine them both. Lauren is right, if that's not the same footwear, it's definitely the same style.

"I'm so confused," I say, and my friend nods.

"So am I. But let's look at the facts... Her name is Suzanne. She's Scott's Facebook friend, but she makes no reference to him being in her real life, does she?"

Lauren looks at me over the top of her glasses. I shrug.

"I don't know, because stupidly I didn't look through every profile when I was logged into his actual Facebook account. I printed off the list to check later, not thinking that I wouldn't be able to find out half as much information if I was looking from my account and not his."

"That's unfortunate," she says. "But then again, if – and it's still an if – she is the side chick, I'm not sure she'd have anything on there that would give her – or him – away. Too dangerous."

"And yet, he's quite openly got her on his friends list." I take a sip of coffee, and know that it will give me a sore stomach soon enough, but I need one today. Oh, how I need one today.

"But in his defence," Lauren says, "he also has some fossil hunters and hikers, too, so that doesn't mean much. If anything."

I sigh. Lauren is right, there's no evidence of anything just because a person is on your friends list. Hell, I have some Babbage Books authors on mine, and that's not because I like them or know them in real life. Far from it. Most of them friended me purely because I'd sent them a random email about their book and they'd tracked down my page. I accepted them without any thought, though after the strange email Sam received, I should maybe be more careful.

"I know that a Facebook friend doesn't mean much, but this..." I poke my finger on Suzanne's Regency Hotel photo, "This is something else entirely."

Lauren picks up a piece of chocolate cake, takes a bite and then rubs the corner of her mouth with the back of her finger. She chews for a moment, and swallows.

"So, here's the million-dollar question."

I'm hesitant to know what my friend is going to ask, but I prepare myself anyway.

"Go on."

"Well, you said you were going to wait until you had more information, before confronting Scott." She dabs at the things in front of her. "Do you think that it's now time?"

"I literally have no idea," I say. "I've gone back and forth with that since last night. When he went to give me a kiss this morning, I almost blurted the entire thing out, but I stopped myself, because I didn't want to confront the situation when he was heading out of the door."

We both stare at each other in silence for a couple of seconds.

"Where is he today," she asks.

"Apparently helping his parents choose a new boiler," I reply.

She rolls her eyes, makes a clicking sound with her tongue, and shakes her head.

"You need to talk to Scott," Lauren says. "It's time."

I nod. Lauren grabs hold of my hand, and squeezes.

"Confrontation is a difficult choice," she says, "but in this instance, I think that having a conversation is a good idea. Then you can clear everything up, get some answers, and then move on – in one way or another."

"I feel as though I've wasted my life," I say, and Lauren rubs my arm.

"You didn't waste it, darling. He did."

I take another sip of my coffee, and gaze out of the window. Thirty-six years together, twenty-five years married, most of them happy, and in the flick of an eye, that is all going to explode.

And I am scared to death.

Robbie Williams' *Heavy Entertainment Show* blasts from my car speakers as I pull onto the drive, but Scott's car isn't there. How long does a fake boiler sale take? I have no idea, and I doubt he does either. Should I turn around and pretend I was never here?

My phone pings. A message from Lauren.

> Good luck. Let me know how it goes.
> Love you.

> He's not here.

> Ugh!!!

I go into the house, make a cup of tea, and then settle at my laptop in an attempt to catch up with some Babbage work. I can't face doing anything, but I haven't been online for much of the week, and I know that Sam will question where I've been. I'm already embarrassed since he received that fake message about me slagging off his company, and nothing will get better unless I can convince him that I am still committed to my job. I open my emails, and I'm shocked. There are way more than I was expecting. Fifteen from random authors, and one from Sam. I open his first.

```
Olivia, I know it's Saturday, but if you
can, please hop on Zoom. Thanks. Sam.
```

Shit. The message was sent at 9.30, and now it's 11.57. I shoot him an email.

```
So sorry! My Wi-Fi has been down. I'll
set up a Zoom meeting now.
```

I create a meeting, send Sam the link, and then wait for him to join. Two minutes later, his face appears on the screen. His red hair is sticking up at all kinds of angles, his strawberry-blond eyebrows are lost against his pale skin, and his glasses look far too big for his face. I've never noticed them before. Does he normally wear spectacles, or is this a new thing? He sits far too close to the camera, and his head threatens to pop out of my laptop screen.

"I'm sorry to talk with you on the weekend," he says. "But I'm afraid we need to have another awkward conversation about your work."

I rub my forehead, and heat rises up into my neck. I know I haven't done all of my work this week, but I hadn't thought it would lead to a telling-off so soon.

"I know, I know," I say. "My Wi-Fi was up and down for much of this week, that's why I wasn't able to log on regularly... But I've got a notebook full of stuff to do this afternoon. I don't mind working at the weekend."

I pick up a nearby jotter, and flash it in front of the camera. In reality there is nothing written in there that is any way related to urgent Babbage tasks, but I hope it will satisfy Sam. He shakes his head, and waves as though trying to flick away the notebook.

"It's got nothing to do with Wi-Fi, I'm afraid. I sincerely wish that it did."

"So, what is it then?"

I squeeze my hands under the table. Surely there hasn't been another strange message about my fictional Facebook posts?

"I'm afraid I've had complaints about you, from some of our authors."

My head swirls while processing the sentence. How could any of them complain about me? I'm always perfectly nice to them, even when they're being complete divas.

"I'm confused. How... What kind of complaints?"

"According to a significant number, last night you sent messages via their websites, criticising their books."

"That's absolute nonsense!" I shout. "Why would I choose to message them through their websites, when I've already got their personal email addresses? If I wanted to criticise them – which I never would – I'd surely get in touch that way!"

Sam takes a gulp of something hot from a *Muppets* mug. It looks completely out of place during this conversation.

"I must say, I did wonder that myself. Look, I know we've had a couple of problems recently, but I do think you're a good worker, and you know a bit about the industry..."

"I know a lot about the industry," I say, my voice barely a whisper.

I can't stop my face from falling. Being an author for all those years, I know more than he'll ever know about publishing. At least I sold copies of my books!

"Yes, you know a lot," he says, "and when you're with me, you do a great job. But these messages..." He thumbs through some printouts on his desk, which I presume are the emails in question. "These messages are awful, and obviously designed to hurt."

"But not by me!" I snap. "I don't want to hurt anyone!"

"That's what I'm saying. I don't believe that you've sent these messages. It doesn't make any sense that you'd do that. So, I must ask. Do you know anyone who would want to ruin your career? Anyone who would send these messages pretending to be you?"

I slump into my chair, and my head spins. I have a roll-on lavender temple oil on my desk, and I rub some on my forehead. A line forms in the middle of Sam's face. I need to stay calm.

"There's nobody who would want to ruin my career," I say. "I'm as confused as you are." In truth, my husband's other woman is probably more than capable of doing that, but I can't help but wonder why would she want to target me? I've done nothing to her at all. I'm the one who should be trying to ruin her life, not the other way round.

"Okay." Sam nods, and manages a smile. "Once again, let's forget about this conversation. I believe you're telling the truth, so let's leave it at that. I'll tell the authors that you've been hacked, or imitated or something. Have a good afternoon."

And with that, my boss hangs up, leaving me staring at the empty Zoom screen.

I spend the next couple of hours working on Babbage stuff, and fuming that someone is trying to jeopardise my whole life. Could it be this other woman? Suzanne? Who knows. I'll probably never know, but it infuriates me all the same. How dare they? How fucking dare they?!

When I'm finished my work, Scott still hasn't come home, so I take some fresh flowers to the cemetery and tell Charlie about my day. Some may say that I'm stupid to talk to my dead son the way I do, but I couldn't care less. His spirit is in his bedroom, his body is in the cemetery, and I'm in both places, making sure that we still have a connection, that he can still feel his mother's love, even if he can't be with me physically anymore.

The wind blows around Charlie's headstone and makes it hard for me to empty and refill the little vase. As my hair whips into my eyes, I grab a bobble from my pocket, and tie it back into a ponytail. It's then that I hear a voice.

"Olivia? Olivia? Hey, I thought it was you!"

I turn and there is Joseph from the Regency Hotel. He's dressed all in black and is clutching a single rose.

"Joseph? You're a long way from home. What are you doing here?"

He comes up beside me, gazes at Charlie's headstone and then gives a tiny smile.

"My great aunt died, so the whole family has come to pay our respects." He signals over to a group of people at the other end of the row. All are mingling, talking, exchanging stories, tears and grief.

Just as we did, ten years ago, when Charlie passed.

"I'm so sorry to hear that," I say. "Was she an old lady?"

"Yeah, ninety-six. To be honest, I only ever used to see her at Christmas, but I wanted to come anyway. I need to keep an eye on all those distant cousins who are hoping for a piece of her inheritance." He looks over at the group, and shakes his head. "Vultures, the lot of them... Anyway, how was the rest of your week? Any news on the husband affair thing?"

I can't help but laugh. My world is imploding, but hearing a youngster refer to it casually as a husband affair thing, is pretty funny.

"Yeah, I think that there's definitely something going on."

"Sorry about that," he says. "Did that photo help you? I wasn't sure whether to tell you about seeing him. Didn't know if it would make the situation better or worse."

The wind riles up again, and I hold tightly to the cellophane from Charlie's flowers, frightened that it will be whipped up and into the faces of the mourners down the row.

"It helped me a lot actually. I was able to uncover at least one other lie, and I identified the woman through Facebook because of the photo. Just call me Poirot."

"Who's that?" Joseph screws up his face, completely oblivious.

"Never mind," I say. "So, how are you? You haven't seen my husband again, have you?"

"Not since Thursday, no. But I'll definitely let you know if I do. As I told you before, I've witnessed what affairs can do to a family. It's not good."

One of the mourners shouts over to Joseph, but the words are carried off by the breeze. He waves to her, and turns back to me.

"I'll have to go, but if you need me again, you have my number. In the meantime, I hope you get things sorted out."

"Thank you," I say. "For everything."

He nods, tips his cap, and disappears back into the bosom of his family.

It's time to go home.

CHAPTER ELEVEN

October is turning into the worst month of my life since 2014. September 2014 takes the biscuit in terms of total despair, and I know I'll never experience pain like that again, since I have no more children to lose. But this, this utter betrayal by the man I love and who I thought loved me... Well, it's too much to bear. It's all just too much.

And while I've never been one for conflict, today is different.

This is the first time since Gabby Haine that I have known for sure that Scott was either involved with, or had a crush on another woman. Yes, there have been times during our marriage when he has mentioned a colleague or a new friend or whatever, and my stomach has flipped, in memory of what happened all those years ago. But this is different. Now, he hasn't mentioned this new woman at all, which in a way I have trained him to do. My reaction to him speaking about random women in the past has been noted, and he's not doing that anymore.

Growth.

Growth is good.

For him.

And now, I sit in the darkened living room, waiting for him to come in. It's 6pm and I've texted him several times over the past couple of hours, but he hasn't seen the messages, never mind answered them. It doesn't surprise me. He's either with this Suzanne woman, or he's stuck in traffic somewhere. Or maybe both.

I turn on the television, and flick on the news, but it's so depressing that I switch it off again. Next, I try *Friends*, but it's the bloody episode where Ross sleeps with the Xerox woman, therefore unleashing the whole 'We were on a break' scenario. The same scenario Scott created when he left me for Gabby Haine, only our situation was worse. First of all because this is me, not someone fictional, and secondly because he left me for way more than one evening.

No, I cannot watch this episode of *Friends*, and I cannot obsess about Gabby right now. This evening is all about Suzanne. I go to switch over once again, but then I hear Scott's car in the driveway, and the hairs on my arms prickle. I turn off the telly, breathe in, and the air hits the back of my throat and makes me cough.

"Don't forget to breathe," I whisper to myself. "Don't forget to breathe."

The front door opens, and then I hear Scott's familiar sounds.

"Hello? Anyone in?"

I ignore him, and then thirty seconds later, he appears at the living-room door, switches on the light, and then visibly jumps, throwing his hands up to his chest.

"Jesus! You gave me a fright! Why are you sitting in the dark? Are you okay?"

I can't speak. I can't even look at him. Instead, I stare ahead at the open-curtained window, while he dashes past me to close it. Open curtains on a dark evening are one of Scott's pet peeves.

Woe betide anyone sees inside our living room. God knows what they might find.

"Olivia! What's going on? You're worrying me now."

Again, I say nothing, and it takes a couple more seconds before my husband pauses long enough for me to know that he's seen the coffee table. There I have placed a copy of the photograph of him and Suzanne in the Regency restaurant, along with a printout of her Facebook page. Not that he needs to see a printout of that, as it has barely any information, but it's there for effect, there so that he knows I've found her. While I have no desire to look at him, I make an exception for this discovery. I want to see every emotion etched into his face.

"What's all this?" He runs his fingers over the printout, his face falls, and then he silently picks up the photo. He turns it from front to back, stares at it for a moment, and his mouth falls. What is he thinking? I have no idea, but whatever it is causes his nostrils to flare, his ears to turn red, and a thick, deep line to appear between his eyebrows. From my place on the sofa I notice his hands are shaking. As they should.

I bite the side of my mouth, waiting for the perfect time to speak. I want him to wonder what's going on for a moment more... Let him realise that I'm onto him... Let him experience the fear, the utter, disabling fear of knowing he's been found out.

He crumples the photo in his hand, and drops it onto the table.

"How did you get this picture?" he asks.

"Someone saw you and thought I should know."

"Lauren?"

"No. Someone who works at the hotel."

"What?!"

The moment the words come out of my mouth, I regret it.

That sentence opens up a whole pile of crap that I don't want to go into right now.

"Don't turn this around to be about how I got it!" I snap. "If you hadn't been there, they wouldn't have had a photo to take, would they?"

"Oh God."

Scott throws himself into the sofa, causing me to shoot up out of it. There's no way I'm sitting next to him. Not today. Not any day. How am I still breathing? I've rehearsed this moment in my mind all day, and now I am utterly speechless. What can I say that will help me in any way? Nothing. So instead, I stand as still as a shop dummy, and thrust my hands in the pockets of my jeans, in an effort to stop them shaking.

"How could you do this to me?" I ask.

That's it. After all the rehearsals, and the thoughts, and the fury, that's the only phrase I can manage. Scott threads his fingers together and looks at the floor, avoiding eye contact, as all liars do.

"It's not what it looks like," he says, as he reaches up to touch my arm. I recoil and slap his hand away.

"What the fuck? How? How can you sit there and say that it's not what it looks like! This isn't like when I found your secret Facebook page you know! You can't say it means nothing. Oh, and I see that you're both friends on there by the way. Is that how you first hooked up?"

"No," he says, but offers no further explanation.

"So how did you meet then? Come on, tell me!"

"We're not involved. We're just friends."

"Bullshit!" I shout. "I've fallen for that one before, and I'm not doing it again!"

Scott shakes his head, and folds his arms across his chest.

"You've fallen for it before? When?"

My mouth falls open, and he suddenly realises I'm talking

about Gabby Haine. He looks away and plays with a loose thread on his jumper. I could quite happily pull that loose thread and watch it unravel in the middle of the living room, just as our marriage is doing.

"So... So, are you sleeping with her?"

I flush, and my eyes sting, but I have to know the truth. I have to know.

"No!" he shouts. "We're just..."

"Before you go on and tell me again that you're just good friends, remember that I've seen a photo of you in the Regency Hotel, holding hands just two days ago! So, no lies, Scott. I'm not interested in them! I need to know now. Are you having an affair with this woman?"

He shakes his head.

"Not anymore."

"But you did?"

"Yes."

Heat rises up into my head, and tinnitus rings in my ears. That's it then. Everything I thought was true, actually is. I knew it would be, and yet – and yet – I prayed so hard that it wouldn't be.

Scott stares at the fireplace, the colour glowing onto his skin. I would guess that he was trying to work out what lie to tell next, but honestly, I think even he knows that the jig is up at this point.

"What's her name?" I know already, and it's quite clear to him that I do, since her Facebook page is printed just feet from him, but I have to hear my husband say it.

"Debbie."

Debbie? The name takes me by complete surprise. Debbie is the woman mentioned in the Regency Hotel visitors book ten years ago, and the blonde woman – Suzanne – is the one who got her photo taken with him on Thursday. How does this make sense? It doesn't.

But then again, nothing makes sense anymore. Not one thing.

"Wait. What do you mean, Debbie. Her name is Suzanne!" I stab at the printout of her Facebook profile, while my head scrambles and spins and tries desperately to find a reasonable explanation.

Scott rubs his temples.

"Yes," he says. "Her name is Suzanne, but she goes by the name Debbie."

"Why would she do that?"

"Debbie is her middle name," he says. "She was named after her grandmother, but thinks it's a bit old-fashioned, so she prefers Debbie... Just keeps Suzanne on Facebook because that's what her family knows her as."

I throw my hands up to my ears.

"Oh God, shut up! I don't need to know her whole fucking life story! I'm not her biographer!"

From where I'm standing, I have a clear view of the Regency key card from 2014, which I had abandoned on the mantelpiece shortly before Scott came in. It's upside down, meaning that the words 'Mrs Collins' ring out like church bells. Is that Debbie the same as the one he was just seen with? It can't possibly be. And yet, and yet I can't help thinking that it is.

"I'm not sure that I want an answer to this, but I have to ask a question."

Scott looks at me with his puppy dog eyes. The same ones he looked through when he told me he'd fallen in love with Gabby Haine. Are we about to have the same conversation?

"What do you want to know?"

His voice shakes, and he wrings his hands. He doesn't want to answer, as much as I don't really want to ask.

"How long have you known her?"

Scott shrugs, and flicks his eyes to the side as though he's working it out. In reality, I am sure he knows the exact moment when he met her.

"About ten years," he says. "We met at a work conference in 2014."

Wow, he's not even trying to pretend. My legs buckle underneath me, and I just make it to the chair before they're gone completely.

"Is she... Is she the woman you went to the Regency Hotel with in 2014?"

Scott's cheeks flush bright red, and a bead of saliva glistens at the side of his mouth.

"What do you mean?"

"You were with a woman in the Regency ten years ago, just a couple of months before Charlie passed away. You both booked in, and she identified herself as Mrs Collins. Her real name, however, was Debbie."

"I don't understand." His cheeks are now so red I fear he may explode at any second. He licks his top lip and swallows hard. He knows exactly what I'm talking about.

"Of course you don't understand," I say. "Well, let me refresh your memory." I retrieve the card from the mantel and hand it to him. He studies the front of the card as though he's never seen it before. "Turn it over," I say, and he does.

"Oh."

"Oh, you suddenly remember what it is, or oh shit, how did she find out?"

Scott throws the card onto the table, and I'm suddenly aware that nowhere on that card does it mention the name Debbie. I pray that he doesn't ask how I found that out. Having to explain that I took a train to Cromer, and broke into the hotel basement archives is not on my to-do list today.

"Are you spying on me?" he asks. "And why are you going through my stuff?"

I laugh through my tears. Why do adulterous, sneaky, lying men always turn things around so that you're in the wrong if you find out what they're up to? It's pathetic.

"Bloody hell, the ego on you! No, Scott, I don't make a habit of going through your stuff. I was looking for donations for Lauren's bloody charity sale. You left that little nugget in the pocket of your old favourite jacket."

He runs his fingers through his hair, causing it to stick up at odd angles. Does Debbie make his hair stick up at odd angles too? I shudder. This conversation is killing me.

"So, is the Debbie woman in the photo the same Debbie who signed into the Regency ten years ago? Just tell me. It's too late to make up lies now, and I deserve to know."

Scott nods, and lets out a long, drawn-out sigh.

"Yes, it was Debbie with me at the Regency ten years ago."

"And you slept with her?"

It's a terrible question, but I have to ask it.

"On that occasion?"

"Fuck me! On any occasion!!"

"Yes."

Scott's phone pings, and he takes a quick look, turns it off and places it face down on the table. I know that it's a message from her, but I don't have the strength to confront him about it.

"And you've been sleeping with her for ten years?"

"God no!" Scott shouts the words as though he's mortified that I could ever think such a thing. "Yes, I made a mistake, I had an affair ten years ago, but I swear to you that I haven't done anything intimate with her since."

"Bullshit!"

Scott throws his arms in the air.

"It's the truth! We slept together a handful of times, but I felt awful about the whole thing and I called it off. It should never have happened, and if I could go back in time, I'd probably change it, but I can guarantee you that nothing romantic has happened between us in the past ten years. Not ever!"

"You're a fucking liar!!" I cannot believe the utter bollocks coming out of his mouth.

"I haven't lied to you about anything," he says. "Except this!"

My husband looks at me, his face as motionless as his real feelings. I do not know this man anymore. I'm not sure I ever did.

"I know about your parents!"

Is this the time to bring up the other lie? Probably not, but the words shoot out of my mouth before I can stop them.

"What about my parents?"

"I know they both died in lockdown, and you've been pretending to go and see them ever since. And I know you spent Wednesday night with Suzanne, or Debbie or whatever her name is, because of the photo that you've been staring at."

Scott jumps up from the sofa, and bumps into the coffee table. The photo falls off and flutters to the ground. He stands on it, and then kicks it away with his stockinged feet.

"Jesus Christ!!" He clutches at his cheeks as though he's about to tear the skin off his face. "What, have you hired a detective or something?"

"No, I have not! Anyone can find out anything on the internet, or did you forget? And how evil do you need to be to not tell your wife that your parents have passed? How cold-hearted you must be to hear that news and yet carry on with your life as though nothing has happened. You're a psychopath!"

"Olivia..."

He goes to grab my arms, but I pull away.

"I never told you about my parents because..."

"Because it meant that you could still pretend to go there while really you were going to see this woman. Correct?"

"No, not really."

Not really. What a pathetic, lying man. Not even a man. Not even a shadow of a man. Not anything. I slump forward and lean against the windowsill to steady myself. The bottom fell out of my world when I found the card just six days ago, but now that it's all confirmed, I feel nothing. I'm completely numb.

"Why did you do it?" I ask. "Why did you have an affair? Wasn't I good enough for you?"

Scott tries to grab my hands, and I push him back. The idea of him touching any part of me is nauseating. Truly nauseating.

"Of course you were good enough for me! You still are!"

I burst into laughter. I just can't help myself.

"So why then? Why would you need someone else ten years ago? Why would you want to play around when you had everything you could ever want, with me and with Charlie?"

He shrugs.

"I don't know. It's just something that happened. You were busy with your books, and the rugby runs, and all that stuff, and Debbie paid me some attention and stupidly I went for it."

The words burn a hole deep into my bones. I was too busy? She paid him some attention? This is bullshit.

"Oh my God, this is 1993 all over again!"

Scott's brow furrows.

"What do you mean?"

"When you fell for Gabby Haine, you said it was because I didn't give you any attention, that I was too busy working on my career. She gave you attention and you went for it, and then twenty years later, you did the same thing with someone else! So, you're blaming me! Again! When in reality, none of it had anything to do with my career, and everything to do with you being so insecure that you need attention twenty-four-seven. You're a fucking asshole!"

My husband doesn't say a word. He knows I am right. He knows that nothing he can say will ever explain why he is the way he is.

"Was she good?"

"What?"

"Debbie. Was she a good fuck? Did she do everything you wanted her to do?"

"Don't ask this." He shakes his head, his mouth a rigid line.

"Why?! Is it a sensitive topic? Just tell me! Was she any good? She seems pretty young, so I'm presuming she's quite flexible... In more ways than one."

He rubs his eyes, and develops a fascination with a tiny frog ornament on the mantelpiece, twisting it one way and then the other.

"She was okay," he says quietly. "From what I can remember."

From what he can remember... The words choke me. He might as well have his hands around my neck right now, because he couldn't possibly strangle me any more than he is already. I whip around and head out of the door, before my husband of twenty-five years can break my heart any further.

"You need to leave," I shout from the hall. "Grab your bag and go to Debbie's. Tell her that I wish her luck."

"Olivia, please! I'm not going anywhere. You need to listen to me. I can explain everything."

"I'm going to Lauren's, and I want you out of here by the time I get back."

I grab my car keys and run to my car. I never want to see this man again.

CHAPTER TWELVE

"So, he was determined that the affair ended ten years ago? In spite of the photographic evidence?"

"Yep."

My hands shake as I nurse a tepid mug of tea. It was hot twenty minutes ago, but I was too busy trying not to throw up, to drink it.

"You need to drink that," Lauren says. "Or do you want me to make you another one?"

Lauren darts off her sofa, but I shake my head.

"No, honestly, this one is fine."

"Well, drink it then. I've put sugar in it, to help calm you down."

"Won't sugar have the opposite effect?"

My friend shrugs.

"I don't know. I always see sweet tea in movies, so I go along with that."

"Well, I appreciate the gesture."

I hold the mug up in a cheers-like way, and then take another sip. Lauren curls her feet underneath her, and scratches her nose.

"It's unbelievable though, isn't it?" she says. "I mean, really! He confesses that he had an affair ten years ago, but then refuses to acknowledge that he's been sleeping with her recently? And what about the parent stuff? Did he even say one word about why he's lied about that for the past four years?"

"No," I say. "He started to tell me, but I cut him off. I didn't want to hear any more lies. When I first mentioned it, he asked if I'd hired a detective, so I can't imagine he was about to tell me the truth. You know men, they're always more interested in how you find out about stuff, rather than addressing their indiscretions."

Lauren's ginger cat jumps onto her lap, and she runs her hand down his back. He arches, and purrs, and rubs his head against her arm.

"True," she says. "From my experience, most men have gaslighter tendencies, if we're honest. But you'd have thought he'd say something. I mean pretending that your parents are alive when they've been dead for four years is a pretty huge thing!" She leans over and touches my leg. "You must be devastated. How do you feel? How do you really feel?"

Lauren loves deep and meaningful conversations, but I can't handle it today. I'm not even sure if I have any feelings. I shrug and play with the tassels on her huge green cushions.

"The truth is, at this moment I'm completely numb. Like, I'm talking to you about him confessing to an affair, but it's only words. They mean nothing. I've been so broken since I found that card on Monday that I'm now immune."

"I can imagine."

"Besides," I say, "since Charlie died, what can devastate me more? I mean, really? What on earth could be worse than seeing your child on a gurney, being rushed to hospital?"

I have not been myself since we lost our son. I am a completely different person, and always will be. I often look at our photos and videos of when Charlie was a little boy, and I have to really concentrate to believe that the happy young brunette woman is me. The woman who wore tight jeans so that her husband could admire her bottom as she went up the stairs... The woman who made disastrous cookies and cakes, but made everyone laugh as she did so. She's gone. Every good part of her has gone, and the only things left are the bones, the trauma scars, and the obsessions.

Is that why Scott decided to lie about his parents being dead, because I'm too neurotic to cope with such news? But that thought has got to be nonsense, surely. I'm not completely deranged. Information doesn't need to be kept from me, as though I'm in a straitjacket, confined to a padded cell.

The vision of Scott in our living room, digesting the magnitude of our conversation, flitters in and out of my mind. Did he want to continue the lies, or to come clean? To be honest, if he had told me he'd slept with every woman who's ever been to the Regency Hotel, it wouldn't have shocked me at that moment. Well, maybe it would have shocked me a little. What I mean is, I'm so jaded from all the lies and all the tales going back ten years (that I know of), that anything else would be noise to me now. Horrendous noise, but noise nonetheless.

"What I can't get my mind around," I say, "is why he's saying that he had an affair because I was too busy for him. I was thinking about it on the way over here, and you know what? We were still going away for weekends together, we still had sex regularly, we had family time, and date nights, and everything. Yes, I was busy with my writing, but not to the extent where I ignored him. I've always been cautious not to do that again."

Lauren shakes her head.

"It's got nothing to do with you," she says. "Truth is, he'd have had the affair regardless. Look at me and Michael! I don't even have a career, just a day job. I would go to work, earn some money, come home, cook his dinner, and dedicate my entire evening to doing whatever it was that he wanted to do. And he still left me for another woman! We can't win."

"Funny, isn't it," I say. "Nobody teaches you how to be a wife or a mother. Everyone is constantly learning and struggling and working things out. I don't think I'm a bad wife. I don't think I've ever been a bad wife. I'm just a human being who is hoping that one day things will all make sense. Unfortunately, the older I get, the more confusing things become."

"What are you going to do now?" my friend asks.

I take a sip of tea, while mulling over my answer. The liquid is so cold now that it takes me all of my time not to gag on it. Lauren notices my discomfort and takes the mug from me. "Leave this. I'll get you a new one."

"I don't know what I'm going to do now," I say. "He'll be gone when I get back – or at least he better be, because if he's not, I might do something I'll regret."

"A patio job?"

Lauren smiles, and I see the humour in her reply, but yes, if I thought I could get away with it, then I'd be digging a new patio, with him in it.

"Do you know where this Debbie woman lives? We could go round there if you like?"

I lift a single eyebrow, and my nostrils flare at the thought of ever seeing the mistress in the flesh.

"Why would I want to do that?" I ask.

"Maybe to see if he's gone there, or to get an idea of her side of the story."

"You mean I should ask her what's been going on? I couldn't! I just couldn't."

That's the truth. While I'm an obsessive internet stalker, I could never entertain the idea of contacting Debbie, or Suzanne, or whatever the hell her name is. Could I?

"I've never told you this," Lauren says, "but when Michael left me for that skank, Tiffany, I went round to her house and had it out with her in the front garden."

"What? I didn't know that!"

"No, you wouldn't! It's not the sort of thing I like to broadcast. Don't judge me, but it got so bad that I ended up covered in trifle! She phoned the police, and I almost got arrested!"

"Oh my God! Trifle?"

After what I've been through, I never thought I'd laugh again, but I guess when something is really funny, there's no stopping a natural reaction. Lauren relaxes into the sofa and laughs too.

"Bloody hell, it's funny now, but it wasn't at the time, believe me! Yes, trifle. The stupid woman was great in the kitchen as well as the bedroom, and she was making dessert when I arrived. The moment I started shouting at her, she threw it over my head, and I punched her. I was so angry, but when I saw the policewoman with her hand on her taser, I calmed down pretty swiftly!"

"I can imagine! Did you eat the trifle?"

I wink, and Lauren scrunches her face.

"Looked a bit vanilla to me. A bit of a basic bitch, like her... But still, I'm glad I went there, because in amongst the shouting, Tiffany did give me a few answers to questions that were burning my brain. The answers were hard to hear, but they did help me to move on... And that's why we should give Debbie a visit. I'm not saying it would be easy, but she could shed more light on everything that's been going on."

I rub my eyes. They're hot to the touch and aching.

"It's too painful right now. Besides, I don't even have her address."

"Have a little think about it," Lauren says. "This is you

we're talking about, and I know that if you want to find her address, you will. So, do that and then we can decide what to do. Me and you, together. Okay? Promise?"

"Okay. Promise."

———

It's late when I get home, Scott's car has gone, and the house is in total darkness. He didn't even leave a light on when he left, which isn't like him at all. Normally, he insists on timers and lamps being on if we're out for any length of time, but perhaps he figured I'd be home. Or maybe he didn't give a shit. Who knows? Who cares at this point?

I switch on the living-room light, and the first thing I see is the printed stuff I left on the coffee table. The printout of Debbie's Facebook page has been torn into three pieces, the hotel card is folded, and the photo is face down on the rug. I pick them all up and put them in the bin. It's pointless keeping them now. They've served their purpose, whatever that was.

I pour myself a glass of wine. It's the first time I've drunk anything alcoholic since our anniversary party, which although only four days ago, seems like a million years ago. The liquid is cold and bitter against my tongue. Far too cold really. The effect of alcohol on my empty stomach is not comforting. If it's anything, it's merely irritating.

So, what now? My husband has admitted an affair ten years ago, and assures me that it is not a thing anymore. But I can only dismiss that as nonsense, given the evidence. If I knew for sure that it had only happened then and never again, then perhaps – perhaps – I could get over it and move on, but the unanswered questions and plot holes dance around my brain until I am utterly worn down.

My phone pings from deep inside my handbag. I reach in

and discover three calls from Scott, and a handful of WhatsApp messages. How I missed them, I do not know, but there they are. He didn't leave any messages from his attempted calls, but the texts are full of self-loathing, and regret.

> You have to listen to me. It's not what you think at all…

> There's nothing going on with me and Debbie, I promise you. I fucking promise you!

> I'm so sorry for hurting you ten years ago, but there's nothing I can do to change that now. I wish there was!

> I've hated myself every day since it happened.

> I'm sorry. Please believe me. Please forgive me!

Forgive him? When I don't even have the full story? Not likely. I can never forgive him for what he's done to me. Even if I ever find out the complete truth, I know that I'll never forgive him.

I switch off my phone and throw it deep into the sofa cushions. It can stay there for the rest of the evening. It can stay there for the rest of my life for all I care. I think about what Lauren said, regards going to visit Debbie. When I was young, I could never contemplate talking to Gabby Haine. I mean, I thought about it in my head many times – her and me having a frank conversation about everything she did, everything he did. But I never did anything with those thoughts, except torture myself. But now it's different. I'm much, much older, and this Debbie woman was carrying on with Scott when he was a husband, and a father. He wasn't just out of his teens. He wasn't still living with his parents. We were a couple. We were a team. We were in love. We were happy.

At least one of us was.

I go upstairs and lie on Charlie's bed. The original smell of his talc and deodorant are long gone, though I'll admit that there have been many times over the years when I have sprayed a little more onto his pillow, so that I can be close to him again. Sometimes it works, if I close my eyes and go deep into my mind. Smells can do that to me. They can take me right back to the past. Which, as it often turns out, is both a joy and a curse. I grab my son's cuddly blue dinosaur, hold it close to my chest, and cry, and cry, and cry.

I open my eyes, and realise that I'm still in Charlie's bedroom. I don't know what time it is, but it's daylight, and I can hear birds cheeping. I must have slept here all night. I pull myself up from the bed, and a pain shoots through my lower back. Sleeping on a child's mattress is not good for my middle-aged muscles. My head throbs from crying, and strands of my hair are dried to my cheeks. Am I dead? I think I am.

In so many ways.

I stretch, and hear the front doorbell jangling. God, it's probably Scott. If he tried to come home last night, he wouldn't have been able to get in, since I deadbolted the door and turned the key. However, I can't imagine he'll stay away this morning, especially as he needs clean clothes for today, and his laptop for work tomorrow. Of course, he might have all of those things at Debbie's house, but if not, then I can expect a visit from him.

And I'm not sure how I feel about that.

I somehow manage to drag myself downstairs and open the door, but it's not Scott. Instead, it's a parliamentary candidate wearing a badge for some party that I have never heard of.

"Good morning, Miss...? Or is it Mrs? It's so hard to tell

these days." He smiles, and his broad mouth takes over his entire face. I have no time for this.

"Not today," I say, and slam the door while he's in mid-sentence. I'm not normally so rude, but today I forgive myself.

I stuff my hand in my pocket in an attempt to find my phone, and then remember that I dumped it onto the sofa last night. Switching it on, I wait for more messages from Scott, but there are none. Instead, there are five from Lauren asking if I'm okay and if I've thought any more about visiting Debbie, and the usual Babbage Books emails that I get every morning, even on a Sunday. I reply to Lauren first, telling her that yes, I'm fine (I'm not), and no, I haven't thought about visiting Debbie (I have, but I still don't know what to do).

It's 10.30am, and even though it is still the weekend, and no matter how much I want to ignore any Babbage work, I really have to check the messages so that I can catch up. Now that Scott and I are in such a precarious place, I'll need every bit of job security that I can get, and while the work with Babbage will never be enough to support myself completely, it might keep the wolves from my door. At least for a little while.

I pour myself a cup of tea, and then open the first message. It's from an author called Victor Victory. His name calls to mind an old soldier in *Dad's Army* or something, but I'm sure it's not real. When I first joined the company, Sam told me that Victor Victory writes World War II novels, set in space, which continues to blow my mind, and not in a good way. But regardless of that, his books are some of Babbage's bestsellers, so who am I to argue? I've never had much to do with Victor, apart from passing along his messages to the editors, so I'm surprised to see that he has written me a message that's much wordier than usual.

Dear Ms Collins, I am in receipt of your unfortunate email, and I must say that I'm quite lost for words. First of all, I am unsure as to why you sent it through my website, except maybe to distance your job from your true feelings about my books. I have no idea, but to say that I'm disgusted by your attitude is an understatement. Your personal views on my bestselling books are none of my concern. I have written for Babbage since 2012, and have seen many staff come and go. I can assure you that none of them have ever sent me anything as diabolical as you did. I will be telling Sam about this. I'm utterly baffled and deeply offended. Yours, Victor Victory, Bestselling Author.

No! Not another fake email sent in my name, not today. My hands shake so much that I can barely hold my phone, and I'm mortified to see that Victor has copied Sam into the email. I don't have much time to wonder if he's already read it as the next message is from Sam himself.

Dear Olivia. After reading the email from Victor Victory this morning, and pondering the others I told you about, I am afraid that I have no choice but to stop using your freelance services in my company. I am aware that you deny sending these messages, and part of me

```
wants to believe that, but even if it is
not you, your overall presence is
causing concern. I am very sorry that it
has come to this, but there is no other
way to rectify what has been happening.
I wish no ill will toward you, and I am
happy to pay what I owe up to the end of
this week. However, from this moment on,
I'm taking over your role as
organisational assistant, and will be
deleting your email account by the end
of the day. I wish you luck, and thank
you for the work you have been able to
do over the past couple of months. All
the best, Sam.
```

I slump into the armchair, and read the message over and over again. I can't blame Sam for doing this, but I know that it wasn't me who sent the email to Victor Victory, or the other authors, and I'm definitely not the one who wrote the terrible Facebook post.

I pick up my phone and dial Sam. It isn't often that I've ever had to ring him – email is his preference, and occasionally Zoom – but today is different. He answers after two rings.

"Hello, Babbage Books. Can I help you?"

I'm confused that he doesn't know who is ringing him, since I'm one hundred per cent sure that he has me in his contacts. Or at least he did, but that was before he fired me.

"Sam? It's me, Olivia."

There's a sigh at the other end of the phone.

"Hi, Olivia. How are you?"

He asks the question, but I'm pretty sure he has no interest in the answer.

"I'm not doing well, at all, actually," I say. "I just received your email."

"I see. Well, as I said in the message, there's nothing I can do I'm afraid. This is not something I took lightly, but given the circumstances – and your apparent lack of interest in your role lately – I had to let you go. I'm sorry."

"Please! Please can we…"

"No. Sorry. Nearly every day this week I have woken up to emails complaining about you. It's not good for my company and it's not good for me either. I do not need the stress of all this."

Asking for sympathy is not working, so I go for a different approach.

"Aren't there laws against this kind of thing? Don't you have to go through numerous warnings before letting an employee go?"

"Ordinarily, yes," he says. "But you're hired by us as a freelancer, not an employee. Besides, I did give you a warning before, so this would be the next step."

I'm sure there's more to the process than he's letting on, but since I've been self-employed for so long, I have no real knowledge of employee or freelancer law. I'll have to believe that what he's saying is true. I'm too exhausted to argue.

"You do know that it wasn't me who sent those emails or posted those comments, don't you?"

Sam laughs, and I can hear him shuffling papers in the background.

"I don't know that at all," he says. "All I know is that you have been ignoring your job as much as you can get away with all week and my business is coming under fire from someone with your name. I'm sorry, Olivia, but I can't take any more risks. My wife is expecting a baby, and I need to know that I can provide for her. To be honest, if I carried on ignoring the situation, I wouldn't have a business by the time the kid is born. I'm sorry."

There is a click, and then he's gone. I stare at my phone, praying for the call to reconnect, but the screen remains black.

So, that's that.

I'm gutted, because before all this drama, I believed I was settling in well with Babbage Books, and Sam appeared to think the same way. As crazy as the company was, I had developed a system, I knew the editors and the proofreaders, and was able to help most of the authors with their problems. Added to that, the extra income really helped, and now that's all going to be taken away, through nothing I've done at all.

In the last ten years I've lost my beautiful child, and my bestselling writing career. Now in the past week, I've lost my husband and my job. Well done, Olivia. That's got to be something of a record.

CHAPTER THIRTEEN

Exactly seventy-six seconds after putting the phone down, it pings. I snap it up. It must be a message from Sam, telling me that he's suddenly realised who the real culprit is, and please, please can I come back! No. Instead, it's a WhatsApp message from Scott.

> Olivia, we need to talk. Nothing is what you think. Or if it is, then just a tiny part is true. I want to explain everything. I can't have you throw our marriage away like this over something so stupid. Let me know. Love you.

I read the text three times… Nothing is what I think? Or if it is, then just a tiny part is true? How does any of that make sense? My head screams at me to ignore the message, and block Scott entirely, but I'm still attached in spite of myself. We've been together since the 1980s. A lifetime ago! I'm ashamed to say that my heart even gives a little jump when it appears that there may be a chance for us, that there might be a logical explanation. These feelings go against everything I've ever believed, but I can't help it. If I speak to him, then at the very least I'll get to know what has been happening. If we break up after that point, then so be it. But until then, I deserve to know the truth.

Okay. Come over this evening.

A reply comes through immediately.

Thank you. Love you.

I ignore that one.

My stomach has shrunk to the size of a peanut, but I'm aware that if I don't eat something soon, I'll likely collapse. I can't even remember the last time I had a proper meal, but it definitely hasn't been in the last twelve hours. I open the fridge and I'm met with a couple of old tomatoes, a bowl of pasta salad that's past its sell-by-date, a block of cheese, and some milk. It's shopping day. We never have anything in the fridge on shopping day, and we're not likely to either. There are some potatoes in the cupboard, so maybe I could do one baked or something. I sniff the cheese, and look all over it for mould. It's fine, but to be honest, I couldn't stomach something as stodgy as a potato. Shit, I'll have to go to the shop.

I'm dressed in my baggy jeans, a hoodie and a Lady Gaga T-shirt. Should I change? I really don't have the energy. It took me all the strength I had to get into those. I examine my face in the mirror. Sunken red eyes with wrinkles at the corners, chapped lips, hair in need of a good wash, and hormonal spots on my cheeks. Bloody hell, I look like a zombie – a heartbroken, damaged, deranged zombie. If Scott is coming over this evening, I need to pull myself together. Despite everything, I do not want him to be relieved that I've thrown him out.

I grab a bobble, tie my hair up into a ponytail, slap some moisturiser on my face and grab my car keys. I'll pop to the small Tesco up the road, grab some bits and be back before anyone sees me. Then after something to eat, I'll shower, wash my hair and throw the entire contents of my make-up bag onto my face.

I open the front door, and there is a figure standing on my driveway. A figure so horrifying that my plans shatter into a million pieces.

"Olivia?" she says. "I'm Debbie. Can I have a word?"

Suzanne 'Debbie' Abbott is perched on my green armchair in the living room.

She is perched on my green armchair in the living room!

The moment I saw her on my doorstep, I did not need any introduction. I may have only seen the woman in photographs, but I knew who she was straight away. Platinum-blonde hair, piercing blue eyes, streamlined figure dressed in expensive-looking jeans and a wax jacket. I knew who she was, and all she stood for.

I should have pulled her hair out by the dark roots. I should have shoved her so hard that she fell into my rhododendron bush. I should have grabbed her by the scruff of her jacket and heaved her over the wooden fence.

And yet I didn't do any of those things...

Instead, when she asked if she could come in, I stepped silently aside and waved her past as though she visited me every damn day.

And now she sits in my favourite armchair, in what was once my safe, cosy little living room, and I am perched opposite her on the sofa, no idea what to say or what to do. I haven't said a word to her since she walked into the house, but she doesn't seem to mind. Her eyes flit around the room, probably seeing things I haven't taken any notice of for years. I'm uncomfortable with her staring at the belongings we've built up over the course of our relationship... The mementoes that have been in this room while she's been sleeping with my husband for the past decade. Probably.

My stomach aches and I discreetly unfasten the top button of my jeans. I'm glad I haven't had anything to eat yet, because if I had, I'm sure it would be all over the carpet by now.

"I'm sorry for dropping in on you like this. I didn't know what else to do."

Debbie's voice goes right through me, and makes me jump. I didn't expect her to speak in that moment. As far as my head was concerned, we were going to sit in awkward silence until she finally decided to leave.

"What do you want?" I manage to say, but I'm so dry that my tongue sticks to the top of my mouth with each word.

"I understand from Scott that you know what happened between us. Or at least, you know about me."

I shuffle on the sofa, wishing that I could slide deep inside it, never to be seen again.

"Yes, I know about you," I say. "You're the woman who has been shagging my husband for the past ten years."

Debbie's mouth drops open, and she takes quick breaths.

"What?! No! That's not true at all!"

I laugh out loud, through a mixture of hilarity and anxiety.

"I'm not being funny," I say, "but you and Scott should really get your stories straight before speaking with me, because he told me in this very room that you had slept together ten years ago. Right before our beautiful son passed away, as it happens."

Her eyes fall, and she plays with the tassels on her coat, swirling them around her shaking fingers. Her nails are painted pink with sparkles, and manicured to perfection. I can't remember the last time I had a manicure. Probably when we got married, and I'm not even joking.

"I'm ashamed to admit it," she says, "but that part is true. Yes, we did have a... have a... relationship, but it never should have happened, and I swear on my life that we haven't been intimate since. Not since we called it off anyway."

"And when did you call it off, exactly?"

"Ten years ago. Shortly after we got together, if you can even call it that."

I watch the postman walk past the end of my drive, and he waves a friendly good morning, as he does most days. Funny thing about situations like this. Lives go on regardless, people walk past regardless, all is normal until it isn't. The postman doesn't come down my path, and I'm slightly disappointed, as I'd have liked some excuse to get out of this conversation, if I'm honest. I lean forward.

"Scott told me that you hadn't slept together for ten years, but I'm not so sure. Either you've both rehearsed these conversations, or by some miracle you're telling the truth, but either way, you're both scum."

Debbie stares at me, her face as blank as a sheet of paper, and I just can't read her at all. I don't know if she's intimidated because I'm at least twenty years older than her, or if that makes her feel better somehow. The younger woman is always the one who thinks she has the advantage, I guess. She may not be there on experience, but she's miles ahead on confidence.

"We are both telling the truth, I promise you." She stares straight into my soul.

Silence fills the room again, and from the reflection of the mirror on the side table, I notice that Debbie still stares at me. What is going on in her mind? As much as I hate this woman, there is no denying that she is beautiful. I was beautiful too, once upon a time, and now here's this other woman, young, pert, her whole life ahead of her. I look at my older hands, wrinkled and bony in comparison to her manicured fingers. I've never really felt old before, but I do now. No number of workouts will ever halt the passage of time.

"Did Scott put you up to this?" I ask.

"What do you mean?"

"Did he tell you to spin me a story about how it only happened a handful of times, and then you forgot about each other? Because believe it or not, I have proof that you have met up as recently as Thursday. On our twenty-fifth anniversary in fact."

Debbie sniffs, and wipes her nose on an ironed handkerchief. Who uses them nowadays? The last time I saw one was when my mum threw all of my dad's into the bin, about fifteen years ago. Debbie stuffs the hankie back into her pocket, and for the first time we make mutual, lasting, deep eye contact.

"He actually told me not to make any contact with you at all," Debbie says. "He's coming to speak with you this evening, I believe. He really wants to make things up to you. He loves you!"

I spring up from the sofa, hands clenched.

"Don't tell me what his feelings are for me! Not you, of all people!"

Debbie grimaces, as though I'm about to strike her. Her reaction sends me off-balance. No matter how angry I get, I've never harmed another person in my life. But I guess there's always a first time. I sit back into the chair, and shove my hands underneath my thighs. I can't do anything that will make this worse. The last thing I need is to be threatened with legal action, or worse – arrest. As easy as it would be to choose violence, I'm not sure that Scott is worth the bother. I'd rather walk away.

"I'm sorry, I didn't mean to insult you," Debbie says. "I just wanted you to know that I'm not here because Scott wants me to be. Quite the opposite in fact."

"So, why are you here?"

Debbie's eyes are damp with tears, and I can't believe it. Over the past couple of days, I've built up such a vision of her in my head that it is hard for me to see her as a human being, with real emotions. She dabs her eyes with her hankie, and sniffs again.

"I wanted you to know my side of things, before you see Scott tonight. I've kept silent for ten years, and now that it's all out, I want you to know that I'm not a bad person. I'm not someone who normally has sex with other women's husbands. It's something that happened, but it's not who I am. I've never slept with a married man since then, in fact."

I laugh, even though I feel like dying.

"It's not who you are, and yet it bloody well is! So, how did you meet? Scott said something about a conference."

"Yes, that's right," she says. "We were both at the same conference at the Regency Hotel in Cromer."

"So, you're in marketing too?"

"No," she says. "I was training to be a marketing assistant back then, but it wasn't for me. I'm a hairdresser now, and that's much more my scene."

"In Cromer?"

"No." She shakes her head. "Sheringham. That's where I live. It's just outside Cromer..."

"I know where that is," I snap. "You and Scott have become regulars at the Regency, haven't you?"

She scratches her forehead.

"We've been there a few times, yes. But I wouldn't say we were regulars... Anyway, there was a get-together in the hotel bar afterwards, and we got speaking and got a little drunk – or a lot drunk if I'm honest."

She swallows hard, and her neck contracts.

"Then what?"

Debbie meets my stare for a second, and then her eyes fall to her hands, twisting uncomfortably in her lap.

"You know what happened next."

"I want you to say it. I want to hear all the details."

Debbie rubs her eyes, and a streak of black mascara smudges under her left eye. Regardless, she still looks beautiful. Bitch.

"The bar closed at 11pm, so Scott invited me up to his room for a couple more. I wouldn't normally put myself in that situation, but I was so drunk I didn't care..."

There's a beat of silence, while Debbie picks at her sparkly nail polish. This woman knows how to fidget, I'll give her that.

"Carry on. You went to his room, you had a drink, and then what?"

"The inevitable happened." She bites her lip.

"Meaning you had sex."

"Yes," Debbie whispers.

"And you knew he was married?"

"Not at that moment," she says. "He wasn't wearing a wedding ring. It wasn't until the next morning that I saw it lying on the desk in his room. When I confronted him about it, he swore blind you had separated, but he still wore his ring because none of his family knew yet. Believe me, if it had been a guy my age saying that, I'd have been suspicious, but this was an older bloke, so the chances of him being divorced or separated were much higher. Besides, I'd already slept with him at that point, so there was no point freaking out about it."

On hearing about Scott's wedding ring, my throat dries up. He had removed his ring. The same gold band that I'd given him when we exchanged our vows. That is the most jarring thing I've heard in this entire conversation. We've been married for twenty-five years, and for most of those, Scott hasn't been able to remove his ring even if he wanted to. Not that he is much heavier than he was when we got married, but somehow his fingers have grown thicker, and the band has stuck in place. It sounds silly, but in a way it used to give me great comfort to know that if he did want to have an affair, or a fling or whatever, he wouldn't be able to hide me from his potential partners, because there I was, all over his finger.

But that comfort was a lie, an illusion, a ridiculous fable.

As was the fact that he couldn't get the damn thing off.

"Are you sure his ring was on the desk? Scott always said he couldn't get it to come off. In fact, he still does."

Debbie nods.

"Definitely. I remember because I picked it up, and he got a bit agitated and took it back off me, and stuck it in his pocket. It's engraved inside, isn't it? I can't remember what it said as I only got a quick look, but there was a date in there."

I manage no words, only a nod. Yes, it does have a date – our wedding date to be exact, and the words, *Always Us, S and O*, next to it. I twirl my own ring around my finger. The same engraving is on the inside of that too.

"And you saw him again after that?" I swallow, knowing the answer, but not wanting to hear it from her lips.

"Yes. For a little while."

"How long is a little while?"

Debbie shrugs.

"A few weeks. That's all."

"And did you always meet at the Regency?"

"Only a couple of times. The rest of the time we met at my flat."

My mind whirrs. Ten years is a long time ago, so piecing together the dates is difficult, but I can only imagine that these overnight meetings were when I was on a rugby trip with Charlie, which was fairly often at that point.

"Did he tell you that he had a son?" I ask.

Debbie smiles.

"Yes, he did. He was so proud of him and his achievements. He told me it was because of your son that Scott wasn't looking for anything serious. He said he was looking for a bit of fun, after his apparent separation, so I promise you, his heart wasn't involved in anything related to me... And vice versa."

His heart wasn't involved. His heart wasn't involved... So, that makes it all okay, does it? I guess on her part it does, if he was telling her that he was separated. Myself, I've never been someone who could have sex with a person that I didn't have a connection to, so that concept is alien to me. I've always been grateful for that, but now... what was the point? It certainly wasn't something that Scott was into. As it turns out.

I want to give Debbie a sarcastic slow clap, but I can't, because I don't think that she is in the wrong here. Unfortunately.

"So, when did you find out he was very-much married?" My heart begs her not to answer, but my head screams for some clarity.

"Just before we called it all off," she says. "He came clean because I asked why he wouldn't tell me where he lived. For a while he said it was because of his son, but I didn't get that, and pushed him for an answer. He finally came clean that you two were still together, and that's when we came apart. I had no interest in being with someone who was still with his wife. I'd never experienced that before, and it didn't seem right to me. It still doesn't."

"Okay," I say. "I kind of believe that it was a short fling, but if that was the case, why did you meet up with him recently? It makes no sense."

"I know, and I'm so sorry that I was with him on your silver wedding anniversary," she says. "That wasn't my intention. It just worked out that way."

Hearing the words 'silver wedding anniversary' coming out of Debbie's mouth is jarring. This woman must have been a child when we got married, and now here she is, sitting in my living room, talking about an affair she had with my husband. It should make my blood boil, and in a way it does, but more than anything I am humiliated, and even embarrassed. Embarrassed because I'm so much older than this person. Humiliated because no matter how much I tried, I couldn't keep my husband satisfied.

And that realisation is destroying me more and more each minute.

"But the funny thing is," I say, "Scott arranged our party for Tuesday evening, which was two days before our actual anniversary. If you didn't mean to meet up on our special date, why would he do that? Why would he arrange everything before then?"

She shakes her head, and shrugs.

"All I know is that he was struggling to get a date when all of your family could get together. But on my part, something happened and I…"

"What could have happened that meant he had to be away on the day of our anniversary? I only got to see him at night!" I'm aware that my voice has risen to a shout, but I really don't care. I've kept everything in long enough.

Debbie runs her fingers through her hair, and it falls

perfectly back into place. She hunches over as if punched, and then launches into a monologue, barely stopping for breath.

"Anthony broke his ankle when playing football. I had to rush him through to A&E, and I couldn't do it alone, so I phoned Scott. When we'd finished, Anthony and I went home, and Scott booked into the Regency. I met him the next morning for breakfast, and that's when he mentioned that it was your anniversary and he had missed it. I'm sorry, I would never have called him if I'd known. I've never wanted to cause problems for you."

My brow furrows, and I rub my eyes. I'm so sleepy that I don't have a clue what's going on, or what she's talking about.

"I'm sorry, but I'm not keeping up with you. Who is Anthony?"

Debbie tucks her hair behind her ear, and her fingers run their way down her neck.

"My son."

Her eyes are wide, and she blinks rapidly.

"Your son? You have a son?"

The words clatter around my brain, but I am incapable of understanding what Debbie is talking about. How can she have a son? I am not stupid, but I cannot force myself to understand what she means. It's impossible. The blankness on my face must speak volumes, because Debbie reaches into her handbag, takes out her phone, and thrusts it toward me.

"Here. This is Anthony."

I take the handset and I'm met with a photograph of my Charlie, when he was about nine years old. Why has this woman got a photo of my son, and why is she calling him Anthony? I enlarge the photo to get a better look, and then realise that it isn't Charlie after all. This boy has the same colour hair, the same build, the same everything in fact, except that two things are dissimilar.

His nose is a different shape, and his eyelashes are short. Charlie's eyelashes were so long that my friends all envied him, but this lad's lashes are stumpy, and much blonder than Charlie's black ones.

"This isn't Charlie," I mutter to myself.

Debbie shakes her head, and takes the phone from me.

"No. No, it's Anthony. Are you okay? You look pale."

Pale? The blood rushes out of my face and straight to my stomach. I must be as white as a ghost. My lips are numb, as though they've been injected by that stuff dentists use while performing fillings.

"So, you are saying that Anthony is your son?"

Debbie nods.

"That's right," she says. "Mine and Scott's son. I'm sorry, but I'm so confused. I thought you knew about Anthony."

I shake my head. Their son? Their son?! That can't be true. It's ridiculous to contemplate such a thing, and I want to call this woman a liar, except for the fact that her son is the spitting image of my own.

"Oh God. No! This can't be true!"

I stand up, and throw my hands to my face in an attempt to hide from this terrible news. Even though the radiators are on, I'm freezing cold, and there's a tightness in my chest that frightens me. The room spins, and I have to put my hands out onto the sofa to steady myself.

"Are you okay?" Debbie asks.

I shoot her a look, but it's impossible for me to remain in eye contact with her. Her figure blurs in front of me.

"No." My voice shakes, and I have to concentrate in order to get the words out. "I had no idea that you had a son. And... and... he's definitely Scott's child?"

Debbie nods, and folds her arms.

"Yes! Surely you know this! I spoke to Scott last night and

he told me that he'd explained everything to you, including Anthony's existence."

"Well, he lied to you, because no. No, he didn't tell me anything about that."

"Shit. I'm so sorry." She throws the phone back into her handbag as though it is on fire. I can't believe what I've just heard. Maybe I could have come to terms with the idea that Scott had had an affair with a mystery woman, but this? This is the worst news I have heard since Charlie passed. As my skin tingles in the discomfort of it all, a thought comes into my mind. Was this child in the world at the same time as my own?

"How old is he?"

"He'll be ten next April," Debbie says.

The numbers rattle in my brain, as I try desperately to work things out. He'll be ten in April 2025, which means he must have been conceived around July 2014. The same time that Scott was at the Regency Hotel with Debbie.

"Wait. When did you find out that you were pregnant with him?"

Debbie's eyes flit up to the ceiling, and she childishly counts on her fingers, as though working it all out. She probably doesn't need to though. Every woman remembers everything about discovering a pregnancy.

"Erm, it was shortly after we'd decided to go our separate ways," she says. "Maybe three weeks later or something? It was very quick, because my periods have always been regular, so I knew something was up as soon as I was a day or two late."

"And when did you tell Scott?"

Debbie rubs her face, dragging her cheeks as she does so. It's an awkward conversation, but I need to know the truth. Her eyes flick to the door into the hall. She's obviously planning a quick exit. She clears her throat, opens her mouth, closes it and then opens it again.

"I... I... I don't remember."

I laugh.

"Debbie, it's been over twenty-five years since I told Scott that I was pregnant with Charlie, and I still remember every detail of how I broke the news, and how he reacted to it. So, tell me the truth. When did you tell Scott?"

She closes her eyes, opens them wide, and then eyeballs me.

"I... I told him on the day your son passed away. That's why you couldn't get him on the phone when you were at the hospital. He had switched it off."

"Oh my God!"

I collapse into the sofa, shaking in shock. I do not want to cry in front of this woman, but I can't keep it in any longer. This is awful. This is bloody awful. When I was in the school car park, watching Charlie being taken away in an ambulance, and when I was sitting in the hospital corridor, waiting for news, and most importantly, when the doctor was breaking the news that our son had gone, all that time, all that despair, and my husband was discussing the arrival of a new son. I'm devastated all over again.

Debbie reaches over to touch my arm, but I swat her off.

"Please don't touch me!"

"I'm sorry," she says. "I didn't want to upset you. When Scott told me he'd explained everything, I thought that meant telling you about Anthony... I didn't think for a second that he would keep that news from you... It's bad enough that he's kept our son secret for the past ten years, and I've told him that many times... That wasn't fair to anyone, most of all Anthony."

She's rambling, putting sentences together as a stream of consciousness, rather than imparting actual information, and her voice pierces through my brain. She finally pauses for breath, and visions of the past ten years spiral through my mind like a train going down a mountainside. All the times Scott had to go away for conferences, all the times he was apparently visiting his parents, all those hiking trips, and all those moments of crying for Charlie after his death. Was he really crying because he didn't know how to break the news to me about his new baby? How do I know that he was ever mourning our son, when he had a replacement, all lined up?

How do I know anything anymore?

"How did he take the news? Was he pleased? Was he shocked? What?"

Debbie rubs her hands together, as though she's trying to thaw them out.

"At first, he was really shocked. We had used... y'know..."

"Protection?"

"Yes. Protection," she whispers. "But it failed. It... it tore... We agreed that I'd take the morning-after pill, but – and this is probably too much detail – I was sure I wasn't ovulating that weekend, so I dismissed the idea. I was young. Stupid. And most of all, wrong, so we were both more than surprised."

The idea of Debbie and Scott discussing ripped condoms, the morning-after pill and even worse, ovulation, brings bile to the back of my throat. It's absolutely disgusting.

"Did he want you to have a termination? Or was he happy for you to have the... the baby?"

"To be honest with you, he was concerned about how it would affect his home life with you and Charlie – this was before he heard the awful news – but he didn't pressure me to do anything. He's not that kind of man."

I grind my teeth as I listen to this woman describe what kind of man my husband is – or is not. The person I have known since the eighties, and been married to since the nineties. How could she know him?

And yet, she does, and I'm not sure I do at all.

And then something occurs to me.

"Wait," I say, and Debbie looks up.

"What?"

"Did Scott tell you that his parents had passed away?"

Her posture loosens, and she tilts her head to the side.

"His parents? I never knew them, never met them or anything like that, but yes, he did tell me that they'd gone. They passed in lockdown, didn't they?"

"Yes, they did, but I only just discovered that. Scott didn't tell me when it happened. He pretended that he was still visiting them. He even told me that his mother was in hospital on the night before our anniversary. So, tell me, was your son really in A&E, or is that another lie?"

Debbie shakes her head.

"Scott might lie, but I don't. Yes, he really was in the hospital, and it wasn't a scheduled surgery or anything like that. He really did break his ankle. He'll be in a cast for a while."

I know Debbie is speaking the truth. She has no reason to lie, except maybe for self-protection, and something tells me that she doesn't need much of that.

"So why did Scott pretend to me that his parents were alive? Did you tell him to do that?"

"No, I seriously didn't know he had done that, until you just told me. I knew nothing about that at all, I swear. I only knew they'd died because he was going to come into his inheritance, and he told me he'd be able to give me more help for Anthony's upbringing."

"He's often told me that he was visiting his parents, even though I now know they were dead. He did that yesterday in fact. He said he was helping his parents pick out a boiler, but I presume he was really with... Anthony."

The child's name struggles to come off my tongue.

"Now that you've mentioned it," Debbie says, "I guess he

must have pretended that they were still alive so that he could spend more time with Anthony."

"Evidently."

Once again, silence descends, and the room seems to get colder and colder. I pull a blanket from the back of the sofa, and throw it over my shoulders. I can't believe what I've been told. It's absolutely staggering.

"Look," Debbie says, "I'm so sorry you've had to find out about my son like this. Anthony is such a lovely boy, and he adores his dad. Despite the circumstances, Scott has always been fully involved in his life. He's been a great father."

That's it. After everything that's been revealed this afternoon, that last sentence is the last straw. I leave my seat and stand on the rug Scott and I bought from London two years ago, but I fear it is about to give way beneath me. I buckle over, and almost hit my face on the coffee table as I gasp for breath.

"Shit. Are you okay?"

Debbie jumps up and flings her arm around my shoulders and I am too exhausted to brush her off. I can smell her perfume. It's Daisy by Marc Jacobs. I know because Lauren wears it. She sits me on the sofa, but I still struggle to breathe.

"Wait there," she shouts, and rushes into the kitchen.

I hear her rustling through my drawers, and a couple of seconds later, she arrives back in the living room clutching a paper bag.

"Here, breathe into this."

She hands me the bag, and sits next to me. I blow into it the way I've seen in the movies, and surprisingly it works. My composure returns.

"Are you okay now?"

I nod, and move away from her. I don't want her anywhere near me at this moment.

"Please could you leave," I say. "I can't do any more of this today."

Debbie nods, stands up and zips her jacket.

"I agree. Look, I'm so sorry I've upset you," she says. "Now I know why Scott didn't want me to come here. He didn't want me to tell you about Anthony."

"Please leave," I say, without looking up.

I close my eyes, a whoosh goes past me, and then the front door slams, announcing her departure.

She's gone.

And so is my mind.

CHAPTER FOURTEEN

"I want to know everything about Anthony. Every little thing."

Scott stares at me as though I've announced that I want him to explain the theory of relativity.

"He's a good kid," he says. "What more can I say?"

My estranged husband sits in the living room, lit up only because of a small lamp in the corner. I know that he'll hate this set-up. Scott is a big light kind of man. He says that he can't see the full picture with a tiny lamp. Ironic really, since he's hidden the full picture for the past ten years.

"Oh, I think there's much more to say. The fact that you've concealed him from me for the past decade, is... is... incredible to say the least. By all rights, I'm his stepmother, and I have a right to know what he's like, and that he actually exists!"

"His stepmother?" Scott laughs, and rubs his eyes. "I knew this would happen. I knew you'd react this way. That's why I never wanted to tell you."

Once again, he turns his indiscretion around as though it's my fault... He falls for Gabby Haine – my fault for ignoring him. He has a secret Facebook account – my fault that I found it. He had an affair ten years ago – my fault, I was too busy with writing and rugby. And now he has a secret son – my fault that I didn't know, because I ask too many questions.

"Oh, fuck off," I say. "Why wouldn't you want to tell me about your own son? Even the most neurotic of wives deserves to be told something that huge."

Scott slams his fist onto the coffee table, rattling the little vase and the coasters.

"I didn't tell you for obvious reasons!" he says. "Like I didn't want you to know that I'd cheated on you for instance! It wasn't one of my finest moments."

"You're telling me!"

He rubs his hand, and wiggles his fingers, presumably checking for any injury. I wish that every bone had broken. He surely deserves it.

"But in addition to that," he says, "you've struggled since Charlie passed away, and I was afraid that if you found out, you'd try and replace him with Anthony."

My solar plexus contracts. I can't believe what he's just said. How dare he assume such a thing? How dare he?!

"Replace Charlie?" I shout. "Are you insane?! I couldn't replace our son in any way, who would do that? Unless that's what you did?"

Scott shoots me a look that could freeze hell, and jumps up from the armchair.

"Don't you ever say that," he shouts. "Our son was the best thing that ever happened to me, and I miss him and think about him every single day."

Scott rarely raises his voice, and when he does, I know that he must be really, really pissed off. Before I can stop myself, I spring up from the sofa, and glare straight into his eyes.

"You think about Charlie every day?" I spit. "Every day? You could have fooled me! The first time I've seen any true outpouring of feelings from you was the other week at the party. You've been a zombie for the past ten years before that."

"Are you being serious right now?!" he screams.

"Yes, I am."

I know I am pushing him, and I'm also aware that what I'm saying isn't the truth, because he spent hours in the early days crying about Charlie. But in this moment, there is a part of me that can't help but wonder if the emotion was for our son, or for the information that he has secretly kept from me all these years. Maybe both. I'll never know.

Scott collapses into the armchair where the mother of his other child sat hours before. He plays with a piece of fluff on the cushion and sniffs.

"So, what do you want to do?"

"What do you mean?"

"You've found out I had an affair," he says, "and now you know that I have a child. I'm presuming you want me to move out." His jaw is clenched, his nostrils flared. He's on a power trip, deflecting his lies and making me out to be the bad one. "Of course, you'll need to get a well-paying job if you want to stay here. Your book royalties aren't exactly setting the joint account on fire, you haven't written anything for a decade, and your little publishing job definitely doesn't pay enough to support you."

I'm confused for a moment, and then I remember that Scott has no knowledge of me being fired from Babbage Books. How would he know? He wasn't here this morning when I found out, and I'm not about to tell him now. But even though he's being sarcastic, he's right, I can't afford to pay the mortgage and run this house even if I still had the Babbage work. I'd have to move out of the home we shared with Charlie, and where his bedroom is still exactly as he left it. No, that can't happen. I can't allow that to happen.

"You shouldn't move out," I say, and Scott's cheeks puff out in confusion.

"You're joking."

"No, I'm not."

A silence hangs in the space between us. He rubs his mouth with the back of his hand, and I notice that his lips are dry and peeling. He can't believe what I said, and neither can I.

"You want to stay together, after all this?"

"Stay together? No, I never said stay together. I said that you shouldn't move out. Not yet anyway."

Scott nods.

"Sorry, I misunderstood. I thought you meant stay as a couple. That's why I was so surprised."

"Well, I didn't mean that," I say, and tears well into my eyes.

The sad thing is though, that even after everything that's happened, I do want us to stay together. Not in our current form, not in this land of destruction. I want to stay as we were just a week ago. Recovering – kind of – from Charlie's passing, but finding ourselves again, driving to the seaside on the spur of the moment, watching ridiculous television shows like *The Masked Singer*, and *The Traitors*. Curled up on the sofa, wearing my *Home Alone* pyjamas no matter what season it is. Popping to Costa for a cuppa and a piece of cake, even though we've got both in the cupboard. Traipsing round shopping centres, buying books, and candles, and yes, tea and cake again. Playing Scrabble on the coffee table, and laughing at the rude words. Looking for Scott's glasses, or his car keys, or both. Making love. Being normal. Being a long-standing couple, traumatised but moving forward regardless.

I want that part of us to stay together.

I want everything I have lost in the space of just seven days.

In short, I want what I now know to be a lie, but even that life is gone.

"I know it's probably not the popular decision," I say, "and likely it's crazy, but yes, I do want you to stay here. If we separated, the house would be sold, and I can't bear the thought of losing all the many years we've invested in this place. So, if that's the only way I get to keep what we once had then I want us both to stay here. We can worry about the logistics later."

My lungs feel heavy, and I fear I'm about to have another panic attack. I sigh just long enough to regulate myself back to calmness. Or my version of it.

"Wow." Scott hunches forward, and a tear falls from his eye and splats onto his jeans. "What's the catch?"

"No catch," I say. "Our marriage might be in tatters – thanks to you – but we've been together too long to just walk away from everything. Except if you want to leave of course. Do you want to be with her?"

Scott moves his head in small, jerky movements, and then laughs.

"With Debbie? Of course not. I told you, that was over ten years ago, it was a mistake and it meant nothing. The only reason I still see her is because of Anthony, and he's the one good thing to come out of it all."

The one good thing to come out of his affair was Anthony. Was Charlie the only good thing to come out of our marriage? He'd never admit it, but it's a possibility. I look at the clock on the wall – a wedding present that we've had forever – and it's only 8.35pm, but it seems like midnight. The only logical thing to do is to give up the fight and throw him out, but I know that if I do that, I'll lose more from my life than my marriage.

"If you don't want to be with her," I say, "then we should stay here, in our home. We've known each other since 1988, and by your own admission the affair was ten years ago, and hasn't been repeated since. Has it?"

"No!" he snaps. "It was just that time."

"In that case, stay."

Scott stares up at me, and in that moment I see the relief in his tear-stained eyes. I'm sad that he's relieved. I'm angry that he thinks I'll forgive him so quickly, so easily, but that's my fault, isn't it? I took him back immediately after the Gabby Haine incident and as far as he's concerned, I swept the whole thing under the carpet, just as he does with the things that cause him pain. Yes, I'm disappointed with the relief in his eyes. I can't win with myself.

"We've travelled a long road together," he says, "and I don't want to give up on us. Not right now. Not like this." Another tear pops over his lower lashes. I hand him a tissue, and he dabs his eyes. "Thank you. It doesn't seem right to throw everything away, but I must say that I'm shocked, because if I ever found out you'd cheated on me, I probably wouldn't be so forgiving."

A laugh escapes from my throat, and I sit heavily into the chair.

"There's no chance of that happening," I say. "I've always been faithful. Loved you too much to ever put you through such pain."

That's true, I never would have hurt Scott. Not because I never had the opportunity, but because I took my vows seriously when we got married. To this day I could never break them, even after recent events.

"I do believe you'd never cheat," Scott says with a smile, and I want to slap him. It would be nice in this moment if he could feel the slightest bit of concern that I might one day have my head turned. It would be satisfying if the seeds of jealousy could just this once puncture his rigid heart.

Maybe I should have told him about the bloke in my office who declared his love for me when Scott and I were 'on a break'. Maybe I should have told him about that old boyfriend who swung into my DMs the moment he found me on Instagram, and asked me out for lunch – even though he was married. Yes, maybe I should have told Scott all of those things, but the truth remains that in spite of any past admirers, I have always been faithful to him because I thought the strength of our relationship wasn't worth even the slightest of flirtations.

"I could move into the spare room if you want me to," he says. "Just until we navigate this new chapter."

"Well, you're definitely not sleeping in my bed. I'm not that stupid."

"I know you're not, and I understand. I'll move my stuff into the other room tonight."

Scott's body buckles under the relief that his wife of twenty-five-years is somehow prepared to try and forget recent events. I'm pretty sure I can't – and won't – but I'm happy for him to believe I can, until I find a way of getting myself back together, and figure out what I want to do. He jumps up from the armchair, throws his arms around my shoulders and hugs me harder than he ever has in the whole of our relationship. His touch is alien to me now, and I do not dare hug him back. My fingers might burn if I so much as touch him. His breath comes in short bursts, and I can feel his tears on the side of my face. It takes all of my energy not to push him away.

"I love you," he whispers through the tears. "I'm so sorry. I promise I won't ever hurt you again."

And then he receives a call, and leaves the room.

***

Later that night, when the silence between us has become too much, I come up to the bedroom, take most of Scott's clothes from the wardrobe and dump them onto the bed in the spare room. The draft causes the papers on his desk to flutter to the ground, but I don't care. He can sort them out himself. He can sleep on top of them for all I care.

When I return to our former marital bedroom, Scott's leather jacket – the jacket that started all of this craziness – stares at me from the bottom of the wardrobe. Hot, flaming rage explodes in my belly, and I grab the scissors from my dressing-table drawer. My intention in that moment is to shred the jacket to pieces. To unravel every stitch, every button, every zip, every creak of leather, and then to start on everything else he holds dear... His car, his computers, his phone, his barely-worn hiking gear... He deserves some revenge. I've held my anger in long enough, and he deserves everything that I can throw at him. Every scratch, every cut, every rip, every tear. I'll destroy it all.

I hold the jacket up by the arm, and as I do so, I catch sight of myself in the mirror on the inside of the wardrobe door. I freeze. My face is contorted into a knot so tight I barely recognise myself. My hair is long, and unbrushed, and in desperate need of a cut and dye. There are bags under my eyes from crying, and although I am wearing a perfectly lovely red woollen dress, for the first time I notice that it is out of style by at least ten years. My eyes scan the rest of my clothes in the wardrobe, and it is then that I realise – apart from underwear and essentials, I haven't bought a single piece of clothing since Charlie passed away. Everything is stuck in 2014. My hair, my clothes, my memories, and now my marriage. My whole being ended a decade ago. Every single part of it.

I stare at my reflection in the mirror. A pathetic woman with gleaming scissors in my hand, ready to destruct Scott's leather jacket in the way of revenge. And it is at that moment that I know. I can't fight back with his belongings. He can quickly replace any and all of those. No, petty revenge is no good for me. It is not who I am, or who I want to be, and it certainly isn't something that I want to be pushed into by my cheating, lying husband.

I once read a quote purported to be from Frank Sinatra, which said that the best revenge was massive success. I always loved that, and held it close when I was building my career in front of those former work colleagues who never believed in me. Now that quote rattles through my head again, and I know that the best revenge I can perform in this moment is to pull myself together, reclaim my life, and remove myself from Scott's.

I slump down on the floor, drop the scissors onto the carpet next to me, and clutch the leather jacket to my chest. I'll be brave in the morning, but for now, I allow myself to cry.

CHAPTER FIFTEEN

Since we decided to stay 'together' (I use the word lightly) two weeks ago, Scott has been the epitome of kind, gracious and reflective. He's done all the household jobs that he'd been putting off, like painting the landing, and changing one of the ceiling lightbulbs in the bathroom that had been out for months. He is still seeing Anthony (which means he also sees Debbie), but instead of pretending that he's heading off for a day of hiking, or going to see his parents, he's been telling the truth about what he's doing, how long he'll be there, and when he'll be back.

The conversations are awkward in that regard, and I know when they're coming, because Scott flits around the room, moving random ornaments, straightening the curtains, that kind of thing. Eventually I'll ask if there's something he needs to say, and that will be his cue to blurt out that he's got a trip to the zoo planned, or a visit to the shopping centre to buy Anthony a new school uniform. After he's told me what he's doing, he always makes out like it's something he doesn't want to do.

"Debbie organised it. I'm so sorry..." Rolls eyes.

"Anthony is insisting I go with them..." Shrugs shoulders.

Every time he has to go out with them, my heart breaks a little bit more, which is strange really, because during the past ten years he's been seeing his new son on a regular basis, so I really shouldn't be surprised that he's still seeing him. Except for the fact that I didn't know about any of it of course. That's the zinger. That's the bit that makes it so raw, and painful, infuriating, and real. Still, I never show any of this to Scott. Instead, I come up with a silly excuse as to why it's all okay.

"Oh, that's good timing because I've got to pop over to my mum and dad's this morning," I'll say. Sometimes I do go over there, but the truth of the matter is it's painful seeing them, because I haven't told them about any of this, but I know I have to. I have to do that soon.

It's Monday morning, which is always a relief, because I no longer enjoy the weekend, either when he spends it with me, or he spends it with Anthony and Debbie. It's all still a lie. It's all still a circus. He says that he loves me, but I question that every time our eyes meet, and I never say it back to him.

What other secrets is he keeping?

Or is that it?

I can't know for sure, and in that regard, for the past couple of weeks – in those moments when I'm feeling strong enough – I have begun to lay the foundations toward trying to sort out my life. I need to gain some independence. I have a little money saved, meaning that I don't need to admit to Scott that I'm no longer working, but it won't last forever. I do need to earn some money, and then sort out my assets, because when this awful lie of a marriage finally implodes, I need to be ready.

Scott has no clue, but whenever he heads to the office, I try to push myself to do a little something, even the tiniest, positive thing. I exercise for hours every day, I am giving meditation a second go, I am journaling and making lists, I am going through old story and article ideas, and I am creating timetables. I bought a couple of new outfits, got my hair cut into a long, layered bob and had it dyed with blonde highlights. Scott didn't notice the clothes, but did see the cut straight away. He didn't compliment it, of course. Instead, he smiled, flicked the hair at the back of my head, and told me it was different. In all honesty, he never liked my hair short, so in that regard, I'm pleased that I did it. A silly bit of revenge, in a haze of muddled thoughts.

In short, I am trying desperately (and secretly) to heal myself, so that I can be strong enough to relaunch my writing career, and maybe – just maybe – regain some of the remnants of the person I used to be. Today, I've edited my LinkedIn profile, updated my Instagram page with photos of my old books, and took a look at the Babbage Books website. It was never the best job in the world, and barely paid minimum wage, but at least it was something. I miss the job and miss the crazy authors I had to deal with every day, which has come as a surprise to me.

The Babbage website looks the same, apart from a couple of new books – ones that I had seen through production a month ago – and the news that they have hired a new me. Her name is Claudia Parker, she looks young enough to be my daughter, and has bright blonde hair, and even brighter teeth. *We welcome Claudia to our team*, reads the announcement. *Claudia is a former primary school teacher, and the proud mother of a three-month-old son, Barney. We wish her lots of luck at Babbage Books!* I smile. Sam has no clue, but I would imagine that the only reason Claudia has accepted that job is so that she can work flexible hours while her son is a baby. The moment he's off to nursery – or maybe even before then – she'll be back to teaching.

"You should have stuck with me," I say to myself, although I'm sure Sam would think differently. That said, I would laugh so hard if the crazy emails and complaints now continued under the new girl's name. That might clear my own name – or add to the conspiracy, I'm not sure which.

I open Instagram again, and I'm thrilled to see that already there are twelve likes on my book post, and two comments.

Brilliant books, someone called Martha says. *God, I wish you'd write another one!*

I got your first novel for my birthday, says a woman called Janet Pickering. *I read it in a day. Currently working my way through the others. Hope there'll be more when I get to the end of them!*

"Maybe one day," I say, as I like both comments. My readers have been so supportive in the past ten years, buying my old books for friends and family, and rereading the ones they already had in their collections, but with no new books coming out, I can't help but notice that my followers are slowly but surely going down. It seems to me that the only new ones I've had recently are either 'American servicemen' looking for someone to scam, new authors looking for a mention on my page, or shifty new accounts pretending to be marketers or influencers. It has come to the point now where if I get a real reader on my page, it not only warms my heart, but it slightly confuses me too.

But whatever I have thought about myself recently, there is no denying that I was once a bestselling writer, and maybe one day I can be again.

Maybe.

As I'm about to be swallowed up by the past, my phone pings. It's Lauren.

Hey, I was wondering if you're up for a catch-up. Fancy a coffee?

Definitely. See you soon.

I upload another Instagram book post, read and reply to the existing comments, and then switch off my laptop.

———

"How's it going? All okay?"

Lauren looks at me over the top of her glasses. Her eyes are narrowed, and her forehead crumpled.

"Yeah, it's okay." I sigh. "We're plodding on."

"Plodding on? Bollocks to that! It's time you chucked him out for real this time!"

An old lady at the next table raises her eyebrows, and Lauren gives her a side-eye. I take a sip of tea. It is hot against my tongue, but not as hot as my friend's words. She knows that nothing is okay. Everything is one long, torturous day.

"In truth," I say, "this situation is bloody killing me. I wake up every morning, and for the first two seconds things are normal, and then it hits me like a steamroller. Somehow, I manage to get through the day, and then I'm back in bed, and the whole thing starts again the next morning."

Lauren leans over and rubs my arm.

"I can imagine. I don't know how you're doing it, to be honest."

"Neither do I," I say, "but for now it's all I can do."

"But you're not thinking about sweeping it all under the carpet, are you? Because I'm not going to lie, I've been worried about that ever since you told me you weren't chucking him out."

I laugh with a mouthful of tea, and it shoots up to my nose, and makes me cough.

"God no! Scott might believe that there's hope for our future, but I can assure you that as painful as it is, there is no chance of anything going back to normal."

Lauren's phone pings, and she takes a look. Her nose crinkles, and she swipes the message off the screen.

"Ugh. Delete!"

"What's wrong?"

"Nothing," she says. "Just this guy I matched with last week. We met up at the weekend, and it was hideous. He was wearing skin-tight stone-washed jeans, and told me that his last marriage broke up because his wife and her workmates caught him watching porn and masturbating when they came back from a work's night out!"

"Jesus. You need to delete whatever app you use to find these people!"

Lauren grimaces, and shoves the phone back into her handbag.

"Anyway," she says, "back to you. Personally, I think you should have broken up immediately, shut the door and let Scott stew in his own juice! That's what I did, and Michael hadn't done half the shit Scott has done!"

"I know," I say, "and I appreciate your concern, I really do, but I need to take my time, to make sure that everything's done to my own advantage, not Scott's."

Lauren shoots me a look.

"And how exactly are you going to do that?"

"I have no idea, but I'm sure it will come to me."

I smile at my friend, and assure her – assure us both – that I really don't have any intention of repairing the tatters of my marriage. However, I will admit that there are times when I get lost in the drama of my relationship. On days like those, I'll lounge on the sofa, and dissect every detail of the last ten years. I go over old diary entries, old texts and messages, and from all of those I have pieced together hundreds of times when Scott has been potentially lying to me. I do believe that his affair with Debbie only lasted a short time, but all the things they did together live rent-free within me, every single day. When Scott left me for Gabby Haine, all I could see in my mind was them having sex, and now it's exactly the same, only with Scott and Debbie.

Naked.

Writhing.

In positions that I've only ever imagined, not experienced.

Strangely, the thing that brings me the most pain though, is the thought of them kissing, or him going down on her, or vice versa. The basic sex act I can just about handle, but the mouth aspect of the whole thing? The nipple-sucking? The thigh-licking? It makes me want to tear my brain out.

And yet I cannot stop thinking about it.

"Hey! Are you listening to me?"

Lauren pats my arm, and I jump.

"Sorry, I was miles away," I say, and I rub my eyes.

"I was talking away to you, and it was as if you were in a trance."

"I'm tired." I stifle a yawn. "I didn't get much sleep last night. Or any night. So, what were you saying?"

"I was telling you that I saw Gabby Haine the other day!"

Gabby Haine. The words burn a hole in my eardrums. I have been so engrossed in my new obsession that I had temporarily – kind of – brushed Gabby aside. Now her name jolts me as it has done so many times in the past.

"You saw Gabby Haine? Where?"

"I went to Norwich with my crochet club," Lauren says. "There was this big conference thing going on, and so we hired a minibus. Anyway, I was minding my own business, looking at the stalls, and I saw this book I fancied... it didn't have a price on it, so I asked the woman behind the table, and it was bloody Gabby!"

"Are you sure?"

The waitress comes over to clear our plates, and we sit back to let her get on with her job. I'm so desperate to continue with our conversation that it seems as though she takes forever. The woman piles the plates and cups onto her tray, gives the table a wipe, and then disappears into the back room without saying a word.

"She wants rid of us," Lauren says. "But yes, I'm positive it was Gabby. She was wearing a badge that had her name on it, and to be honest, I probably wouldn't have recognised her if not for the fact that you'd not long shown me her Facebook page. She looks a lot older than her profile pic by the way. It's either a really old photo, or she's used a filter, but either way, yeah, she looked a bit different. It was definitely her though."

Lauren pulls a tissue out of her pocket, dabs her nose, and then sniffs.

"And she was on a crochet stall?" I ask, my mind a whirr of activity.

"More of a craft stall, really," she says. "She was selling books and patterns. Not her own, I should add, but there were a lot of bits and bobs that she'd made herself. She was also doing her own crochet when I spoke to her, but I never let on that I knew who she was."

I laugh. For thirty-odd years I've thought of Gabby Haine as something akin to a red-outfitted horned vixen, who spends her time hunting for attached men to have her wicked way with. The idea of her enjoying something as wholesome and normal as crafts and crochet is mind-blowing. I would have guessed that her hobby was more on the lines of scheming and lying. Politics maybe, but certainly not crochet.

"Blimey. What did you say to her?"

Lauren shrugs.

"To be honest, I was so surprised to see her that I couldn't think of anything to say at first. I just stared at her like a right weirdo. But she was quite decent actually. Friendly enough. I asked how much the book was, and she told me and I bought it. That was about it, really. I didn't want to ask any specific questions in case she worked out that I know you and Scott. Oh, but she did give me this…"

Lauren rummages in her bag and pulls out a small card. It's a sickly pink colour with gold writing. My friend hands it to me, and the gold letters catch the light, causing them to sparkle.

"'Gabby's Joyful Crafts. Crochet, knitting, sewing and special gifts, to live, to gift and to love'."

Underneath the words is her phone number, and Instagram name.

"Awful, isn't it?" Lauren laughs. "It's all ridiculously corny, from the colour to the font, to the words."

"Yes, it's horrible. Looks like some kind of medicine advert… Can I keep it?"

"Why?"

"Not sure. Maybe I'll take up crochet."

Lauren rolls her eyes.

"I was going to throw it away once I'd shown you, but if you want to keep it, you're welcome. Just don't do anything stupid with it. Like show Scott, for instance. You don't need to add this bit of the past to all the other crap you're dealing with."

"I won't show him anything," I say, and I stuff the card into my pocket.

We leave the restaurant, Lauren gets into her car, and then my phone rings. I'm surprised to discover that it is Joseph from the Regency Hotel. I hesitate to answer, frightened that he might have found out something else, but curiosity gets the better of me. I swipe to accept the call.

"Hello?"

"Hey, Olivia. It's Joseph here. You know, from the Regency."

"Hi, Joseph! What can I do for you?"

Lauren drives past and gives me a wave before disappearing round the corner.

"I wanted to let you know that I'm not at the Regency anymore," Joseph says. "I left yesterday."

"You did? How come? I thought you enjoyed that job."

Joseph coughs on the other end of the phone.

"I did. Well, you know, it wasn't my dream or anything, but it was a job and I was glad to have it."

"So why have you left?"

The wind whips around my legs, and a drop of rain plops onto my cheek. I scramble into my car as the heavens open.

"I was fired," Joseph says, and I can just about hear him over the sound of the rain on my car roof.

"What do you mean, you were fired? Why?"

"Gross misconduct. It was from that photo. The one I took of your husband and his mistress. Somebody reported me for taking it, and I was hauled into the office."

Scott. It must have been Scott.

My hands sweat as I clutch the handset to my ear.

"Oh God," I say. "This is my fault. I accidentally said something to my husband during an argument about his affair. He must have made the complaint. I'm so sorry."

"Aww, don't beat yourself up about it," Joseph says. "It's my own fault. I should have minded my own business and not said anything to you. My mum always says I should learn to keep my mouth shut."

"No, what you did really helped me. If you hadn't told me about it, I would probably still have been in the dark about everything... Look, let me phone the Regency and explain. I'll say that it was all my fault..."

There's a long puffing sound on the other end of the phone, and I imagine Joseph letting out a long stream of cigarette smoke.

"You don't have to do that," he says.

"Yes, I do. This is so wrong. I made you take that photo. You didn't want to, and I forced your hand. Leave it with me, okay?"

The line goes dead, and I look at my screen. No service.

Shit.

I type a quick message to Joseph in the hope that it will eventually send, apologising for everything. I can't seem to do anything right these days, but maybe I can rectify this. I start my car, and drive home in the rain.

CHAPTER SIXTEEN

The house is dark when I get back, and there is no sign of Scott. He told me this morning that he was going to make spaghetti Bolognese for both of us this evening, and while I've been trying to cut pasta from my diet, I was quite happy to let him. But there is no sign of cooking in the kitchen. The pots are still in the cupboard, the pasta is still in the container, and the tomatoes are still in the fridge. I check my phone and there are no messages, so decide he must be running late, and make myself a cup of tea.

It works out quite well that Scott's out, however, as it means I can call the Regency in peace. I don't know for sure if it was my dear husband who reported Joseph, but who else could it have been? I wouldn't put anything past him at this point, and I feel awful that he has chosen to attack a young man not much younger than our son would have been. Not that Scott knows that of course, but still...

At first, the Regency receptionist refuses to put me through to the manager, but once I explain who I'm calling about, she relents. Apparently, she has a soft spot for Joseph and feels it is unfair that he's been fired. That we can agree on.

When the manager picks up, his voice is booming, and loud and intimidating, and while normally I'd be distracted by such an attitude, I have gone through so much recently that it doesn't faze me. I explain the situation to him, and at first his stance is uncaring and complacent, but I've got a lot of experience of talking to all sorts of folk in my writing career, and I put my skills to good use now. I tell him that if anyone is to blame, it's me, and by the end of the seventeen-minute call, the manager has calmed down. He has even admitted that Joseph was a fantastic employee, and while he can make no promises about the cocky waiter's future at the Regency, he is willing to at least think about options.

Progress. After my cuppa, I fire off a message to Joseph, telling him that I've done my best. He thanks me, and then a little later, messages again to tell me that the Regency has been in touch. There are no guarantees, but there will be a meeting and an opportunity for discussion. I smile, and send him a heart emoji. It warms me somewhat to be able to help somebody who is a similar age to my son. I like to think that if Charlie had survived, people would want to help him too.

That all done, I make the most of being on my own, and whack the heating up to eighteen degrees. Ever since the gas bills went up, Scott has insisted that we go no further than fifteen, but if he's not here, he'll never know. Hell, secretly turning up the heating is nothing compared to the secrets he's kept from me. I make another cup of tea, and send him a message.

> Where are you? Do you want me to start
> dinner? It doesn't bother me, but you did say
> that you were making spaghetti tonight. Is that
> still the plan?

A message comes back three minutes later.

> Oh shit! I'm so sorry, I forgot to tell you. It's Anthony's parents' evening, so I've taken him and Debbie to the school. We're having pizza afterwards, so I don't need any dinner, but I can bring you something back if you like? So sorry I forgot to tell you. I'd much rather be home, believe me. See you soon. Love you.

I slam my mug so hard that the tea splashes over the side and dribbles onto the table. I grab one of Scott's clean shirts off the radiator and mop up the mess. In spite of the promises of no more lies, this is yet another outing I didn't know about, another story kept from me, even though the line was supposedly drawn under ten years of deceit and sabotage.

I put my phone onto silent, stick a ready-made curry in the microwave, grab the business card that Lauren gave to me, and stare at it. It is a bizarre feeling that Gabby Haine has touched this card. It has been in her hand, it has been in her bag, it has been in her home.

And now it is in mine.

It's repulsive, but I can't let it go.

Gabby's Instagram page is as pretentious as she makes herself out to be. The theme is pink and gold, and almost every photo has the same colour scheme in the background. The pictures themselves are made up of different items that she's crafted herself. Textile Christmas decorations, felt teddy bears and dolls, crochet blankets and knitted sweaters. She's certainly got some skills, I'll give her that, and to be honest, if she wasn't Gabby Haine, I might be interested in buying a sweater or two.

But I can't do that of course.

It would be like wearing the skin of the woman who once fucked my then fiancé.

A shiver rises through my back, but I continue to scroll Gabby's page. It's like watching someone fall in the street – awful, but you have to look. She has a fairly respectable 2,476 followers, and she follows 1,302. I click on both and search for Scott's name, but I can't see anyone who could be him, which is something of a relief.

There are very few photos of Gabby herself, but the ones she has published are almost always of her wearing one of her sweaters, or holding a crochet blanket. There are some of her in nondescript places, like against an interior wall, or with a closed curtain behind her. But one of them is rather interesting. It was posted on a hot day in July 2023, and shows her standing in a garden, leaning against a gigantic conservatory. She's wearing a knitted summer hat, a T-shirt with flowers all over it, and skin-tight pink jeans the likes of which I haven't seen since the 1980s. She's holding a glass of rosé wine, in a long-stemmed glass. The caption is a corny tribute to the summer months:

Beautiful day to be in the garden, but protecting myself from the sun's rays with my knitted hat. (Please DM me for price.) Long days, short nights, a glass of wine, a good book, and the sound of birds and the river bubbling past my back fence. The village teddy bears' picnic is on later, and I've got my teddy ready! Bliss. Total, utter bliss. Have a beautiful day, everybody. I know I will!

Bliss. Bliss it may be, but the caption is also far more revealing than she ever intended it to be. The mention of a river next to her back garden, for instance, and the teddy bears' picnic. While on the subject, who on earth goes to a teddy bears' picnic when they're in their fifties? Maybe she has grandchildren, but there is no trace of them on her Instagram page if she does.

I take a screenshot of the photo, and then come out of Instagram for fear of accidentally liking one of her posts. I log on to my newspaper archive account and search for teddy bears' picnics in July of last year. There are a few results, but I filter my search to only include those relevant to Norfolk. I could be wrong, but if she was at a craft fair in Norwich, then I'm going to imagine she still lives in our county.

The filter narrows the search to two results. One near Great Yarmouth, and another in Storley-on-the-Water. Storley is the biggest clue of where Gabby now lives, so I go onto Google Earth and search. Sure enough there is a river heading straight through the middle of Storley, and it takes me only a few seconds to find a row of houses next to it, and one with a large conservatory on the back. I flick onto street view, and before I know it, I'm virtually standing outside of what appears to be Gabby Haine's house, at the top of a quiet cul-de-sac.

Bingo.

There are no random photos of her walking up the road, or looking out of the window, but outside the house is a pink Beetle car, and there are cerise-coloured curtains hanging at her bedroom and living-room windows. Evidence of her living there would never hold up in a court of law, but for me – for now – it is enough. I google how far she lives from us, and it's just over thirty minutes. Not too far, but far enough to ensure that I'm not likely to bump into her – unless I have a sudden interest in craft fairs, teddy bears' picnics or riverside walks of course.

Until then, she can stay far, far away from me.

<hr>

Scott gets in around 8.30pm, full of apologies.

"I can't believe that I forgot to tell you," he says. He tries to give me a hug, but my whole body tightens at the very touch of his fingers. "In my defence, I had forgotten about it myself until this morning. Debbie kind of sprung it on me a couple of days ago, because Anthony had forgotten to give her the letter."

He rolls his eyes, as if it's a funny faux pas that frequently happens. Maybe it is. The idea of my husband going to some kid's parents' evening is diabolical, but I hold my feelings in. I can't let myself be vulnerable. I need to stay in this position long enough for me to find my feet again.

And then I'll be gone. Or he will be.

"It's okay," I lie. "I understand. Tea?"

"I'd love some. The tea at the open evening was horrendous. Looked like milk in lukewarm water."

He sits heavily into the armchair, and takes off his boots. I hate it when he doesn't take them off in the hall. I hate the thought of him walking germs into the house, and I especially hate that he's walking in school germs. School germs from his secret son's school, no less. I can't believe how nonchalant he is about going to a parents' evening, but then it occurs to me. Maybe this isn't the first one he's been to. Maybe it's something that him and Debbie have been doing regularly over the years.

"Have you been many times before?"

"Eh?"

"To parents' evening. Have you been to many parents' evenings?"

He places his boots neatly next to the fire, and shrugs.

"I've been to a few. Not many. Debbie was doing them on her own when Anthony was at infant school, but now that he's heading toward secondary, I'm a bit more involved."

"Of course. It's good to be involved." The words almost choke me.

Scott smiles, completely at ease with my gentle attitude. He's so bloody stupid. As if I would forgive him so easily for what he's done to me! For what he's doing to me! He should know by now that I forget nothing, no matter how much time has passed.

I make the tea, and he takes a mouthful. I hope it burns his tongue and his throat, but instead he runs the back of his hand over his lips, and sighs.

"Lovely. I needed that."

"I can imagine." I sit on the sofa opposite him, and curl my legs under my body.

"No tea for you?" he asks.

"I've not long had one."

"Good, good. So, what have you been up to this evening?"

I'd love to tell him that I've spent most of the night having a good gander through Gabby Haine's Instagram. *Yes, my dear, I found her pink-and-gold page, had a laugh at the corniness of it all, oh, and then I found out exactly where she lives. Yes, that's what I've been up to, while you were with your other family.*

I chuckle at the thought, and Scott looks up from his tea.

"What's funny?"

His face beams and he smiles broadly, as though expecting some kind of hilarious anecdote. I shake my head.

"Oh, it's nothing really. Just a stupid joke that Lauren told me earlier. I met her for tea today."

"Ahh."

He gets back to his drink, uninterested in anything Lauren had to say. He's never been particularly fond of my friend. In the early days of our relationship, she was a bit too involved for his liking. She was my best friend and so if Scott and I had a fallout I'd tell her everything, and she'd often comment her displeasure within Scott's earshot. He couldn't stand that, especially when it came to the Gabby Haine situation. Days after we broke up, Lauren bumped into Scott in the pub and told him exactly what she thought about him leaving me – and especially the way he'd done it.

"It's not my fault," he said, shirking all responsibility. "I did everything I could, but the only thing she's interested in is her career."

Lauren hated him from that moment on.

"How you ever put up with that floppy-haired twat is beyond me," she told me afterwards. "This is a silver lining. You deserve more than him." I nodded and agreed, and all the time hid the fact that I was breaking inside, and desperate for him to return to me. When we eventually did get back together, Lauren was raging.

"How the hell can you take him back after all he's done to you? He's a walking red flag!"

"I know it's not ideal," I cried, "but I love him. When you fall in love, you'll understand."

It took my friend a long time to forgive Scott, though in the years since Charlie's passing she has mellowed to the point where she'll talk to him, and even defend him if she thinks I'm being a little dramatic. In retrospect, I maybe should have taken her earlier advice, studied those red flags and ran far away from Scott, but if I had, I'd never have had our beautiful son, and he was surely worth every moment of the pain Scott wielded on me.

Charlie gave me fifteen years of beautiful life, and for that I'm forever grateful that I reunited with his father. But now he's gone, and another boy has arrived, and it pains me so much that this new child has no place in my life at all, except for having to listen to Scott talk about him.

For now.

An hour later, and I'm about to head upstairs when the front door goes. It's 9.30pm, and every instinct tells me not to open it, that somehow it will be an incarnation of Jack the Ripper, or some kind of scam artist, hoping to find a sucker. However, when I look at the Ring footage on my phone, I'm shocked to see that it's my mum and dad.

I head to the door, but Scott gets there just before me. He swings it open, and a whoosh of cold air bites through my clothes.

"Ken! Carol! To what do we owe the pleasure?"

Scott stands back and my parents push past him, shaking their jackets off and laughing.

"We were on our way home from seeing a production of *Shirley Valentine* at the theatre," my mum says. "Since we have to drive straight past your house, we thought we'd pop in."

My mum hands her coat to me, and my dad hands his to Scott. We both stare at each other for a second, and then decant the jackets onto the newel post at the bottom of the stairs.

"You weren't in bed were you?" Dad asks, oblivious to the fact that neither of us are in pyjamas.

"No, not yet," Scott says. "Won't be long though. I'm knackered." He pretends to yawn, and I know that even if he is tired, there's no way he'll be trotting off to bed before 10pm. No, he just wants rid of my parents, and their unexpected visit.

"Come through," I say, and usher them into the living room. Whenever I've seen them since finding out about the affair, I've had to gear myself up so that I don't accidentally tell them what's going on. Tonight, however, there's no opportunity to do that. I'm just going to have to wing it, and see how it goes.

"I'm just popping to the loo," I say, and Scott avoids my eye as he follows them into the living room. By the time I've gathered myself together in the bathroom, my parents are safely ensconced on the sofa, talking animatedly about the play.

"Oh, Olivia!" my mum says. "I was just saying to Scott that the production of *Shirley Valentine* was extraordinary..."

"Yes," my dad adds, "the production was second to none."

"And we know it's an amateur play and all that, but honestly, you could never tell."

"No, you could never tell!"

Words go back and forth between them as though they're playing conversational tennis, during which time my mum thrusts the programme into my hands and points out the cast, the crew, even the adverts in the back. I can't help but remember that they never had this much enthusiasm for theatre or acting when I wanted to be an actress. In fact, I do believe that when I showed them a brochure for RADA, my dad threw it across the room and told me I was being ridiculous.

Scott smiles, and nods and does his best to integrate himself into the conversation, but I know he'd rather be anywhere but here in this room, with my too-enthusiastic parents. My eyes flit between him and my dad who is sitting next to him, and that is when I see it.

Anthony's school report.

Right there on the coffee table, between us. I didn't notice it before, but Scott must have thrown it there when he came in this evening. It is blue, with a photograph of the school on the front, and the words *Parents' Evening, Forest-Newton primary school.* Underneath are the words *Anthony Collins, 6A,* in capital letters.

Scott wipes his mouth on the back of his hand, and stares at me. He knows it is there, but it is impossible for him to do anything about it without my parents seeing him. Shivers land in my solar plexus, and I know that I should be keen for my parents not to see it. I should throw a magazine on the top of it, or pretend to clear something from the table, and accidentally knock it underneath. Yes, I should do all of these things, and yet I can't bring myself to do any of them, because it gives me too much pleasure to see Scott squirm.

How will he get out of this one?

My arm tingles, and Scott's eyes are wide, begging me to intervene. Begging me to get rid of the report, or my parents, or both. I smile, and give him a little nod. His demeanour relaxes, his shoulders soften, and he smiles back.

I reach forward, discreetly scoop up the school report, and then hand it to my dad.

"Look at this wonderful report," I say. "We're both so proud!"

My mum stops talking about the leading lady's hairstyle, and strains to see what I've just given to my dad. I stare into Scott's face, and it is ashen. His eyes are so wide I fear they may pop out of his skull, his mouth is slack, and even from this distance, I know that he's holding his breath. He can't believe I've just given the school report to my dad, and that makes me want to laugh out loud. My heart pumps in my chest as my dad stares at the cover.

"Forest-Newton primary school? What's this then?" Dad slides his reading glasses onto his nose. "Anthony Collins? Is this your nephew, Scott?"

My mum tuts.

"Scott is an only child, Ken. You know that." She leans further forward to get a better view. "What is it?"

Scott ignores my mother's question, and sinks deep into the sofa, his fingers playing with his top lip. As our eyes meet, he shakes his head. An instruction not to explain, not to go any further. I take the report from my dad and hand it to my mum. She looks briefly at the front cover, and then opens it up.

"Oh, it's some kind of report card, is it? Who is it for? Who is Anthony?"

The question hangs in the air for a second, and I lick my lips, and rub my cheeks.

"Actually," I say, "Anthony is Scott's son."

My mum and dad exchange looks, while Scott shuffles in his seat.

"It's Charlie's report card, did you say?" My dad's brow furrows. He goes to take the report from my mum's fingers, but she leans back in her chair, and flicks through.

"No, not Charlie's," I say. "It's Anthony's."

"Anthony?" My dad's eyes flick up to the ceiling, as though he's trying to work out if he's somehow forgotten we had another son. My mum closes the report and lays it onto her knee. I can feel Scott eyeballing me, but I refuse to be drawn to him, or his displeasure.

"Anthony," she mumbles. "Anthony? How is he...? How can he be...?"

"Scott's son? Quite easily really. You see, your beloved son-in-law had an affair around the time Charlie passed away, and the result was Anthony."

"I don't understand." My dad sits upright in his chair and looks from me to Scott and then back again.

"Olivia," Scott says through gritted teeth. "Don't do this."

"Don't do what? Which bit don't you want me to tell them? That you found out about this kid on the day our own son died? Or that you hid him from me for ten years? Or, oh, maybe you don't want me to reveal that you forgot to tell me your own parents had died, just so you could spend more time with your other kid? Which bit don't you want me to tell them? Best let me know, before I blurt it all out!"

The last part of the sentence drops out of my mouth far louder than I expected it to, but it sends shivers of unexpected joy up my torso. My dad's nostrils flare, and my mum grabs at her neck. If she was wearing pearls, she'd surely be clutching them right now. Scott laughs, a strange, strangled, unbelieving laugh, and then jumps out of his seat.

"Thanks a million, Olivia," he says, and then storms from the room.

"You're welcome!" We all watch him go, and then I turn to my parents. "So, come on then... what do you want to know?"

My mum silently drops the report back onto the table as my dad stares across the room, lost in his own thoughts.

"Well, Ken," my mum says, "now do you agree that we should have just picked up a Costa, and driven straight home?"

An hour later, and my parents have left, with more answers than they ever expected or wanted to receive. Scott never came back, and as I enter his room, he is sat on the side of the bed, phone in his shaky hand. He looks up, barely recognises my presence, and then gets back to whatever it is he's doing.

"Happy now, are you?" he asks. "Happy that you told your parents all my business?"

I shrug, and loiter at the door like some kind of trespasser in my own home.

"All *your* business? I think you'll find that it's my business too... But yes, they needed to know." Scott rolls his eyes and I laugh. "What did you expect? That I would keep it a secret from them for another ten years? No way. No way am I keeping any secrets from anyone, let alone my parents."

"There's a time and a place for sharing news, and that wasn't it. I should have told them in my own way."

"Well, you didn't, so I sorted it for you."

Scott leans back into the pillows. I notice that the pillowslips he's used are the ones we bought last year when we were at a designer shopping outlet. I hate that he's used them. He should be sleeping on the old, thin ones like the dog that he is.

"What must they think of me?!"

He shakes his head, and snorts.

And there it is. The concern not for what Scott has put us through, not for the embarrassment or the heartbreak he's thrown in my direction, but for himself, and how he looks to my parents.

"You'll have to deal with their feelings as they come," I say. "But on another note, I want to meet him."

"Who?"

Scott stares at me, his forehead furrowed. Who the hell does he think I mean?

"Anthony. I want to meet Anthony."

My estranged husband squirms on the bed, and pretends to fish some imaginary debris out of his sock. As for me, I'm not sure why I suddenly blurted out that I want to meet his son. It is something that has been on my mind recently, but I had been prepared to wait for an introduction, but now that it's all come out to my parents, my mood has changed.

"I'm not sure that's possible," he says. "Not yet anyway. It's too soon."

I laugh in spite of myself.

"Too soon? It's been ten years! You've had more than enough time to get used to the idea, and I have every right to meet him. He's your son after all. Does he even know where you live?"

Another squirm. Another fake, imaginary piece of fluff in his sock.

"He's seen a photo of where I – we – live, and he's seen it on a map, but he doesn't really know where it is."

That breaks my heart. When I was a little girl, my dad was my hero. I used to watch for him coming in from work every night, and the sound of his voice in the kitchen was a comfort, a blessing, a warm, welcoming hug. If I only saw him for a couple of hours a week, and couldn't even visit his home, it would have destroyed me. But now here Anthony is, not even knowing for sure where his dad lives. That has to change.

"Does he know about me?" I ask.

"He knows I have a wife, yes."

"A wife? Does he even know my name?"

"I think so," Scott says. "Yes, I think he does, but Debbie and I have always been very discreet. Her family know that there are... complications."

So that's what I am? A complication. That doesn't fill me with joy or confidence. I suspect that I've been as much a secret to Anthony as he has been to me. I can't help but be sorry for this young lad. Despite everything, he's just a kid and didn't ask for any of this to happen. A little like myself.

"Well, it's time he gets to know me better," I say, "and I don't care what you think about it. I am your wife – even if it is only by name at this point – and Anthony deserves to know who I am, and where we live. Sort it out."

"I will if I get the chance," he snaps.

Scott's phone buzzes, he looks at it for a second and then throws it back onto the bed.

"Was that her?"

"Yes," he says. "She wanted to let me know that..."

"I couldn't care less what she wanted you to know, but there you go – there's your chance to tell her that you'd like Anthony to visit."

I point to his phone, expecting him to promptly pick it up and dial.

"I don't know how to bring that up," he snaps.

"Well, if you have any intention of saving this marriage, you'll find a way."

"I'm sorry, but it's not a good idea to introduce you to Anthony right now. It will only confuse him, and that's the last thing I want."

Debbie scowls at me from the other end of the kitchen table, while Scott's eyes flit between the two of us. It's just days since I told my husband that I want to meet Anthony, and now here we are, thrashing out the details of our new reality. We've been here for the past thirty-four minutes, and I'm knackered. It seems like all I've done so far is to tell Debbie that I'd like Anthony to visit us every other weekend, and she has brushed my words away at every turn.

"Look," I say, "I know that this is a difficult situation, and nobody is as disturbed as I am, believe me. But despite my grievances, Scott is Anthony's father, and we all deserve to be involved in his life."

Debbie looks from Scott to me. My husband, meanwhile, stares at the beach-themed place mat in front of him, and rubs his nose, avoiding all eye contact. The ironic thing is that this man is to blame for everything in this scenario, and yet he wants nothing to do with sorting it out at all. Debbie wasn't the one to make a vow to be faithful to me, although that doesn't mean that I don't hate her just the same.

"I understand that," Debbie says, "and I'm more than happy to have Scott involved in Anthony's life. He has been there since the beginning." She stares at me and then at Scott. "Tell her, tell her that you are very involved in his life!"

Debbie shakes Scott's arm, and I have to resist the urge to fly over the table and rip her fingers off. My husband jumps at her touch, but I'm unsure if that is in surprise that she's done that, or shock that she did it in front of his already agitated wife.

"Yes," he says, "Olivia knows that I am involved in Anthony's life, but she just means that she'd like us to do it as a couple. No more hiding the fact that I'm visiting Anthony, and also letting him see where I live occasionally... Stuff like that."

His eyes make contact with me for a second, and then flit back to the place mat. What a coward.

Debbie sniffs, and pulls out a handkerchief from her handbag. It is embroidered at the corner with her initials, and a tiny red butterfly. She dabs at her nose, but still manages to roll her eyes. This version of Debbie is more bolshie than the one I met the other week. Perhaps because Scott is here, or maybe because she now realises the stakes are high, and she is no longer in control of the situation.

"I'm more than happy for you not to hide the fact that you're visiting your son," she says. "That was never my idea in the first place."

Scott sniffs, and throws his hands in the air.

"We didn't really have a choice though, did we?"

"I didn't," she snaps, "but you did. You should have come clean from the moment you found out about the pregnancy. Then we wouldn't be in this situation, and Anthony would never have been a dirty little secret."

"He was never a dirty little secret!"

Scott bangs his fist on the table, the cups rattle, and Debbie jumps, gives her head a wobble, and straightens her shirt.

"If you think you're going to intimidate me into agreeing with you, then you've got another thing coming!" she shouts. "Your priority might be to protect your reputation, but mine is to protect my son, and no matter what you say now, you have never, ever been open to telling anyone about him, especially your wife. So, don't pretend that it was ever a decision we made together. You made the decision! You did!"

"For fuck's sake!"

Scott flies up from the table so quickly that his chair falls backwards and crashes against the fridge. He storms out of the room, and slams the door behind him, leaving Debbie and I nursing our tepid cups of tea.

I am shocked by Scott's emotional outburst, but I am also enthralled. It brings me nothing but joy to see these former lovers, and consistent liars, now arguing amongst themselves. Any worries I may have that they're still enjoying an illicit fling are pretty much out of my mind, and that's got to be a good thing.

"I know I shouldn't defend him," I say, "but in fairness to Scott, your pregnancy was announced the day our own son passed away, so there's no way he could have even thought of telling me about it. It probably wasn't a big thing on his mind, given the circumstances."

That barb is unnecessary and maybe even cruel, but I'm past caring. I stare at my younger rival to see if my words have any impact, but her face is as unmoving as a rock. She gazes into her cup for the longest time, and then looks at her watch.

"I've got to go," she says. "Anthony will be finishing school soon, and I need to get him to his grandparents' house. We go there once a week for spaghetti. It's his favourite."

"That was my Charlie's favourite too."

Debbie touches me on the arm, as she did with Scott, minutes before. The feeling of her fingers on my sweater is uncomfortable, but something inside me refuses to brush her off. Instead, I am dying for Scott to come in and witness this moment of solidarity between the two women in his life. He doesn't though. Of course he doesn't.

"I'm so sorry about what happened to your son," she says. "It must have been terrible for you, and I don't know how you ever moved on. It must have torn you to shreds."

Her words burrow under my skin.

"It is still tearing me to shreds."

Debbie nods.

"I can imagine."

Yes, imagining is the only thing this woman can do. She's never had the experience of losing a child. Not like me.

She gets up from the table, and slings her dainty handbag over her shoulder.

"Debbie?"

"Yes?"

"Anthony might have been a secret for the past ten years, but he isn't anymore. I'd very much like it if you could consent to him coming over here."

She stalls for a moment, opens her mouth as though to speak, and then leaves the room. I hear the front door close, and then a flutter of voices outside the front window. Scott and the mother of his child are having further words, but I can't hear or understand a single word they're saying. The only thing I can make out is that the voices are getting louder.

I watch, rooted to the ground as Debbie tries to walk away, but Scott grabs her arm, and shakes her. I have never seen him like this, and it both horrifies and intrigues me that he is so passionate in his actions around his ex-mistress. Still, the last thing I want is for the neighbours to think we're running some kind of soap opera in our driveway, so I leave my place at the window and head down the hallway, toward the front door.

Just in time to hear Scott's car engine.

Just in time to hear a screech of tyres.

Just in time to hear Debbie screaming.

Just in time to hear her being hit by Scott's car.

And then.

Silence.

"Fucking hell! Fucking hell! I didn't do this! She just stepped out from nowhere! I thought she'd gone. She said she was going!"

Scott twirls around in the driveway, his fingers threaded through his messy hair. I race to the back of the car, and there is Debbie, lying halfway under it, her body a tangle of misshapen bones. I touch her neck, but there is no sign of a pulse. Instead, a single stream of blood trickles from her ear, and soaks through her hair and onto the tarmac below her.

"Oh my God!" I shout. "What happened? What did you do?!"

My husband stomps to the end of the drive, looks left to right, and then comes back to me.

"Scott! What did you do?"

"Nothing!" he shouts. "She said that she was leaving and went off down the road. I don't know why she came back! Why the fuck did she come back?!"

With shaking hands, I dial 999, and ask for an ambulance, but Lord knows I'm aware that it's too late. The woman on the phone asks me to check a pulse, to see if there is any sign of life, but while I am sure there isn't anything at all, I don't think she believes me. The operator says that an ambulance is on its way, but when the paramedics arrive, they confirm my suspicions. Two minutes later, a police car screeches to a halt outside our driveway, and a red-headed policeman jumps out and starts questioning my traumatised husband.

"I didn't do it on purpose," he cries. "I would never do this on purpose."

"Nobody is saying that you did," the policeman replies. "I know it's hard, but we need you to calm down so that we can get a better understanding of what happened. Okay?"

Scott nods, and sits heavily on the front step, his eyes never leaving the sight of the paramedics and police gathered around Debbie's once beautiful and now wrecked body.

"First of all, can you tell me who the victim is? Is she a friend? Family member?"

My husband shakes uncontrollably, his face a shade of grey I have never seen before.

"I can't... I can't..."

"Mr Collins, I know it's hard, but please, if you could let us know who this woman is, then we can start filling in what happened to her."

"She is the mother of his child," I say.

"Thank you." The copper writes something in his tiny notebook. "And you are?"

"I'm his wife."

CHAPTER SEVENTEEN

TWO MONTHS LATER

The days and weeks after Debbie passed away were fraught and full of questions. First, from the police and medical personnel, and then social services, the coroner, Anthony's maternal grandparents, teachers and goodness knows who else. After much discussion, consultation and studying of the Ring doorbell, the matter was deemed a tragic accident. Yes, there was footage of Scott and Debbie quarrelling, but there was also proof that she had left the driveway before my husband banged his car into reverse. It wasn't his fault she had returned, and while one could argue that he should have been paying more attention, even I had to admit that my husband didn't kill her intentionally. A lying, scheming dickhead he may be, but a murderer? No.

We needed everyone to know that Anthony would be safe and loved in our home, and after more discussion – mainly between Scott and myself – it was decided that this would be the best place for the child. Luckily, Anthony agreed with the decision. Having lost his mother, he wasn't anxious to lose anyone else, least of all his father. Not surprisingly, he had lots of questions about his mum. How did she die? Why was she at our house? Where is she now? Is there a heaven? What if there isn't a heaven? Where would she be then?

I left most of the explaining to Scott, because I had only just met this child, I did not know him, and he did not know me. Because of that, I wasn't sure if it was any of my business to tell Anthony about his dead mother, especially given the circumstances. However, recently, when his dad is out of the house and Anthony asks me a specific question, I do my best to give him some kind of explanation, even if it is just to tell him that everything will be okay.

And it will all be okay. One of these days.

So, now Anthony is with us full time. I'm not going to lie, it took a while for him to settle in, and that's still an ongoing learning curve for us all. For the first weeks, Anthony cried for his mum every day, and it broke my heart to hear him sob. The tears would become more frantic at bedtime, when he was tucked up in bed, his blue teddy bear hidden from view but clutched in his little hand. I wanted to hug him during that time, but I didn't know if I was allowed to. I'm not his mother, and Scott laughed when I referred to myself as a stepmother, so I wasn't sure what I was, except somebody who could perhaps offer this little boy some love.

One evening he was quietly sobbing, and I sat on the edge of his bed, and stroked his hair as I used to do for Charlie when he was upset.

"I'm nearly ten," Anthony said. "I don't want to cry, but I can't stop it."

"It's okay," I assured him. "I cry sometimes, too, and I'm nearly fifty-five."

He turned over to look at me, wiping his nose on the sleeve of his football pyjamas.

"What do you cry about?"

I handed him a tissue.

"I cry because I lost my little boy."

"Charlie," he said through snuffles.

"Yes, Charlie."

"My brother."

"That's right. Your brother."

In those moments of pain, we somehow managed to bond, in spite of how he came to be here. I would never say that I replaced his mum, or that he replaced my child, but on some level we have connected. We are both wounded souls, flowers with roots out of the soil. Two broken parts, not quite fitting together as we should, but somehow making up a whole. A whole what, I don't quite know yet, but a whole nevertheless.

I discovered quickly that Costa hot chocolate and the occasional cupcake were Anthony's favourite treats, mainly because his mum never allowed him to have any when she was alive. I make the most of that knowledge, particularly when he's feeling sad, or scared, or discombobulated.

"Debbie doesn't – didn't – like him having too much sugar," Scott complained one afternoon as I slipped my shoes on for another Costa run.

"It's a couple of hot chocolates a week," I retorted. "Let him eat vegetables for the other five days." My husband was far too traumatised by the situation to argue with me, and since then, like it or not, he has – for the most part – sat back and let me get to know the child who was kept hidden from me for the past decade.

The idea of having a child in my life again is warming. Of course, some people – my parents included – thought that it was a tremendous mistake to get involved. They can't see Scott at the moment, let alone entertain the idea of his son. A week after Debbie's death, my dad bumped into Scott and I in Tesco, and told my husband that he is a massive disappointment to them, and that they always knew I should have sent him away in 1993. Scott didn't reply, but his puppy dog eyes and downturned mouth gave me a buzz. He's wanted their approval ever since the Gabby incident, and has gone out of his way to impress them, hoping that by now they had forgotten all about his indiscretion. Now, after all that hard work, the only thing he's done successfully is repulse them. Oh well.

Apart from the Tesco encounter, my parents have stayed far away, though they send messages every morning to ask how things are. I always reply nonchalantly, sticking to the weather, and general chit-chat. They never ask about the state of my marriage, or the new addition to our family, and that's okay with me. I'm sure before long, Mum will find some reason to come over here with a list of questions, but for now things are very much on a need-to-know basis.

Another development is that me being close to Anthony seems to piss Scott off on some level. That in turn gives me a definite sense of satisfaction. Since birth, the child was my husband's special secret, and now he has to share all of their moments with me too. Scott never says anything about it, but there are times when Anthony and I are doing a jigsaw, or watching television, and we're so engrossed in our new friendship that Scott quietly exits the room. He'll appear later with a cup of tea, or a slice of toast, and he'll sit ten feet away, close enough to be able to say that he spent time with his son, but not close enough to really be spending time with him.

Does Scott miss Debbie? Does he long for the time he was able to spend with her and Anthony as a family? Is he traumatised by what happened to her? Now he has to raise his son with me, instead of her, and maybe that makes him sad. I would like to be able to ask if he misses her, but at the same time, I'm afraid that he'll say yes. Because despite the fact that I no longer have much to do with Scott, I still want him to want me. I do not want him to be in love with a memory, in love with a ghost, in love with the mother of his other child.

I want Scott to be in love with me, regardless of how I feel about him.

Meanwhile, Anthony is such a sweet boy. Shy. Concerned about wildlife, and nature, and the polar bears not having enough ice to live on anymore. His favourite colour is yellow, and he likes to play something called Roblox on the Xbox. He doesn't like *SpongeBob* like Charlie used to do, but he does enjoy the old classics like *Scooby Doo*, and *The Flintstones*. That's thanks to his father, who apparently introduced Anthony to those shows as soon as he was old enough to watch them. He doesn't play rugby, nor has he even watched it on television, but he does like looking at Charlie's sports memorabilia in his room.

"And my brother won this when he was my age?" he asks, while pointing to a cup Charlie won for best player of the season when he was ten.

"Close to your age, yes. He loved playing rugby. He was really good at it."

"Maybe I'll play it one day," Anthony says, though that makes me grimace. He knows that Charlie passed away because he had a poorly heart, but he doesn't know the exact circumstances. He doesn't know that Charlie had been warming up for a rugby match when he died, and that no matter how hard I tried, I couldn't ever go near a sports field again. Too many memories. Too many awful memories.

"Well," I say, "I'm not sure your dad would like you playing rugby, and I don't know that I would either. You might hurt that beautiful face of yours. Maybe stick to jigsaws."

I gently bop him on the nose, and he scratches it. This boy loves jigsaws so much that I have already bought him at least twenty to work on. I'm aware that nothing can replace his mum, or the hurt he feels after losing her, but keeping his mind busy is surely a good thing. He's very clever at puzzles, I must say. Scenes from movies, cars, novelty photos like bees or beans, anything and everything cut into a jigsaw shape is Anthony's favourite thing.

Right now, my favourite thing is Anthony.

"That boy loves a puzzle," I said to Scott, after he'd been with us for a couple of weeks. My husband laughed and told me that he'd bought him all kinds of puzzles and brain-teasers over the years, not just jigsaws.

Comments like that hurt me beyond all reason. It boils me up inside to know that while I was mourning our child, my husband was busy raising a new one. I spend hours lying on my bed, thinking about it...

When I was hugging my son's old teddy bear... Scott was buying Anthony a new one.

When I was forcing myself to eat to stay alive... Scott was bottle-feeding his new son.

When I was listening to sad music and crying... Scott was listening to nursery rhymes and laughing.

When I couldn't get out of my pyjamas... Scott was picking out baby clothes.

Basically, when life as we knew it had ended, Scott was able to pick everything up and start again. For ten years he has been able to channel his love into a new scenario, a new existence, a new family, but now I know all about it, and for the first time in a long time I am comfortable.

For the most part.

Not because of Anthony – although he is a super kid – but because I now know that there is literally nothing my husband can do to break me any more than I once was. The knowledge of that makes me stronger and more determined to get back on my feet, earn some money and rebuild my life.

Success is the biggest revenge, I keep telling myself...

Success is the biggest revenge.

"Olivia? Do you think I could play with Charlie's Transformers for a while?" Anthony's voice is soft and calm, but brings me away from my thoughts and back into the room.

"Of course you can. But be very careful with them, okay?"

He nods his head, and picks up the Bumblebee Transformer.

"I will. I like this one the most because it's called Bumblebee, and it's yellow."

"It's a good choice," I say. "I'll go and remind your dad that we're going to Costa soon, and then I'll be back." Anthony licks his lips, and I leave him playing with the toy in the middle of Charlie's old room.

Anthony has settled into his new school, but he sometimes tells me that he misses his old friends, misses his old teachers, and his old house. I nod, and hug him and tell him that I know how he feels. It's not a lie. While I'm not in his position, I do miss my old life, so I can totally identify with him on that. Scott drops him off most days on his way to work, but I get the pleasure of driving down in the afternoon to collect him. It's the same school I used to go to every day when Charlie was little, and it's odd but somewhat comforting to be there again.

The playground where I used to stand has been transformed into another car park, which seems strange, and forces all of the parents to stand in the street instead, but that's okay. I park the car five minutes away from the gates, and then walk the rest of the way, taking in the surroundings. The trees where Charlie would collect conkers, the path where he would play tag with his friends, and occasionally chatted with a cat, or rescued a bee, placing it carefully onto a flower. It's strange being back there again, and I'm aware that some people might assume I'm Anthony's grandmother, given the fact that I'm in my mid-fifties, but never mind.

When I'm not looking after and bonding with Anthony, I'm busy trying to get more work. Scott still doesn't know that Babbage Books let me go, and I'm currently living off the bit of savings I have left. When he's working from home, I pretend to do Babbage work in my study, and even make up the odd crazy story or two, to keep him from the truth. But when he's in the office, I don't have to pretend at all, and it's something of a relief. Regardless of whether he's at work or at home, when I'm in my study, I'm emailing editors, letting them know that I'm still alive and able to work again. My mind is in a much better place than it was, and I know that if someone has a project for me to do, I'll be able to take it on without any problems.

Sometimes I hear back from the editors, assuring me that they'll keep me in mind for future books, and declaring how happy they are that I'm doing better in my life. Other times I'll receive a return-to-sender message, as the editor I once worked with has now left the company. If that's the case, I'll google to see where they are now, and message them at their new place. Sometimes they reply, often they don't, but at least I know where they are, should I need to contact them again in the future.

My current life situation with Scott and now with Anthony is not what I would have ever wished for, and it's certainly not ideal. However, it's the hand I've been dealt, and I'm dealing with it day by day. And though my career remains fairly dormant for now, I'm still determined, still persevering, and still pushing on.

Success is the biggest revenge...

Say it louder for the people at the back.

CHAPTER EIGHTEEN

Sometimes I like to go to Charlie's grave, and sit with him for a while. Not for any particular reason, like it's not his birthday or anniversary or anything, but I have to be there. Today is one of those days.

The cemetery in January is a bewildering place. Desolate because of the bare trees and freezing wind, but at the same time, beautiful because of the frost on the bushes, and the grass crisp beneath my feet. I park the car, wrap my long, red scarf around my neck, and make my way to Charlie's grave. His headstone is black marble, with gold lettering, and tiny rugby balls etched into the top. The words, *Beloved Son, Missed Forever*, hurt my soul. A mother should never have to say goodbye to her son, especially when he's fifteen and has the whole world to explore, and so many adventures to experience.

The roses I put here two weeks ago have withered and died, so I throw them away and refill the pot with the brightest of flowers – a combination of roses, carnations, and baby's breath. I'm sure Charlie would never appreciate being gifted flowers in real life, or at least he never would have, aged fifteen. Now he would have been twenty-five, and perhaps flowers would have brought colour to his apartment, or his little doer-upper house.

I spend a lot of time imagining what he would have been doing now, if he'd had the chance. I think he would still be playing rugby, though probably not professionally. While he loved the sport at school, perhaps he would have found professional sports to be a little too competitive. He'd have grown into other interests eventually. Maybe.

"Hey."

A familiar voice echoes around the cemetery, and I jump. It's Scott, standing behind me, his arms full of the same kind of flowers that I've just delivered.

"Hello." I brush the random pieces of soil and petals from my trousers, and stand up. He waves the bouquet at me, and laughs.

"Great minds," he says, pointing toward my flowers in the pot.

"Indeed."

Scott places the flowers on top of Charlie's grave.

"I can get another pot to put these in," he says. "The little shop at the office sometimes has them."

"Don't worry, I've got a vase in the car, I'll get it in a minute."

We both stand in silence, staring at Charlie's grave, and Scott reaches out and holds my hand. It is the first time he has properly touched me since everything imploded, and it feels alien, a little awkward, but not altogether strange. I would normally shrug him off, or pretend my fingers were cold and push them into my pockets, but this time I go with it. The moment is fragile, and fleeting, and while it might sound silly, I really don't want Charlie to see that his mum and dad are damaged. If he can somehow see us in this cold, unforgiving cemetery, then I don't want him to see anything that would cause him to worry.

"I miss him."

Scott sniffs, and I look up and study his face for the first time in months. The wrinkles under his eyes seem deeper, and the skin around the area is mottled, and dark, as though he's cried a thousand tears.

"I miss him, too," I say. "He was my whole world."

"Mine too."

I bristle at hearing those words. There's no disputing that Scott loved Charlie dearly, but his whole world? No, I don't believe that. If he could turn his attentions away from his family, put work before almost every family event, have an affair with a woman barely out of her teens, and conceive a baby while his son was still here, then no, Charlie was not Scott's whole world. He was merely a slice of it.

"Do you ever think about what he'd be doing now?" I ask.

Scott laughs.

"Yes, I like to think that he'd be a famous professional rugby player by now... Helping to take us to the World Cup, or beyond. What about you?"

"I'm not sure. I don't think he'd be playing rugby professionally, but it's nice to imagine that. Maybe something creative would have come his way though. He always loved art."

"True. Remember that huge picture he drew when he was little – the map of Charlie-Town?!"

I laugh, in spite of myself.

"Yes! He taped together about thirty pieces of paper, and it ran all the way up the hall and into the kitchen. Didn't you step on it, and he had a meltdown?"

"A meltdown is an understatement. But I stand by my opinion that a size ten boot print brought a bit of colour to Charlie-Town."

The memory of Charlie-Town makes me smile. It took up far too much room, even when rolled up, but it was full of imagination, of cars, and streets, and houses and a whole infrastructure in fact. It even had ducks on the pond, and children in the park.

"You'll be glad to know that Charlie-Town is rolled up underneath Charlie's bed."

Scott's mouth falls open.

"Really? I never knew that. I'll have to take a look at it again. It was very good though. Maybe he would have been an architect... Given the chance."

An architect. I could see that. He could have his own modern apartment, with one of those tall, arty table things next to the window, and a pot full of pencils. Yes, a pot full of pencils is a much better option than a pot full of flowers. He would have definitely preferred the pencils...

"I wonder what he would have thought about Anthony."

Scott's comment takes me by surprise. He has never addressed this before. At least not with me.

"He would be confused," I say. "He would have wondered why his dad had gone out and got himself a new family."

My husband shuffles from one foot to the other.

"I'd have explained everything to him," he says. "He'd have understood it all eventually."

The bitterness that has buzzed away inside my mind for the past months threatens to fizz out of my mouth, but I somehow manage to hold it in. I do not want to create a scene. Not here, not at Charlie's resting place.

"We'll never know," I say. "But I suspect he would have been mortified. He was fifteen years old, after all. That's not an age that generally radiates forgiveness and understanding, especially when it comes to knowing that your parents have had sex – with or without each other."

I look at Scott from the corner of my eye, hoping for a reaction to my barbed comment, but there is none.

"Regardless, as you say, we'll never know. I wish we did… Oh, God! It's all fucking awful. I miss him so much."

Scott gasps, tears his hand away from mine, and throws both up to his face. It has been so long since I comforted him. Should I do it now? Would he be accepting of it? Would I? When I see his face crumpled and folded in grief, I leave behind any feelings of disdain, and weave my hands around his arm.

"It's okay," I say. "It's all going to be okay."

"But I feel so responsible. I can't cope with it."

"I know, I know. I'm the same way, but it's not our fault. It's just something that happened, and we couldn't help it. We couldn't help it at all!"

Scott steps away, as tears land on the collar of his jacket.

"It wasn't your fault, but it might have been mine."

His words pierce through my brain.

"What do you mean, it might have been your fault?"

Silence, and then Scott shakes his head.

"Nothing."

"Scott! What do you mean it might have been your fault?"

He wipes his eyes on the back of his sleeve, hangs his head forward, and sniffs.

"A few weeks before Charlie died, he told me that he'd been feeling dizzy sometimes, mainly after he'd been playing rugby or taking some kind of exercise. He said that sometimes it was hard to catch his breath, and he had pains in his chest."

I have no idea what Scott is talking about, and my mind races, searching for answers. There are none.

"What do you mean?" I ask. "Since when did he have pains in his chest? He would have told me. He would have told me if he couldn't breathe! Or at the very least, you would have!"

Scott pulls out a tissue from his pocket, and blows his nose. His eyes glisten with tears.

"No, he didn't want me to tell you. He didn't want me to tell anyone because he was worried that he'd be told to give up his rugby. So, I said it was probably nothing, but I would make a doctor's appointment, just to be sure."

I open my mouth, unsure if I can get any words out. When they do come, they're stilted, and full of pain.

"And did you? Did you book him a doctor's appointment?"

Scott shakes his head, and avoids my eyes.

"No. I got waylaid, and forgot about it."

His casually cruel words sting my soul. He got waylaid? What?!

"You forgot about making a doctor's appointment for our son? Are you insane?! Why? Why wouldn't you make an appointment for him?"

Scott's mouth falls at the corners, and his hooded eyes narrow. He says nothing, and yet reveals everything.

"You forgot to make an appointment because you were too busy having your fling with Debbie, weren't you? Weren't you?!"

My legs are freezing, and it is as if the earth is moving around me, swallowing my body, swallowing my mind, swallowing everything I thought I knew about my poor boy's death. Meanwhile, Scott looks at the ground, and eventually nods.

"Yes, I was busy with... with her, but not in the way you think. I wanted to break up at that point, but she was quite emotional about the whole thing... and I also had this huge work project, and the hours weren't ideal for phoning the doctor."

"Oh my God!"

I can't believe what I'm hearing. My husband – Charlie's father – knew that he hadn't felt well for goodness knows how long, but had done nothing about it because he was consoling his mistress and busy at work? It's too much. Out of everything that's been revealed over the past couple of months, this has to be the worst of all.

"You monster!!" I scream. "Our son could have been saved, but instead you were cavorting with another woman, and trying to let her down gently?! And don't get me started on the work stuff. Why has your career always come before anything else? Why?!"

"It hasn't!"

Scott goes to grab my arm, but I swing him off and slap his face as hard as I can. An older lady tending a grave thirty feet away, gasps, and then crouches, pretending not to see us, not to hear us. Scott rubs his face, and I can feel his tears in the palm of my hand. I scrub them off on my jeans, and then head for the car.

"Olivia! Olivia, don't go!"

"Do not come after me!" I shout, and to his credit, he doesn't.

It's been ten days since Scott confessed that he had been too busy to tell me or the doctor about our son's illness. Ten days since he basically told me that his actions could have caused our son to pass away. Ten days since I realised that no matter how much time goes by, the lies keep coming.

And I don't know how deep they go.

Or if they will ever stop.

I try to keep myself together for the sake of Anthony. It's bad enough that he lost his mother, and his dad is a deadbeat, without seeing me dissolve before his eyes. Together, we watch old television shows, and I introduce him to 1980s classics, like

The Golden Girls, and *Only Fools and Horses*. He likes both, though Scott doesn't think either of them are appropriate for an almost-ten-year-old.

I don't give a shit.

His actions killed my son.

No amount of 1980s sitcoms will ever do that to Anthony.

Scott has tried to make conversation with me, tried to explain how awful he has felt for the past ten years, and how much he's wanted to confess. It has shattered him. Apparently. It has haunted him every single day. Apparently. It has been the darkest, deepest secret he has ever kept. Apparently. It seems to me that every moment of every day since 2014 has been a mirage. The grieving, the healing, and finally putting together the pieces. It's all bollocks. Utter, utter bollocks. How much more is there to come? Nothing, according to Scott, but how do I know that for sure?

The only thing I know is that he helped to kill my son, and I'll never forgive him for that. It's the last straw. The information that finally shattered my brain into a thousand microscopic pieces. He might as well have killed me too because that would have been less painful than what I'm going through now.

I talk to Scott, though only enough for him to think there is still a chance for us. The longer he thinks that, the more time I have to get my life back together. Anyone in their right mind would know that we've reached the point of no return, but I've come to the conclusion that my estranged husband is not in his right mind, therefore it does not apply to him. Outwardly, things continue as they are, and I'm polite, flash the odd fake smile, and keep the household running, but inside, I've checked out.

When Anthony is at school and Scott is in the office, I continue my quest to gain independence through my work. I've been commissioned to write an article about grieving parents, which will bring £350 into my bank account, and I've renewed my domain name, and hired the IT-savvy teenager down the road to create a website for me. He even uploaded a store for my books, and I sold five signed copies on the first day, and seven the day after. I couldn't believe it when I saw the orders slide into my messages, and yet there they were, reminding me that I was once a writer. Reminding me that I am still a writer. Reminding me that maybe, just maybe I am still relevant and still talented, and still loved.

And that's not the only thing. The acting dreams I have had since I was young have come back to me, thanks to an online course, which I found purely by accident when I was scrolling Facebook. A London drama school was advertising a ten-week part-time course, which was to start that week. I clicked the link and stared at the description... Online, once a week, the study of modern and classic texts, improvisation, voice exercises... My heart buzzed in the way it had all those years ago, before Scott encouraged me to give up my dreams. I did give them up because the only thing I wanted to do at that time was to please him, but now I don't have that desire.

Before I knew it, I had clicked the link and enrolled myself. And you know what? The moment I got the acceptance message through to my inbox I felt true happiness for the first time in years. The first time I linked into the Zoom class, my heart exploded. There in front of me were ten fellow students, some young, others older than me, but all of us with a story to tell about how we've always wanted to give acting a go, but never had the chance. We've only had one class so far, but it has reminded me of the girl I once was, and brought me back to a time when I truly felt that the universe could open up for me. And while I don't expect to ever get a paid acting job, or become the next Dame Judi Dench, it gives me tremendous joy to be feeding the arty teenage girl who lives inside me. It feels so good.

I share none of this with Scott because he hasn't done anything to warrant the knowledge of his wife getting her career and her life back together again. It's all a delicious secret, which I happily share with Anthony. He doesn't comment much on my acting dreams, but he thinks it's terrific that 'Aunty Olivia' wrote books before he was born.

"How many did you sell today?" he whispers when he comes in from school one day.

"Eight," I say, and Anthony fist bumps.

"That's one more than yesterday," he says. "This time next year we'll be millionaires!"

We both laugh at the *Only Fools and Horses* reference, and the fact that if things keep going as they are, I might not be a millionaire next year, but I'll definitely be in a better financial position.

And that in itself fills me with joy.

CHAPTER NINETEEN

"Do you think that my mummy is looking down from heaven?"

Anthony sticks his spoon into a big bowl of Rice Krispies, and looks at me, his blue eyes wide and inquiring. He has asked this question several times before, but how do I answer? I go for the gentle approach.

"I'm sure she is," I say, as I pour him a glass of milk.

"What does it look like?"

"Heaven? I'm not sure, but I like to believe that it is bright, and happy, with no worries or upsets."

"Do you think that Mum has met Charlie up there?"

The words catch in my ears. That has never crossed my mind, and the very idea of Debbie and Charlie hanging out together – wherever they are now – is not a pleasant one. Tears pool into my eyes, but I don't want Anthony to think that he's upset me, so I blink them away, and then place the glass of milk in front of him. He gulps at it, as though it's the first drink he's ever had.

"Well, your mum and Charlie didn't know each other," I say. "So, I doubt they have met. But maybe they've given a quick wave over the clouds, or a little smile."

"Maybe they've texted each other," Anthony says, and I laugh. As much as I hate the idea of Debbie and Charlie having any contact with each other, I do love the idea of being able to text the afterlife. How lovely that would be. How comforting.

As I sit down with my slice of toast and jam, Scott appears in the kitchen, and slings his tie over his neck, late again. He grabs my toast and takes a bite out of it. It's staggering to me that he can claim partial responsibility for our son's death, but still hold on to the thought that I like him enough to let him have my toast. He doesn't even mention his confession anymore. It's been swept away, like so many other things.

"Hey!"

"Sorry," he says. "Running late. You don't mind, do you?"

He smiles, and I shake my head. I do mind, but I'm not going to give him the satisfaction of knowing. I still need to keep up appearances.

"If I did, it would be too late now." I stick another slice of bread into the toaster.

"Bye, champ," Scott says, as he kisses Anthony on the top of his head.

"Bye, Dad," he replies.

Scott then kisses me on the cheek, wishes me a happy day, and heads out of the door. As he reverses off the drive, I can still feel the tiny thread of his saliva on my cheek, and I discreetly wipe it off before it makes me vomit.

One morning when Scott is in the shower, his phone rings. He normally takes his phone with him, but he hasn't today because it's charging in the bedroom socket. I pick it up, don't answer the call, but I do log the number. Later, when he's gone to work, I google it, and I'm surprised to discover that it's a local estate agent. Scott has said nothing about why he would need one, but then again, this is the man who kept his son's birth and his parents' death secret for many years. In that regard, I wouldn't put anything past him at this point.

I could come straight out and ask Scott why he's contacted an estate agent, but I decide against it, mainly because he'll know I looked at his phone... But at the same time, I need to know what is going on – the real truth, not the Scott truth.

I need to log in to his emails.

In spite of the fact that recent events have turned me into something of an investigator, I've never had access to Scott's email account, and have never searched for his password, purely because if he was having an affair, it surely wouldn't be conducted over email. But now that I've found out he has been talking to an estate agent, it's a different matter. They would maybe converse over WhatsApp or text for appointments, but for anything official, I imagine it would come as an email.

I wait a couple of days, and then a rainy Saturday morning arrives and Scott takes Anthony to watch the local football team. I wave them both goodbye as they head down the driveway, and then I head straight to his desk. Luckily, his laptop is switched on, but unfortunately his Outlook has been logged out. Shit. All I know is Scott's email address and his provider, since we both share the same one, but that is it. I hesitate to input random words for fear of being frozen out, but in the end, I don't have to, because as I contemplate my next move, my hand brushes against a piece of paper stuck to the underside of his desk. I get on my knees, and of course it's a list of passwords not only for Scott's emails, but also for Facebook, Instagram, Amazon and Zoom. Hiding them under a desk is the oldest trick in the book, but I have to be grateful for my husband's lack of originality.

Armed with this information, I log in to Scott's emails and

discover not only messages from one estate agent, but three. There are also letters from solicitors, and all are in relation to one thing – the sale of Debbie's house. Yes, it turns out that the house Anthony lived in with his mother is owned outright by my husband, and the purchase was made in 2021, shortly after he sold his parents' home.

I sit back in my chair and wring my hands. His parents' house sold for £295,000 with no mortgage to pay off. He then went straight out and bought his ex-lover and son a comfortable little cottage for £174,000. I guess that left enough money for Scott to treat himself, and his second family, without me ever knowing about it.

Until now, of course.

From what I can gather from the emails, the house has just gone on the market, and two couples have already toured the place, but turned it down. A quick visit to the estate agent website reveals photos of every room in the house. The cream-and-white living room (how could she keep it so clean when she had a child?), the light-blue-painted hall with navy carpets, the tiny but fully functional country-style kitchen, Anthony's old bedroom, and finally, Debbie's pastel-green bedroom, complete with pine furniture, a white duvet and flowery curtains. I'm intrigued by the décor. It looks more like my parents' taste than a young woman's, but who am I to judge? I'm not exactly an interior designer myself.

The photos were obviously taken before the house was cleared out – a multiple-day event Scott had apparently undertaken to protect Debbie's parents from the stress of it all. I thought that was uncharacteristically thoughtful, until I realised he probably wanted to take back anything he could potentially sell. I didn't volunteer to help, nor did I ask how it went. Instead, I took Anthony to school as normal, and then helped him find a home for all the toys Scott brought back with him that evening.

While my husband has not told me anything about owning Debbie's house or selling it, I am not going to mention it. Why? Because when things do get to the point where I'm able to file for divorce, a good lawyer might be able to get me half of whatever Debbie's house eventually sells for.

In that regard, I am willing to keep quiet about it all.

And away from all the lies, the secrets and the despair, it is now Scott's fifty-sixth birthday. He insists that he wants a quiet day, just me, him and Anthony.

"It doesn't seem appropriate to celebrate so soon after Debbie's death," he says, which grates me to the core. I want to remind him that she was his mistress, not the love of his life, but then I remember that I'm probably not the love of his life either, so I let it go.

And quietly die inside.

But it doesn't matter what I think, because Anthony is determined to give Scott the happiest birthday ever. While I just buy him a small box of Thorntons chocolates, I begrudgingly dive into my flagging savings and buy some multicoloured trainers from Anthony.

"I had my eyes on these when we were shopping before Christmas," Scott says.

"I know you did. That's why I – I mean Anthony – bought them for you."

"Do you like them, Dad? I donated my pocket money too!"

Scott turns the footwear from left to right as Anthony beams up at him.

"I love them," he says, and then kisses his son on the cheek.

"Anthony, let's get the cake," I whisper, and off we go to the kitchen. We retrieve the blue frosted sheet cake, with the words *Happy Birthday, Dad* in white icing.

"Shall we put fifty-six candles on the top?" Anthony asks. "Or will that burn the whole house down?"

I laugh, and take out four candles from the cupboard.

"Yeah, that would be a fire hazard indeed. Here, let's use these instead. We'll tell Dad to times them by fourteen, and he'll get fifty-six."

"That's quick maths," Anthony says, as he sticks the candles into the soft, creamy icing. I ruffle his hair as I used to do with Charlie. It sticks up at angles, but he doesn't care. All he wants to do is present his dad with the cake he carefully picked out himself.

"Come on, let's light these candles," I say. That done, we carry the cake into the living room, where Scott is trying on his trainers.

"These fit perfectly," he says and looks at us. He clocks the cake and smiles broadly. "Hey, what's this? A birthday cake for me?"

"I chose it, Dad," Anthony says, as he thrusts the cake under Scott's chin. "We got it from Tesco this morning!" The candles reflect an orange glow underneath my husband's face, and he blows them out before they manage to singe his chin.

"You did a good job," Scott says. "Blue cake is my favourite."

Scott takes the cake from Anthony, who then claps his hands together.

"I know, I remembered!" he says. "I remembered when Mum made you a blue cake last year!"

Scott lets out an embarrassed laugh, and then looks at me from the corner of his eye. Debbie made him a cake? I swallow heavily before my mind races back to his last birthday. How did he manage to slip off to see Debbie and Anthony on his special day? I remember that we spent the morning together, and then went out for lunch at the Italian restaurant in town, but what did we do after that? I can't remember.

And then it comes back to me.

Scott received a phone call from his mum, asking him to

pick up his card and present, and off he went for the next three hours. I remember because I had an influx of people popping over with cards and presents, and Scott wasn't there to greet them. When he got home, he was full of stories about how his mum had brought out the photo albums and had insisted on telling the story of how Scott was supposed to be born in the hospital, but snow meant that he came in the back room instead.

I had rolled my eyes and mentioned that it was the same story she'd been telling for the past thirty-odd years that I'd known him. Of course, now I know that there were no stories, there were no photo albums, because she had passed away years before that. No, my darling husband was visiting his ex-mistress and his secret son, while I collected gifts from friends and wondered if he'd be home in time for the movie we had planned that evening.

Another event to add to the bank of unwanted memories.

I open my mouth to say something profound or sarcastic, but before I have a chance, the doorbell buzzes.

"That will be Lauren," I say. "She said she'd pop over with your card."

I smile, thinking about the conversation I had with my friend two days ago, where she contemplated whether or not to even give Scott a card this year.

"He doesn't deserve one," she said. "He deserves a stiletto in the balls, that's what he deserves!" But I knew she would cave in. I knew she would bring around a card, purely because although Lauren now hates Scott, she does not want him to hate her. She doesn't want anyone to hate her. She's a bit like my husband in that way. Sure enough, when I swing open the door, there she is, wearing a hot-pink dress, and carrying a huge yellow envelope and a bottle of whisky.

"Hey!" She kisses me on the cheek. "Don't worry, the drink

is for us, not him. I just thought we could have a glass before I go on my date."

"You have a date?" I take the bottle from Lauren's cold hands and head into the kitchen.

"Don't sound so surprised," she says, laughing. "It's not really a date, to be honest. Just some guy from yoga who has taken a shine to me. He's very flexible, so I thought what the hell?"

Scott appears from the living room, followed by Anthony. This is the first time Lauren has seen my husband for a while, and the way she shuffles her shoulders and tilts her head back confirms that despite the birthday card she hasn't forgiven him for all his indiscretions.

I don't blame her.

"Good evening, Lauren." Scott sounds like he's in one of his Zoom meetings. My friend nods, looks over at Anthony, smiles, and then hands over the birthday card.

"There you go. It's just a card, so don't get too excited."

Scott stares at the yellow envelope, with his name scrawled over it in blue biro.

"That's very kind of you," he says. "I'll open it in the living room. Come on, Anthony, you can help me."

Anthony stares at Lauren, his lips turned up at the corners, and then he disappears back into the living room.

"So, that's the famous young lad, is it?" she asks, and I nod.

"That's him. He's not normally that quiet, but he's a bit wary of strangers."

"I don't blame him. I'd be wary, too, if I suddenly had to live with Scott... Now come on, let's open that bottle before I have to go. I'm meeting Reginald at eight."

I take the bottle, and frown.

"His name is Reginald? You're going out with someone called Reginald?"

"Yes. But as I told you, he's very flexible, so we forgive him."

───

Two hours later, Lauren is long gone, Anthony and Scott have both headed to bed, and I'm still sipping the whisky. It's not often I drink hard liquor, but after the time I've had lately, I think I deserve a little tipple. I'm not drunk, however, just a little bit fuzzy around the edges. Warm, but still in control of all my faculties.

Kind of.

I lie on the sofa and log in to Instagram. There are half a dozen comments on my latest book post, and I click to read them.

Someone called @DandyMandyMoony has written the first comment.

Does anyone know why Olivia hasn't written anything in years? Her books got me through post-natal depression, and that was over ten years ago! Such a shame, because I loved her books!

A woman called @Betheney23 has responded.

Her son died some years ago, so she's probably still healing from that. But you're right, it is a shame. I would have thought she'd have written something by now, but who knows what's happened in her life in the meantime.

Nothing bad, I hope, @DandyMandyMoony has replied, to which @Betheney23 has added a shrugging shoulders emoji.

Hope not, she says. *But who are we to know? Maybe she'll pop on here and tell us what's going on.*

Her comment has been liked thirty-two times.

I rub my eyes. It's absolutely astounding to me that complete strangers can be discussing what has been happening in my life and why I haven't written anything in years. The fact that they care enough to talk about it blows my mind.

I could ignore the conversation, and let everyone believe what they want. Or I could reply and say that I have some ideas, and there could be something new coming in the future. I don't know if it's the whisky talking or what, but I choose to do neither. In this moment, I want to tell the truth.

I want to tell my truth.

I sit up, straighten my hair, and press record.

I wake up to the sound of my alarm going off. I turn over to grab my phone, and my head bangs. Shit. I must have drunk way too much whisky last night. Much more than I thought I had. My eyesight is blurred, and I can hardly make out the words on my phone notifications, but even so, there are a lot of them, mostly from Instagram and TikTok, and then one on WhatsApp from Lauren. I tap on that.

> Oh My God! That video! Wow! I know I said previously that talking would help, but I had no idea you were planning to tell the whole story on your socials! Go You! Hope you sell some books because of it! But hey, your parents don't have Instagram do they? After the shock they had with the school report, they could lose their minds over this!

I stare at the screen, and my eyes narrow. What on earth is she talking about? What video? What story? I can only imagine that Lauren drank so much last night that she's seeing things.

> What are you going on about?

I reply, and then come out of WhatsApp.

When I open Instagram, the first thing I see is a woman who looks exactly like me, and even though the sound is off, it's clear that she's talking about something she's enthusiastic about. I rub my eyes, give my head a wobble, and switch the sound on. Then, and only then do the memories begin to return.

The whisky.

The video.

The story.

The upload.

Oh my God, the upload. All nine minutes forty seconds of it.

To Instagram, and TikTok, too.

My stomach contracts, as I watch the video version of myself unfold every little detail about what has been going on between Scott and I. I talk about the hotel card, the finding out about his parents, the photos in the hotel, the discovery of Debbie, and then Anthony, and finally, the death of Debbie at the – albeit accidental – hands of my husband. My philandering, lying husband is laid open for all to see. The only thing I don't mention is my thirty-year-old obsession with Gabby Haine, which is something to be thankful for, at least.

I scramble to delete the video, but then I notice how many comments it has garnered. One thousand in under twelve hours. One thousand people saw my story and posted their thoughts on it?! Surely not?! And yet it must be true, because there it is, printed for all to see. Not only that, but the video has had 5,679 likes, and 480 people have saved it. I click over to TikTok and the views have been almost the same, which is so strange because I normally struggle to share my posts on there.

I go back onto Instagram, rub the sleep out of my eyes, click on the comments and start to read.

Bloody hell, this Scott bloke sounds like a right wanker.

What a minute, isn't he the guy she's been married to forever? I thought they were happy.

Yes, it is him! Just shows you, you never know what's going on behind closed doors.

I wonder if he knows she's posted this! LOL!

She once posted a pic of him running a marathon for a heart charity. Obviously he was hiding his sins behind his charitable endeavours. What a shock.

Is she filing for a divorce or what?

Surely, she's not staying after all this. An affair would be bad enough, but a secret kid as well? Nah, no thanks!

Hang on, is this the woman who was a fairly famous author before her son died?

Yes. Hasn't written anything for years, but maybe she'll get a novel out of this crap. Sounds like it should be a novel, to be fair.

I scroll through as many comments as I can, but there are more and more being added before I'm able to come to the end of them all. I click on the three little dots at the top of the post, and my finger pauses over the delete button, but I just can't bring myself to get rid of it. I have spent the past ten years wondering if my career is over, and despite trying to get people re-interested in my work, this post has had more traction overnight than I could have ever hoped for. Any damage has already been done, so could it be more harmful if I kept the video up for a couple more hours? I doubt it. Besides, Scott doesn't even like Instagram (that I know of), so the likelihood of him seeing it is pretty low.

I keep the video up.

Scott leaves early for yet another important work meeting, so I agree to do the school drop-off. On the way, my phone pings from inside my handbag. My stepson picks up the bag, and thrusts it in my direction.

"Your phone is beeping, Olivia," he says. "You want me to see why? It might be more book orders."

I shake my head.

"No, no, that's okay. I'll check it when I drop you off. It's probably just junk mail anyway."

I know it's not junk mail of course. It's Instagram notifications, hundreds of them, all adding to the ones I received during the night, and early this morning. Flutters of... what? Adrenaline? Anxiety? I'm not sure, but whatever it is, it flies across my shoulders and into my chest. I am a fairly private person in the grand scheme of things, and yet I have just spilt my guts out to tens of thousands of strangers. Would I have done it without a drink in my belly? Probably not. Definitely not. But I did, and it's out there, and there's nothing I can do about it now, apart from seeing where it leads.

I haven't had a day like this for years. Probably since my last book was released, on the day my sweet Charlie passed away. On that morning, before the awful events of the afternoon, there were interviews and social media posts, and blogs and all that kind of thing, but while it hasn't happened quite the same way today, I've been so busy with social media that I haven't even had time for a proper lunch.

Lauren comes over in the afternoon, and after grilling me about why I uploaded the video, she settles into my sofa with a strawberry juice and a chocolate chip cookie.

"How many views has it had now?" she asks.

I grab my phone.

"Bloody hell. 120,345. This is crazy."

"Not really," Lauren says. "One time my niece uploaded a video about Minecraft, and it got like a million views in a couple of days. Social media can be wild."

I roll my eyes. A viral video about a popular game is one thing, but surely my little story of scandal and lies won't gain that many. Will it?

"Not all of the viewers have written comments," I say. "But many of them have."

My friend shakes her head and laughs.

"As your best friend, I should be telling you to delete it immediately, but first of all, I suspect it's way too late for that, and secondly, I'm far too invested!"

Lauren loves a bit of scandal, so long as it isn't about her, and while I know that it probably wasn't my best move to share such personal information, the views are intriguing, and the comments even more so. Some of the viewers have already said that they're going to revisit my books, while others say they've never read one of my novels, but they're going to download one or two immediately.

"To be honest," I say, "when I first saw the post, I was going to delete it, but then I saw the comments and changed my mind."

Lauren places her glass onto my coffee table and I scramble around for a coaster.

"When I looked earlier," she says, "there was someone who said they'd downloaded your entire back catalogue because of the video. You can't buy this kind of publicity."

She's right, and that's exactly why I will keep the video up. If I'm going to leave this sham of a marriage, then I need to sell more books and earn more money. In addition to that, the idea that my husband's sordid, sorry tale is out there after years of him hiding it, gives me a little buzz of excitement. After revealing everything to me, the story has now become my own, and in that regard, I'm fully entitled to share it.

Which is exactly what I have done.

I make lasagne for dinner, and while we're eating, Scott announces that he's up for promotion at work. He's full of brash excitement as he details how the boss took him into the office and revealed next year's plans. The company is expanding, a large – but so far secret – contract is coming their way, and Scott will be promoted to Director of Marketing, with a bigger team than he's ever had before. Of course, the promotion will come with a substantial pay increase, as well as some major bonuses and added holidays.

"You know me," he says, "I probably won't take the extra days, but it's always good to know they're there..."

After much bragging from Scott, a handful of whoops from Anthony, and a steady dose of fake oohs and aahs from me, father and son go to the park for a kick-around. I haven't mentioned anything about the video to my errant husband, and he thankfully hasn't asked, which confirms my hunch that he is unlikely to ever see it.

Until I log in to Instagram.

The first thing I notice is that the views, comments and likes have almost doubled since this morning, and the amount of people who say they're going to check out my books is staggering. Added to that, there are questions from some viewers, and others begging for a follow-up video. I'm not sure if I'm up for answering anything that I haven't already discussed, but you never know, maybe one of these days.

I idly flick through the comments, making sure that I don't like any during the process, and then I see it... A comment from somebody called @Joannabananas67.

Funny story – I watched the video this morning, and showed it to my sister just now. She almost choked on her salad, cos the guy in question is her boss! LOL! She couldn't believe it. No one knew about this at all, but I'm sure they'll all know when she gets back to work tomorrow!

Shit.

I read the comment over and over again, to the point where I persuade myself that it's probably made up, but then I notice that there are a whole range of comments underneath:

Yeah, of course your sister knows him... Things that didn't happen, part 362.

If she knows him, where does he work? Also, I'm going back through years of posts from Olivia, and can see photos of her husband, but not his name. Anyone else know?

You should have gone to Specsavers. Olivia mentions him all the time – or at least she did until recently (interesting!). His name is Scott. Presumably Scott Collins, unless Olivia uses a pen name.

And at the end, another comment from @Joannabananas67:

No, Olivia doesn't use a pen name, and yes, his name is Scott Collins. He works at The Norfolk Marketing Company. Won't post the exact address here, but if you want to know more, you can always google them. They have a HUGE social media presence!

The comment has had 237 likes, and a do-gooder has tagged Scott's company in a comment.

A chill passes between my shoulder blades, and rises up my neck. Someone has recognised my husband in real life... Someone has named him and his employer, and someone else has tagged them. Dear God, I had not expected that. I take a screenshot and send it to Lauren, who responds straight away.

> Oh dear. Are you going to take the post down? And has Scott said anything?

> No, he doesn't know yet. Or if he does, he hasn't let on. He was too busy bragging about his job promotion.

I don't respond to her question about taking the post down, because even though I'm horrified that people now know where Scott works, the vengeful part of me is secretly thrilled. This man slashed my life into a million frayed remnants, and then continued to live his own life as though nothing had happened at all. Maybe it's about time he got a taste of despair at my hands. All my adult life I've done everything I can to keep my husband happy, and he's repaid me with infidelity, secrets, lies and humiliation.

Now it's his turn to see how that feels.

The next morning while making breakfast, Anthony asks how many books I've sold on my website, and it occurs to me that in all the video drama, I haven't thought to check.

"You know what? I don't know, but that's an excellent question. Hang on, you butter your toast and I'll take a look."

I hand Anthony the knife, log in to my website, and my mouth falls open. Four hundred and thirty copies sold in the past twenty-four hours. Four hundred and thirty!

"What the...?"

"What's wrong?" Anthony looks up from his toast, and I

hand my phone to him. He stares at the screen, and turns his mouth into an O shape.

"Oooooh!!" he gasps. "Four hundred and thirty copies? That's way more than it was last time we checked. I thought sixteen copies was good, but this is... this is... way more!"

He gives the phone to me, and claps his hands, having given up on trying to work out the maths in his head. Four hundred and thirty copies. Do I even have that many to sell? The answer to that would be a firm no. I have about thirty random copies of my rom-coms in my study, and a couple of boxes of my psych thriller in the garage, but four hundred and thirty? No way. I'll have to order more from the publisher, and I'll have to do it soon.

Just as I'm trying to work out the logistics of suddenly selling so many copies of my books, Scott arrives in the kitchen. I turn off my phone, place it face down on the counter and put my finger to my lips so that Anthony knows not to mention anything. Scott ruffles his son's hair, and kisses me on the top of my head. It takes all of my power not to wipe it off with the nearest tea towel. He grabs a banana from the fruit bowl, turns it over in his hands and then puts it back.

"You want some coffee?" I ask, my hand on the machine. Scott shakes his head.

"No, you're okay, I'll stop at Starbucks on the way to work. Oh, also, I've got a meeting this afternoon, so if I'm late I apologise."

Scott ruffles Anthony's hair again, grabs his bag and is out of the door. Of course, he didn't mention if it was a work meeting, a secret get-together with the estate agent, or another sordid indiscretion. I'm surprised, however, to discover that I don't really care.

And that brings me some welcome relief.

I drop Anthony off at school, and then head home to phone my old publisher. It's been such a long time since I've spoken to anyone there, that I imagine everyone I once knew has long gone. However, if I'm going to get all these orders sorted out, then I need to speak to someone, and can only hope that all of my titles are still in print. Otherwise, I'm screwed.

As predicted, my previous contact has moved on, and instead I'm put through to a woman called Andrea, who answers with an enthusiastic squeal.

"Olivia Collins! Your name seems to be the only one I've heard this morning! How are you?"

I'm confused, and my first thought goes to the usual – *what have I done wrong?*

"I'm fine, thank you," I say. "But I'm confused as to why you've been hearing so much about me. Should I be worried?"

Andrea laughs, and I can hear a rustle of papers.

"Of course not! No, according to our sales people, they've had orders come through for so many of your books that we've had to send almost all titles to reprint."

"You have? I don't understand."

A reprint? After not writing anything for over ten years? Surely, that can't be because of my video? A few hundred copies ordered through my website is phenomenal enough, but there wouldn't be enough interest to order a whole new printing. Would there?

"That video you posted has really brought a renewed interest to you as a brand, and now that the *Daily Mail* has picked it up, it's only going to get better."

"Wait. What do you mean the *Daily Mail* has picked it up?"

"You haven't seen it? Oh, they've written a whole article

based on the story you shared in the video. Didn't they tell you?"

I shake my head, completely aware that Andrea can't see me through the telephone. The *Daily Mail*? She must have got that wrong. Why on earth would a national newspaper want to report on my video, let alone write a whole article on it? It doesn't make sense.

"This is the first time I've heard about it," I say. "I'll have to check it out."

"You do that," Andrea says. "But first, what can I do for you?"

I talk to Andrea for a good twenty minutes about the books I need to order, and during that time her colleague tells her that my psychological thriller is currently number 22 in the Amazon bestseller lists. My books have barely sold in the last few years, and now one of them is inching toward the top twenty? My mind is blown, and all I can hear is Lauren telling me that you can't buy publicity like this. I think she's right.

"Look," Andrea says, "you go and deal with your renewed fame, and I'll keep you informed of any more developments."

"I will," I say, my hands hot against the phone.

"Oh and, Olivia?"

"Yes?"

"You should start thinking about your next novel. The people buying your books for the first time today will be looking for something new before long. We'd love to look at a new project, as soon as you have one."

I thank her, and hang up. I can't believe what's just happened. I have spent so long trying to get attention from publishers and editors, and aside from the odd lukewarm message, I haven't had much luck. Not in the grand scheme of things. But now, thanks to a video uploaded through a haze of whisky, my old publisher wants to see something new? Wow. I wasn't expecting that at all.

I flick onto the *Daily Mail* website, and only have to scroll down for a moment before I come face to face with a photograph of Scott and I, taken from my Instagram. Above the picture is a headline:

THE AUTHOR, HER HUSBAND, HIS DEAD PARENTS, AND THE OH-SO-SECRET SON.

My throat dries to a crisp, and I bite my lip so hard that a metal taste descends into my mouth. I click and read the article, which – as Andrea said – is more or less a retelling of my video, complete with screen grabs and photos of me taken not only from my Instagram, but Facebook and X, too. At the end are the words, *Mr Collins has been contacted for comment.*

My face burns so bad I think I'm about to throw up. I grab a glass of water and drink it down in one go. What do they mean they've contacted Mr Collins? How? Where? Do they have his phone number? Surely not. But then I remember the person who outed him as working at The Norfolk Marketing Company, and I know that's where the reporters will have tried to get him.

Before I can read the article again, my phone rings, and my stomach lurches when I see that it's Scott. I decline and then he tries again. And again. And again. Each time I refuse the call, until finally a message comes into my WhatsApp.

> Why have I got the Daily Mail on the phone, and a local reporter in reception? They've said something about a video? What the fuck is going on?!

I wouldn't know what to answer even if I wanted to, but just as I'm trawling my mind, my phone pings again. It's an Instagram DM from someone called Sean, who works freelance for women's magazines. He wants to write an article about my story for *Closer* magazine, and wonders if I'm up for an interview. I scroll past, and then notice similar requests from other reporters, all telling me how intriguing the story is and how it would make a terrific feature for this Sunday newspaper, or that Saturday magazine. Two minutes later, another message from Scott, this time telling me that he's had more than a dozen messages from my readers, all calling him a wanker, or a dickhead, or similar.

> What is going on?

He asks again, and I shrug as if he can see me.

I power off my phone, place it in my desk drawer, and grab my notebook. I need to write down some notes for my next novel.

"Have you any idea what you've done? You've ruined everything!" Scott growls at me as he comes in the front door, and throws his bag in the corner of the hall. I've spent the past couple of hours rehearsing what I'll say to him when he gets home, but I hadn't counted on him being here at 3.05pm.

"Why are you home so early? I thought you had a meeting?"

"It was cancelled! Along with everything else I've got to do this week. Apparently, they don't think it's advisable for me to take care of marketing for my clients when I can't even deal with my own life. Or my wife, come to that!"

It would seem that Scott has watched the video.

He kicks off his shoes, and I expect him to stomp into the kitchen, but instead he stands right in front of me. Arms by his side, mouth clenched.

"I'm sorry that your work has been dragged into it," I say. "I really had no idea that would happen!"

"What the fuck did you think would happen?" he snaps. "You posted a video, revealing all our private business, and then wonder why people are interested? Why the fuck did you post it in the first place? You're going to ruin me!"

I shrug. What does he expect me to say? That I'm sorry? That I regret it all? Yes, he probably does want that, but I'm not going to say it, because after dealing with his crap, and discovering that it has actually helped my career, I regret nothing. Nothing at all. I might change my mind tomorrow, but for now, I'm just too excited about the book sales.

"Whisky was the reason I posted it," I say, as calmly as I can. "But I don't take responsibility for ruining you. Definitely not."

Scott leans on the bottom of the banister. His hands shake, and I'm not sure if it's nerves, despair, or anger. Maybe all three.

"What do you mean?" he asks.

"Perhaps if you gave it a little thought, you could work it out! But if that's too hard for you, I'll explain. It was you who ruined everything, ten years ago, when you screwed another woman!"

He throws his arms in the air, and his wedding ring catches the light coming in from the glass on the front door.

"For fuck's sake. I made one mistake!"

I know that he's trying to dismiss all of this as something that I'm unnecessarily hanging on to, but he's not getting away with it this time. He's done it one too many times, and the attention I've had today has buoyed my confidence.

"Hmm, not quite one mistake though, was it? You went back for more, and more, and more!"

"Not this again. No wonder I didn't tell you at the time. You're a freaking psycho."

He pushes past me into the kitchen where I find him filling up a glass with the spring water I keep in the fridge. It annoys me, because he never drinks that water. He's a fizzy water kind of guy. Always has been.

"If you need a reminder of everything you've done, you could always watch the video. It even includes the bit about you secretly buying a house for your mistress and kid!"

The words slip out of my mouth before I can stop them, and Scott stands motionless, breathing heavily onto the kitchen units that we picked out just two years ago.

"How did you know about that?"

"An estate agent tried to call you one day, when you were in the shower." I don't add that I found out about the actual house sale by logging the number and hacking into his emails. He doesn't need to know that part.

"Are you getting off on this?" he says through tight lips. "Is that it? Is it some kind of ridiculous revenge or something?"

He turns toward me, and for the first time I notice a little vulnerability in his demeanour. His eyes appear sunken, and his skin is pale. My husband's career has always been the most important thing in his life. More important than me, than our relationship, and yes, even our son, and now it's been threatened because of his own actions. I should care, and a year ago I would have killed anyone who made him so unhappy, but not anymore, or ever again. I feel empowered for the first time in many years.

"Am I taking revenge?" I say. "I don't know. Maybe. I mean, it's not revenge in the traditional sense, like keying your car, or slashing your trousers up and stuff. It's just a little video that I put out there after having one too many to drink. I didn't think it would go viral, and I certainly didn't think anything about it being vengeful at the time. Now, however, I'll admit that it has made me rather happy to get the truth out there, instead of holding it all inside. So, in that sense, yes, keeping it uploaded is a bit of revenge, if that's what you want to call it."

He takes a glug of water, tips the rest away, and then drops the glass into the sink. It smashes into a million pieces, each one glinting under the kitchen lights. That glass was part of a set we bought from IKEA several years ago, and seeing the sharp, broken shards glisten in the basin rocks my confidence a little, but I hang on.

"Well," he snaps, "whatever you did it for I hope you know that you've completely humiliated me. You do know that everyone in the office saw it, don't you? The PAs couldn't look me in the eye, the woman on reception stifled a snigger when I arrived, my colleagues were whispering when I walked into the morning meeting and even Mike Dickens has watched it! His fucking granddaughter showed it to him!"

I know the last one will have crushed him. Mike Dickens is the CEO of the company, and Scott has always worshipped him.

"I'm going in the shower. Take the fucking video down!"

He pushes past me, but I don't follow. As he stomps up the stairs, my phone pings, and I flick open my emails. There are messages from various shops, telling me about their sales and special offers, but in the middle of them all is one from an editor at a London publishing house, wanting to talk to me about writing a book about my recent life. Let's set up a meeting, she writes, and my heart leaps.

Yes.

Yes, let's do that, indeed.

The next morning, Scott takes Anthony to school, and then I hear him tap-tapping on his laptop. By his own admission, he doesn't have anything to do at work this week, because of the video, so I don't know what he's doing, and I don't really care. I go to my desk and open Instagram. Much to my surprise, the first photo I see is one of Scott and Debbie, taken from afar in what looks like a school hall. The description reads, *I took a photo of my son at his recent open evening, and didn't think much about it at the time. That is until I read about that author's cheating husband. Can't believe I managed to capture him and his mistress in the background of my pic! God rest her soul.*

Underneath, there are a variety of comments. Some discuss the possibility of Scott killing Debbie on purpose, others describe sightings of the couple anywhere from Scotland to Australia. Most of the comments are absurd, and while I recognise the human instinct to wonder if Scott deliberately ran Debbie over, I can't get on board with that. A cheater and liar my estranged husband might be, but a murderer? No.

But it doesn't harm my career to have people wonder…

I check my website shop, and discover that there are close to seven hundred signed book orders. My stomach trembles at the logistics of putting all of them together, but the excitement far outweighs my nerves. I print off my latest list of sales, and when I turn back toward my desk, Scott is standing at the door. I jump, and drop the papers onto the desk.

"Jesus, you scared me. What can I do for you?"

Scott's face is emotionless, and his blond-and-salt-and-pepper hair uncombed. He's normally first to the mirror in the mornings, but not today.

"You didn't take the video down," he says.

"No. No, I didn't."

"Why?"

I shrug, but don't reply. Let him wonder. Let him squirm just a little more.

"Did you see the latest fallout from it?"

I presume he means the murder conspiracy theories, but I'm not about to confirm that.

"What fallout? There's been so much attention, I can't keep up."

I smile, and Scott's mouth falls even further.

"There are memes," he says.

"Memes?"

"Memes. You know, photos with funny captions and stuff."

"I know what memes are, Scott. I'm not that stupid."

He shakes his head, and opens his mouth to say something else, when his phone rings.

"You better answer that," I say. "It might be a reporter."

I probably shouldn't get such a kick out of antagonising my husband, but I can't help it. Seeing him so embarrassed is almost as satisfying as seeing my book sales shoot through the roof. He rolls his eyes, and heads back to his room. Two minutes later, he's back.

"This will please you," he says. "My promotion is off for the foreseeable. Mike Dickens thinks that with everything going on, now is not the time to raise my profile further. So, thanks for that. Thanks a bunch."

He retreats back into the hall before I can say a word about it. Just months ago, I'd be devastated to hear that Scott's career was imploding, but now? Now, this news gives me a certain sense of satisfaction that I never thought I'd feel again.

I go back onto Instagram, and the first thing I encounter is one of the memes that Scott was complaining about. It shows a photo of him walking out of The Norfolk Marketing Company.

The description reads, *Walking out of your PR job cos you couldn't handle your own PR. #Awkward.*

The author of the meme obviously doesn't know the difference between marketing and PR, but I click like anyway, and then I switch off my phone.

A week later, and the video views continue to grow, podcasters have swung into my DMs, blogs have been published, and the news of my husband's infidelity and lies has hit social media as far away as New Zealand and even Japan. Strangely, Sam from Babbage Books has even messaged to say that he'd read all about my video, and wishes me the very best of luck with the renewed interest in my career. As if that wasn't enough, a couple of hours ago, I gazed out of the window and I could swear that there was a woman with a camera loitering at the end of our driveway. I closed the curtains and got back on with my work, but still, the ongoing fallout from the video is astounding. At least to me.

Away from the drama, I've been working hard on the proposal for a tell-all book, making notes for a new novel, and liaising with my fiction publisher regards releasing a special edition of my old psychological thriller, *Love to Hatred Turned.* It will be my first hardback, complete with blood dripping down the edges, as well as the end papers. It all sounds like a dream, and I'm so busy replying to her email that once again, I don't immediately see that Scott has appeared at my study door. I should put a bell around his neck at this point.

"Hey."

I jump, and then close my laptop.

"Hey."

"You busy?"

"Kind of. Yes, actually. Trying to deal with a million things at once."

Scott sits himself down on the armchair in the corner of my study, and rubs his eyes.

"Glad to see that someone is busy," he says. "All I've done this morning is take down my LinkedIn page. I've been bombarded with so many messages and comments that my whole page is a wreck."

"Oh dear."

I pretend to grimace at the very thought, but in reality, hearing that his LinkedIn page has been destroyed is not a surprise. Many of my readers have commented on my posts that they've been leaving messages, and while I haven't condoned any of this, at the same time, I don't consider it my business to tell them to stop. It will be killing him though. Scott has spent years building his LinkedIn, sharing his LinkedIn, preening over his LinkedIn. It's the only social media he actually enjoys.

Because it's work-related.

"Do you need help with anything?"

I almost laugh out loud. Why is he asking if I need any help? He's done enough, if only he realised it.

"No, you're okay, thanks," I say. "I'm quite happy working by myself."

He picks up a book from the pile next to the armchair, thumbs through it and then puts it back.

"Looks like your book sales are picking up," he says. "Are these all being sent out?"

"Yep."

"Great."

We both fall into silence, and I wonder if he's going to say anything else, or will he quietly wander back out into the hallway? I pretend to write something in my notebook, and then gaze up at him. It's only then that I notice his eyes are red and swollen.

"Have you been crying?" I ask, and my words prompt him to burst into tears. My first reaction is to head over to him, but then I remember that his tears are no longer my business, so I stay exactly where I am, and say nothing.

"I just can't believe what's happening," Scott says, wiping a tear away from his cheek. I don't know why, but his apparent disbelief rattles me far more than it should.

"What part can't you believe?" I ask. "The affair? The secret son? The fact you didn't call the doctor when our son felt ill? The fact that you contributed to his death? Or pretending your parents were still alive?"

Scott pulls a tissue out of the little box I keep on the windowsill, and dabs his eyes.

"All of it. But this video business has been the breaking point. At least before that happened, it was all contained. It was nobody's business but mine."

Of course, it's the video that's bothering him so much. That was something that affected his career, and we all know that comes before everything in his life. Any empathy that may have been creeping into my mind, evaporates, and I drop my pen onto the desk.

"It was my story too," I say. "And I was quite within my rights to tell it."

He sniffs, and then throws the tissue into the wastepaper basket next to the chair.

"Take me back," he says with a straight face.

"What?"

"Take me back. Let's move on, draw a line under everything that's happened, and create a new life together. You, me, and Anthony."

A tiny laugh escapes my lips.

"You're joking?"

"No, I'm deadly serious. Let's start again. Start everything again! I never stopped loving you, and we've spent nearly forty years loving each other..."

"And yet you left me for one woman and had an affair with another. So much for loving me."

Scott rubs his eyes. It must be awful for him, knowing that he can't possibly deny the affair, since the evidence of it currently sleeps in our spare bedroom.

"The affair was the biggest mistake of my life," he says. "Apart from Anthony... And you've said yourself that he's a great kid."

My heart leaps a little when Scott mentions Anthony. Several days ago, the boy told me that some kids at school had been laughing at him and calling him a dirty little secret. He wanted to know why, and it took all of my strength not to burst into tears. In the midst of all the good stuff happening in my career, and the remarkable breakdown of Scott's, it hadn't occurred to me that the video would reach the halls of Anthony's school. But social media reaches everywhere, unfortunately, and his school is no exception.

I'm normally one for honesty, but the moment Anthony told me, my mind went blank, and I had no idea what to say. So, instead I brushed it all away, told him to ignore the boys, and prayed that he wouldn't mention it again. Later, I heard Scott talking to him in the kitchen, and my husband told the child that I'd done something crazy on Instagram. Thankfully he didn't explain what it was.

"Olivia isn't like your mum," Scott said. "She doesn't think before she acts. She doesn't have the intelligence, unfortunately."

I fizzed on the other side of the door, and my head longed to burst in there and demand that Scott apologise for his words.

However, my heart demanded I stay quiet for the sake of Anthony. That day was the first time I had been forced to think about the effect the video could have on him and I did – and do – feel sad in that regard. Thankfully, however, our beautiful friendship has continued regardless, and he still watches television with me, laughs at my jokes and remains the brightest spark in this house.

"Olivia! Did you hear what I said?" Scott's voice shakes me out of my daydream, and I nod.

"Yes, he is a great kid," I say. "The complete opposite of his father."

"Then let's stay together! We'll raise Anthony, and rebuild everything we once had."

Scott launches off the armchair and before I know it, he is on his knees on the floor next to my chair. He grabs my hands with his own tear-soaked fingers, and I think back to the man he used to be. So confident, so self-assured, so full of his own self-worth. Now here he is, a pathetic bundle on my study floor, scrambling around for a semblance of his old life, while I build my new one. The fact that it used to be the opposite way around is not lost on me.

"I can't do that," I say, and he takes a breath in.

"You can! Please!"

"No. Sorry."

"Why not?"

He stares up at me, his eyes wide. His demeanour pathetic and deflated.

"Because you contributed to our son's death. Plus, you tried to break me on at least two occasions, and I have too much respect for myself to let you do it again. And besides that, I can't help but wonder if your career hadn't just imploded, would we even be having this conversation?"

Tears threaten to spring into my eyes, but I hold them back. No more tears will be shed because of this person. I'm done.

And so is he.

"Please just hear me out," Scott says, without addressing my career comment. "We could get back together, maybe renew our vows, and then you could make a video about that! Show the world that we've recommitted to each other. That we're happy and raising a family. What do you think? I think it could work!"

He stares up at me, a small, desperate smile on his lips.

"I can't get back together with you, nor can I renew our vows," I say.

"Why?"

"Because I want a divorce."

Scott drops my hands.

CHAPTER TWENTY

THREE MONTHS LATER

The fallout from the viral video continued for many weeks. The *Daily Mail* did a follow-up story, with quotes from unnamed colleagues, neighbours and friends. Even my parents provided a quote, which my dad assures me they didn't mean to do. The official line is that they didn't realise the reporter was actually interviewing them, but I can't help but believe that their cooperation was a little bit of revenge for their son-in-law's sins.

Thankfully, everyone interviewed conveyed their shock at finding out about Scott's secret life, but all of them denied that they had heard any hint of it during the time they'd known him. I was pleased to hear that. It would have been horrendous if they'd all come out and said that they'd kept the secret for as long as he had.

The *Daily Mail* wasn't the only newspaper to cover the story though. There were several local papers that got in on it, too, along with various other national and international newspapers, including some in New York, Los Angeles, and even Australia. Dozens of blogs also popped up, podcasts discussed us, the memes kept coming, and even the *This Morning* show did a marriage-counselling segment, inspired by the saga. I was asked to go onto that, and various other media outlets, but I turned down all interview requests. The editor I'm talking to says that if we are to sell the idea of a tell-all book to her colleagues, then I shouldn't get too involved with the media at this stage. That can come later, when the book actually comes out. God willing.

While the video views have dropped in the past month, and everyone has moved on, my followers continue to climb, my novels continue to sell, and three of them are currently in the top one hundred on Amazon. I was in Waterstones the other day, and the paperback of my psychological thriller, *Love to Hatred Turned*, was sitting right there on the table next to the window. I don't think I've ever seen my book on the top table before, except when I placed it there myself. One of the shop assistants spotted me, grabbed my arm, and begged me to sign their copies. I couldn't do it quick enough, and she was thrilled to know that there will soon be a special edition.

Scott went back to work after a couple of weeks, but his new-found and unwanted notoriety proved too much for him. His promotion was continually held back – happily-married clients, and those who expressed their support for the sanctity of marriage all took away their projects. Colleagues continued to stare... and talk... and predict what would happen next, and they all became mute whenever Scott walked into their vicinity. The company received so many emails and phone calls that they ended up releasing a statement, distancing themselves from the scandal. In spite of that, however, they then tried to turn the whole thing into a bit of publicity for the company, but that backfired when social media turned on them for hypocrisy and trivialising cheating.

In the end, Scott had enough of the whispers, the stares and the laughter from fellow colleagues. He handed in his notice, and as yet, hasn't found another job. As we speak, he is living off his savings and wondering what his next move will be. Who knows what he'll do next. Who cares? Certainly not me. I'm too busy with my own career.

My estranged husband sold Debbie's old house, and that enabled him to buy a little place around the corner from our family home. For now, he hasn't mentioned selling our place, but I know that conversation will come eventually, especially since I've now contacted a divorce lawyer. I'm hoping that by the time our assets are split up, I'll have enough money to buy Scott out of the house. I live in hope.

But for now, here we are. My husband's suitcases and boxes are in the hall; a sad and random collection of belongings from twenty-five years of marriage. Badminton racquets from games we never played, hardbacks that I've never seen him read, old trainers with their laces missing, and framed photos of relatives that we've never hung on the wall.

And in the middle of it, Anthony's little boxes of toys, books, and his prized jigsaws. The beautiful boy that I had no idea existed until so recently is moving out with his dad. When Scott and I first spoke about him leaving after the video went viral, the shattered part of myself hoped that he would choose to let Anthony stay with me. The mature, sensible part knew better, of course. The child who I have come to love over the past few months is not my own. My child passed away over ten years ago, and I know that the hole left by him will never heal. It is as raw and vacant as it ever was, but maybe Anthony has helped soften some of the jagged edges.

For that I am grateful, and in line with that, I took Lauren's advice and agreed that it was time to let go of Charlie's bedroom once and for all. Together, we gathered up his clothes and toys, donated most of them to charity, gave some to Anthony, and kept a box full of Charlie's favourites, along with his sports trophies. I now realise that my late son is always with me, regardless of where I am, and what I'm doing. In that regard, I don't need his bedroom to be a museum piece, and I think that he would approve of that decision.

I pick up the library book that Anthony has been reading for the past couple of evenings, and hand it to him. He takes it, but does not look at me.

"Thank you," he says, and I detect the anxiety in his voice. I touch his shoulder, and his muscles relax.

"Don't worry," I say. "You're only moving down the road, and your dad has promised both of us that you can visit whenever you like."

He nods, and flicks the pages of the book with his thumbnail.

"Can I come and watch *Only Fools and Horses* with you?"

"Of course you can. You can watch whatever you like. I'm not going anywhere, and your room will always be here, just in case you ever want to stay over."

Scott walks out of the living room, and eyeballs me. I know that there's no way he'll want his son staying here, after all the trouble we've managed to stir up between ourselves. However, I also know that Anthony lost his mother just months ago, and whether Scott likes it or not, I have stepped up as some kind of matriarchal figure, and I'll always be here for him.

"Are you ready, sport?" Scott picks up a bag, and throws the handle over his shoulder. Anthony nods, but his eyes remain on the floor. I hug him to me and rub his back.

"I'll see you soon, okay? Now, don't lose that library book or you'll be getting a fine!"

Anthony opens the book and stares at the date.

"I've got five days," he says. "I should finish it by then."

"Of course you will. You're a quick reader."

Scott looks from his son, to me, and then back to his son.

"Right, come on then. I told the estate agent we'd be at the house by five." He gazes over at me, and in that moment, I want to grab him, to bury my face in his chest, to smell his aftershave, to let him stay, and to apologise for everything I've done in the past couple of months.

But then I remember that none of this is my fault. Not one single, solitary moment of it. And so, I keep my mouth shut, and allow Scott to walk out of my life, just as he did in 1993.

"Goodbye," I mouth to myself, and the words sting my eyes.

EPILOGUE

It's funny, but I spend a lot of time beating myself up for things that I should have said or done, back in the day. I was only twenty-four the last time I saw Gabby Haine, but I still visualise it, and wish I had said something to her when I had the chance.

It was 1994, and the christening of Scott's colleague's twins. I only knew the workmate in passing, but since Scott and I were now living together and came as part of a package, I was invited too.

I knew that Gabby Haine would be there, since she still worked in the same company. However, according to Scott, they were now just mates, and had firmly put everything they'd done together behind them. That morning, I put on my best outfit – a green taffeta number with padded shoulders, which sounds horrendous now, but it was the 1990s, when pretty much anything went. Having studied magazines like *Jackie* and *Blue Jeans* as a teenager, I was always something of an expert at applying make-up, so I got up early that day to make sure that I looked as good as I possibly could. There was no way I was going to be intimidated by Gabby Haine, so that day I envisaged myself as a reincarnation of one of those golden age actresses, like Marilyn Monroe, and off we went.

We sat toward the back of the church, and the place was busy by the time Gabby arrived. I can't recall exactly what she was wearing, but I do remember there was a purple shirt, and her long red hair – curled for the occasion – bobbed from side to side as she bounced down the aisle. She was with a female friend since she didn't have a boyfriend of her own at that time. While outwardly I smiled at the thought of her being alone, inwardly I panicked that she was not attached to anyone. It was only a year since Scott's fling with her, and my emotions were still raw and painful. This woman had slept with my fiancé for at least four weeks. They had shared secrets and lies, and stories, and bodily fluids, and now she was single again.

Bile rose up in my throat, and while Scott squeezed my hand, I wanted to punch him. I watched her throughout the christening, wondering all kinds of things about the relationship she'd had with my fiancé, and by the end of it I could barely function. As she walked back out of the church, I caught the first real sight of her since it had all kicked off the year before. Her bulbous nose, her skin so pale – more corpse than Snow White – and her eyes made up in a series of purples... Purple eye shadow, purple eyeliner and purple mascara. I kept my eyes on her as she went past, but she never looked anywhere but ahead. If she had smiled at Scott, I'd have ripped her face off, though that probably wouldn't have gone down well in the church.

Scott's colleague and his wife were a bit on the pretentious side, so they had arranged a fancy party after the ceremony. We nipped home in between, and I cried, and shouted at Scott that I still didn't understand what he'd seen in her, and why he'd ever wanted to leave me for her. I don't remember what he said about that – I suspect nothing at all – but I do recall that he asked if I wanted to skip the party and stay home instead. At that point he wanted a quiet life, but I didn't want to stay home. I wanted to go to the hotel reception and feel the pain. Experience the bloody agony of having to sit in the same room as Gabby fucking Haine.

Once there, Scott and I found our seats on a long white table reserved for all the workmates. Gabby Haine was on my side of the table, about five or six chairs away, and she spoke animatedly to her fellow colleagues, laughing and joking, and dancing to that 'Cotton-Eye Joe' song that required everyone to do an impression of a crazy line dance. I was always fond of dancing, and generally first on the floor, but with Gabby and her cronies boogieing away, I could do nothing except sit in my corner seat and try to remain calm. It was one of the hardest things I'd ever done.

When it was time for the buffet, Gabby was in front of me in the queue. To this day I can't remember where Scott was, since I was so focused on her. As she grabbed her plate and started piling it up with sausage rolls and quiche, I wondered if I should tap her on the shoulder and ask if I could have a word. My hand quivered at my side, and I fiddled with the strap of my handbag as I contemplated what I would say to her.

Or what I would do to her.

She was so close that I could have grabbed the back of her purple silky shirt. Even better, I could have reached out and pushed her into the christening cake, squished potato salad into her ridiculous hair, or thrown her head-first onto the dessert trolley.

I could have done anything.

But in the end, I did nothing, except let her fetch her food and take it back to the table without a word being said at all. Twenty-four-year-old me was a gentle, shy person who wanted no trouble. Fifty-four-year-old me on the other hand, would have torn out every wavy red hair from her smug, round head.

When Scott came home from work the following Monday, he had a message for me.

"Gabby thought you were very pretty," he said. "Quiet... but pretty."

Quiet, but pretty...

Quiet, but pretty...

The nerve of that woman. The utter, utter nerve of her.

It was at that point I realised that the quiet but pretty girl should have said something while she had the chance.

So, now there's only one thing left to do, before I move forward into my new life. Rightly or wrongly, my mind has been full of Gabby Haine for my entire adult life, and as time has gone on, the visions in my mind have become larger, and more vivid in pattern and colour. Strangely, Gabby infuriates me even more than Debbie, and maybe that's because Gabby attacked my life when I was a young, naïve woman, trying to make my way in the world, trying to figure out who I was, and where I was going. I wanted so badly to build a career and fulfil my dreams of having a happy home with Scott, but the moment she laid her eyes – and then her body – onto him, that part of my life was irritated, like a piece of grit in a pearl shell.

And now that my relationship with Scott is over, I need to see Gabby. I need to see this woman who helped to destroy my relationship and my confidence when I was barely out of my teens. Because as my spring and summer years have evolved into my autumn ones, I've come to the pathetic realisation that I have never fully recovered from Gabby Haine's presence in my life.

And I need to put that right.

I need to heal.

Once and for all.

Shortly after my video went viral, I messaged Gabby on Facebook, on the pretext that I thought she should know that Scott's new-found fame may send reporters to her door. It was nonsense, of course. Why would they want to interview someone Scott had been with for four weeks in the early 1990s? They wouldn't, and they didn't. But the thought of it was enough for Gabby to write back to me, two and a half days after she read my message.

I know who you are, she messaged. *I remember you.*

That was it. No hello, no goodbye and just eight words to sum up the long years of hurt. I had hoped that the message would be substantial, that she'd give me information on their past relationship, but she didn't. Instead, we messaged back and forth for several days, a sentence here and a sentence there. Very rigid on her part. Maybe even suspicious, but at least she had the balls to reply.

That was that, until a couple of days ago when I messaged her to propose a meeting. I pondered telling her another lie, about how there were media things going on behind the scenes regards Scott and my story, but in the end, I told her the truth: I wanted to get some things off my chest. She was hesitant at first – didn't reply for fourteen hours – but eventually she agreed. That shocked me, as I didn't really expect her to come back in the positive, and I'll admit that for the first twenty-four hours after her acceptance, I went back and forth with myself. Should I ignore her message? Should I send her questions by email instead? Should I ask Lauren for advice? I decided against that one, however, as I knew exactly what my friend would say.

"Don't even think about it."

I spent a lot of time staring into space, contemplating every scenario, but in the end, I thought about the heartbroken twenty-three-year-old girl who still lives inside me, and decided to have the meeting for her. To heal. To grow. To move on. To live.

As expected, Gabby didn't want to meet at her home, likely because she didn't want me to know where she lived. I didn't have the heart to tell her that I'd already traced her home using Instagram and Google Earth, but in any case, I agreed that we could meet at the river, which is about forty yards from her house. Not that she told me that. I knew already, of course. The river would be the ideal place for our conversation, and in preparation, I studied Google Earth for hours, looking at every little detail. There were a couple of benches scattered around, and maybe the odd dog walker, but at 10.30 on a Wednesday morning, I doubted there would be much of anything going on. I was prepared to take a chance in order to bury the old ghosts that have haunted me for so long.

There is no parking at the river, so I park up at the end of Gabby's street instead of her house, for fear of being seen by the Neighbourhood Watch. I know that there is one in the cul-de-sac because I've been to their website, and anonymously joined their mailing list and read the minutes of their meetings.

I know everything about the area. I even know the name of the bichon that belongs to old Mrs Potter in the far corner. It's Archie, for anyone who is interested, and he frequently pisses off the neighbours by standing at the back gate, barking at anyone and anything that happens to go past. Mrs Potter is deaf. I know that too.

There was a time when I knew nothing about anything.

But now I know it all.

I keep my head low and saunter up the grassy lane that leads to the river. It is overgrown by bushes, and I'm careful not to let the stinging nettles swat at my legs. I may be wearing trousers, but those sneaky things can get through everything, as

I've discovered in the past. The lane is surrounded by trees, all revealing their new spring buds, and above my head there are tweets and chirps of all kinds of different birds. My Charlie would have identified the noises immediately. He knew the names and sounds of every bird imaginable. He loved to learn. He loved to discover. And I loved him so much that it still makes every inch of me ache.

I reach the end of the lane, and it opens up onto a large area of greenery, with the river running in front of me. It's flowing fast this morning, the result of a rainy month – far rainier than expected in springtime.

I walk into the clearing, and see Gabby in the flesh for the first time since that christening in 1994. I feel dizzy, my stomach churns, and for a second I wish that I hadn't come. What is going to happen? What is the worst that can happen? Could she reveal the news that her and Scott have never stopped loving each other? Does she have a secret child to him too? I shake the thoughts from my head. Two mystery children would be too obscure, even for Scott.

Physically, the first thing I notice is that Gabby is slightly heavier than in her infrequent social media photos, and while her hair is still strawberry blonde, the remnants of pastel-pink highlights are duller than they appear in her pictures. But then I guess we're all duller in real life, aren't we? I suspect I am, though I hope in this instance I can persuade her that I'm not.

Gabby sits on one of the park benches, located near the riverside, and as I approach, she looks up and gives a hesitant smile. She's in her early fifties now, and without the aid of Facebook filters, she looks it. There are deep lines at the corners of her eyes, and her skin looks as though she puffs away on fifty cigarettes a day.

Her thin lips are painted in the darkest red lipstick she

could possibly find, and unbelievably, her eyes are still framed with the same shades of purple... Purple eyeshadow, purple mascara, and purple eyeliner.

"Hi," she says. "I wasn't sure if you'd come."

Her voice grates on me, and takes me by surprise. It's high, and constricted, and seems to come straight from her nostrils, which is not something I remember from the fleeting meeting with her at the christening.

I take a breath in, open my mouth and pray that something sensible comes out.

"I could say the same about you. I wondered if I'd end up sitting here alone."

"I'm not that rude," she says, and smiles again.

"Well, I've waited for this moment for over thirty years, so I wasn't about to miss it now."

I sound like a Bond villain, but if Gabby thinks I'm being corny or sarcastic or both, she doesn't let on. Instead, she moves her pink sparkly crochet handbag from the bench, and motions to the seat next to her.

"We could go for a walk if you like," she says. "Or we could sit here."

"Here's fine for now. Thanks."

I sit, and our bodies are so close that her aura must surely be mingling with mine. I am sitting next to Gabby Haine. The same woman who took my fiancé all those years ago, and has ruined my self-confidence ever since. I swallow hard. I must not cry. Not here, not now, not anywhere.

The wind blows at my trousers and cuts through my coat. It's no longer scarf season, but still, I wish I'd remembered to bring one with me. My neck is exposed and cold, and goosebumps send shivers toward the back of my head. Maybe it's because after all these years, this purple mascara woman still intimidates me, and I hate that about her. I absolutely hate that.

And yet here I am.

"So," she says, "what did you want to speak to me about? I never did get any reporters at the door, by the way. Thanks for keeping my name away from them."

I inwardly cough. Of course, I wasn't about to give Gabby's name to a bunch of journalists. Wasn't it bad enough that Scott cheated on me during our marriage, without adding a vintage fling into the mix?

"That's okay," I reply. "They did ask me if I could put them in touch with any women from Scott's past, but to be honest, I wasn't sure if you'd count. It was such a long time ago, and you only went out for a couple of weeks."

That's a bitchy thing to say, but Gabby laughs. It is shallow and weak, and comes straight from her upper chest. I hope it chokes her.

"Time is strange, isn't it?" she says. "We only went out officially for twenty-seven days, but we were emotionally involved for much longer than that."

My face tingles.

"Yes, I know you were. I knew that at the time."

"You did?"

"Of course I did. No man goes on about another woman's love life, her favourite colour and her new dress without having some kind of attachment to her. I figured out where his heart had gone, long before he left."

"You were too busy for him," she says, and her words hang in the air like haunted bats. "You were always working on your newspaper column, that's what Scott told me."

She's right. I did ignore him up to a point. But I've come to realise over the past year that there was no malicious intent implied. The only thing my young heart wanted to do was build something special in my life. I wanted to be somebody. I wanted to be a success. Just like Scott wanted for himself. If I was doing something wrong, and if he had wanted more attention, he didn't need to go to such extremes to get it. He could have just asked.

"I was trying to establish a writing career," I snap. "There's nothing wrong with that."

She shrugs. Obviously she believes otherwise.

"Well, you made it. I've seen your books in Waterstones, and that big shop in London. Foyles, isn't it?"

I'm shocked. The idea of anyone seeing my books in a shop has always been delightful, but the idea of Gabby Haine seeing them? I'm not sure how I feel about that.

"You've seen my books?"

"Yes," she replies. "I bought a signed one while I was in London about fifteen years ago. I even read it, but it was weird to know that you'd once touched it." She laughs. "But I guess after the Scott stuff I should be used to touching something that you had first."

Until now I've been trying to avoid looking at Gabby while we talk, but that revelation, and the accompanying giggle, pisses me off. How dare she even mention touching my then fiancé? How fucking dare she?! Her cheeks are flushed with the cold, and she rubs at them with her hands. Now all I can think of is how she once touched my fiancé with those hands and how her mouth once met his. I need to change the subject.

"Which book did you read?" I ask, and her brow furrows, causing a straight, vertical line in the middle of her forehead.

"I can't remember what it was called, but it wasn't one of your rom-com things. It was more of a thriller, I'd say. Something about a woman who kills her husband's lover by throwing her into a river. Ironic really, since here we are, sitting next to a river. Would you like a chewing gum?"

Gabby offers me a stick of gum, and I shake my head. She

unwraps one and sticks it in her mouth, folding it in half with her tongue and her thin, red lips.

"*Love To Hatred Turned.*"

"Pardon?"

"The name of my psychological thriller. It was – is – *Love to Hatred Turned.*"

"Oh. Well, I'm glad the writing stuff worked out for you," she says, slapping the gum against her teeth. "What are you working on now? Haven't seen a new one from you in quite a while."

Small talk. Polite, ridiculous small talk that has no meaning in this conversation. I hate that she's brought up my lack of recent work, but I'm secretly thrilled that she read my book about the wife murdering her husband's lover.

It was inspired by you, I want to tell her. It was all about you!

"I haven't been very busy in recent years," I say. "But things are picking up."

"Great," she says, with no conviction at all. "I imagine it was hard for you to write, after your son passed. Charlie, wasn't it? He sounds like he was a great kid too... I never had children myself. Been married twice, and briefly engaged another time before that, but I didn't have kids with any of them."

She rolls her eyes and shakes her head, but her words are like acid, and they burn my heart. How could my son's name come out of her mouth? What business has she to even know about Charlie, never mind talk about him?

"How did you know that my son had died?" I expect her to squirm, but instead she looks up to the sky, runs her tongue along her top lip, and then flicks it back into her mouth.

"You wrote an article about it, didn't you? Must be about ten or eleven years ago now. My mum had the magazine and kept it for me."

"She kept it for you?"

"Yes, she always saved stuff she thought I'd be interested in, and she knew that we had a... history. Bless her, she's gone now, so no more articles for me."

"I'm sorry to hear that," I say, but in reality, I'm not sorry or surprised at all. I only ever knew Gabby's mother by name, but I've known for a while that she died. I found the woman's obituary on the funeral director's website, when I was researching her wretched daughter.

Gabby either doubts my sincerity, or doesn't care for my good wishes. Either way, there's a pause in our conversation while we're both lost in our own thoughts.

"So, what do you want to talk about?" she asks. "I have to be back at work in an hour, so I can't stop long."

Work. Yes, of course. I recently discovered that Gabby Haine has given up office work, and when she's not flogging her craft goods is now a teaching assistant at the local primary school. Judging by the photos of her on the school website, it looks as though she's some kind of classroom angel, but we both know the truth.

"To be honest," I say, "I wanted to get some closure on stuff that happened between you and Scott."

She scratches at her hair, and hangs her head. I've made her uncomfortable. Goal achieved.

"Jesus, I can hardly remember it after all this time. As you say, it's been thirty years."

"Thirty-one," I remind her. "Actually, coming up for thirty-two."

"You're still counting? That's commitment."

She laughs and pops another chewing gum into her mouth. The nerve of this woman. She has literally just told me that she's kept tabs on my career over the years, and her mother even collected articles for her, but she can hardly remember her time with Scott? Well, if that's true (which I doubt), it's a good job I've got memory enough for the both of us.

I forget nothing.

But sometimes I wish that I could.

"So, what do you want to know?" she asks.

Gabby leans forward, the toes of her pink trainers touching. She turns her head to stare at me, her thin eyebrows knitted together. There is a hardness about her. I felt it the first time I ever saw her outside Scott's workplace, but now it's evolved. Time, marriage, divorce, heartbreak, life lessons... All of those things mould us, shape us, harden us. Sometimes they even kill us.

Or worse.

I am aware that this will be the first and last time that I speak to Gabby Haine. She has haunted me for more than half my life, and now this is it. The only opportunity I'll ever have to find out why. Why she is what she is. Why I am what I am.

"Why did you go after him, knowing that he was engaged to someone else?"

Gabby sits back on the bench, and clenches her hands.

"We got on really well at work," she says. "He was in marketing as you know, and I was on the reception. He'd pass me every time he went to the canteen, or the vending machine, or whatever, and we'd have a chat."

"What did you talk about?"

"Gosh," she says, "you really do want to know everything! I'm not sure what we spoke about to be honest. If I'd known I'd need to recollect those memories three decades later, I'd have written them down."

A swan swims on the river, gliding effortlessly, but paddling so hard underneath the water. What a metaphor for this conversation, and for the last ten years of my life.

"Oh, come on," I say. "I'm sure you can remember far more

than you're making out. I can tell you some of the things you spoke about, if that helps."

"Really?"

I take a deep breath. The air is thick and cold at the back of my throat.

"Yes, for some reason Scott thought I'd enjoy hearing about your conversations. Let's see... Well, your boyfriend, ex-boyfriend, whatever, was one thing you spoke about, and your current method of contraception was another."

Gabby's eyebrows shoot up toward her hairline.

"My contraception?"

"Diaphragm and spermicide, if you need to be reminded," I snap.

Gabby takes her gum out of her mouth, wraps it in a tissue and throws it into her handbag.

"That's shit that he spoke to you about that. Shit for you to know it, and shit for him to gossip about me in that way. Degrading really. Weirdly, I don't even remember telling him what contraception I used. Until we... you know."

"Yes. Yes, I do know."

"Anyway," she says, "one thing I do remember is that after a while of talking, he began going on about his girlfriend – you. He said that you were heading for a break-up because you weren't spending any time together, and when you did, you'd only argue. He was really unhappy."

This conversation – as important as it is – makes me want to bawl my eyes out, but I can't let Gabby see me cry. Not after all these years.

"Go on," I say.

She fiddles with her hair, and I notice that her nails are yellow, short and bitten. One of Scott's bugbears has always been women who bite their nails. Did Gabby bite hers when they were having their fling? Did he push aside his distaste, just for her?

"He would go out for a sneaky ciggy in his breaks," she says, "and I started going out too. I didn't smoke then, but I enjoyed spending time with him. He was funny, and he made me laugh. I presumed nothing would come of it, but I probably made it a little too obvious that if he wanted to see me out of work then I was available. In the end I even broke up with my boyfriend because it seemed like a waste of time to be with him, when I'd fallen for someone else."

A dog walker rambles past, and his spaniel sniffs at our legs, before trotting on. The owner has no clue of the significance of this conversation. He does not know that this is the first time we've spent any real time in each other's company. His life goes on. He'll go home, he'll take his cap off, he'll give his dog a treat, and then he'll have a nice cup of tea, still completely oblivious to the history he just witnessed on the river pathway.

"Were you happy?" I ask.

"What?"

"When you were together. Or even when you were fooling around. Were you happy?"

"I thought we were," Gabby says. "I know I was. For a while."

"And you didn't feel guilty that you had taken someone else's fiancé?"

She shakes her head.

"I really didn't feel as though I had stolen someone else's boyfriend, or fiancé, or whatever. I was young – I was twenty-one – and I thought I'd met someone who truly liked and wanted me. What I discovered, however, was that like any bloke, all he really wanted was some attention. You didn't give him any, and so he came to me because I was happy to give him it. But I think I could have been anyone. He didn't care where he got the attention from, as long as he got it."

"Scott always did enjoy attention," I say. "He still does... so long as it's on his terms."

Gabby opens her handbag and brings out a cigarette. She offers me one, I shake my head and she lights up. She takes a long drag and then flicks the ash onto the ground, narrowly missing my trousers.

"Men are funny really, aren't they?" she says. "Like, I've been on this earth for over fifty years, but no matter how old I get – or how old the men I'm with get – they're all the same. They're all just boys looking for someone to be enamoured with them. I flattered Scott, it fed something in him, and then when he was full up, he went back to the person he really wanted to be with. You."

I laugh.

"Well, he wanted to be with me for a while."

She blows out a stream of smoke, and it takes me all of my strength not to swat it away from me. I know that when I get home, the smell will have enveloped my clothes, a reminder once again of her presence in my life.

"He wanted you enough to marry you, and have a kid with you," she says. "I'd have married him too, given half the chance."

"Think yourself lucky you didn't," I snap, "or you'd be in the same position as me right now."

"What? A successful author? Yeah, that must be a terrible place to be."

Gabby spits out the words, as if they were seeds stuck between her teeth.

"No, I meant in the middle of a messy divorce. And being an author isn't as glamorous as it sounds, you know. It's bloody hard work."

She shuffles in her seat.

"I don't know about that, but no matter what, at least you've got something to leave behind when you're gone. When I go, that'll be it. All of me will disappear. And people love your books. I've seen all the love for you on social media."

I blink rapidly. This woman looks at my social media? Is she a follower? Does she interact with my posts and view my stories? Surely not. And yet, I think she might.

"You follow me?"

"No," Gabby says. "I just kind of float around your Instagram sometimes. I can't visit too often because it does my head in. Especially before, when you seemed happily married to Scott. Whenever you posted photos of you two together, I would study them for hours and ask, why you? What did he see in you, that he didn't see in me? Why was it me who got played? Why couldn't he stay away from you?"

I can't believe it. All those hours I've spent worrying about this woman. All the days, weeks, months, years I've spent being intimidated by her, and it seems that she feels the same way about me. How is that possible?

"Maybe it's time for you to move on," I say. "You're still young enough to find someone else."

Gabby laughs, and she launches into a long, frenzied rant.

"Been there, done that, didn't make a success of any of them." She slouches forward, throws her cigarette onto the ground, and sighs. "To be honest, my hang-up maybe isn't even about Scott as a person anymore. Maybe it's about the humiliation. The fact that I loved this man – the first person I ever loved, in fact. I invested in him and felt sorry for him that his girlfriend was more interested in her career than him. And I gave him everything I had, everything he said he didn't get with you, and I treated him so well, but still he went back to you. He would rather be ignored by you, than loved by me. That's the stinger. That's what's so shit about it all. And to make it worse, you didn't even fail at being a writer. You made it work and became a success. That ate me up inside. I didn't understand any of it. Still don't, actually."

I am shocked that these words are coming out of Gabby Haine's mouth. This conversation is the complete opposite of how I imagined it would go.

"Are you going to write another book?" she asks randomly.

"I think so."

"You should," she says. "Write about all the shit he's put you through! I'd definitely read it."

I open my mouth to thank her, and to tell her that yes, I am indeed going to write about this awful situation, but then I remember who I'm talking to, and our history prevents me from sharing myself with her. It prevents me from even trying with her.

"I'll think about it," I say, and she smiles.

"Definitely do... Besides, I thought you were terribly wasted in that job you had with those publishing people. Babbage Books, wasn't it? They have some terrible books on their website. I ordered one by some bloke called Victor Victory or something, but it was so awful I returned it."

The mention of Babbage Books is startling. This woman really has kept tabs on me. All the time I was trying to find her on social media, she was right there, watching, stalking, discovering, judging.

"You know I worked for Babbage Books? How? I never spoke about that on my social media."

"You can find anything on the internet nowadays," she says, laughing, and I can't argue with that. "So, now that you've been fired, you can go back to writing. It makes sense, really."

My blood freezes.

"Wait. How did you know that I was fired?"

Gabby sticks another piece of gum into her mouth, but doesn't reply. And then suddenly, everything becomes clear.

"Oh my God, it was you, wasn't it?"

"What was me?"

"It was you who sent the hate mail to the authors, wasn't it? It was you who left the terrible comments and got me fired! It was all you!"

Gabby shuffles in her seat, and her dull hair catches glints of the sun.

"I have no idea what you're talking about. I didn't do anything... Not really."

"Of course you didn't."

She spits her barely chewed gum onto the grass beside us, and throws her hands in the air.

"Okay, I thought that you deserved it," she barks.

"Deserved it? Why? How?"

Gabby shakes her head, and clenches her mouth.

"Why should you have so much when I have absolutely nothing at all? How is that fair?"

"I..."

I don't have any chance to finish my sentence. I have no chance to ask how I have it all, when my beautiful son passed away, and my marriage broke up in a blaze of scandal. I have no chance because Gabby's on a roll, and there's no point of return.

"When you were working at Babbage," she says, "I had no idea you were going through a break-up with Scott. As far as I knew, you were still very much together, all those years since he used me, and then threw me away like a piece of crap. And you know what? I honestly think Scott is the only person I have ever really loved, and thirty years later, it still pisses me off. Everything about you pisses me off, and I just wanted to punish you a bit. Just a little bit of revenge... I thought it might make me feel better."

"And did it?"

A tear appears in the corner of Gabby's eye, but she doesn't answer my question. And in that moment, I can honestly say that for the first time in my adult life I am not threatened by this woman. Any power she may have had over me belongs firmly in the 1990s, and now here she is, unhappy, bitter, and still engrossed in what could have been.

What a fool she has been.

What a fool I have been.

What a fool we have both been.

A whoosh of something – relief maybe – swirls around my stomach. This is it. It's all over.

"You know what?" I say. "Ever since you and Scott had your fling, I've felt intimidated by you, and what you both did to me. I came here today, thinking that I'd likely end up slapping you, or pushing you into the river or something."

Gabby's wet eyes shoot wide open, and she sits upright in her seat.

"Don't worry," I say, "I'm not going to do anything to you. But for years I've imagined destroying your life, and believe me, if I wanted to I definitely could. But now, I realise for the first time that you're not the vixen I painted you to be in my mind, and to be honest, you're really quite pathetic. So, in that regard, it's probably crueller to not do anything to you at all; to leave your pitiful little life exactly as it is."

I laugh, stand up, straighten my jacket, and offer Gabby my hand. Her nostrils flare, and her mouth hangs open. She is embarrassed, startled, shamed even, but then her shaking hand takes mine.

"Goodbye, Gabby," I say. "I wish you all that you would wish for me."

And with that, I stroll back down the river path, leaving behind Scott, Debbie, Gabby, my demons, the ghosts of my past, and everything I ever believed to be true.

It's time to reclaim my life.

Finally.

THE END

ACKNOWLEDGEMENTS

In 2022, I was diagnosed with breast cancer, and I had no idea if I would get out of the other side, or ever write again. I am so grateful to have come through it, but I'm not ashamed to say that I have been left significantly traumatised by my experience, and there was a time when I truly believed that my career was over. Through writing this book, however, I have begun to mend. Olivia's trauma is different to my own, but by working through her fears, worries and obsessions, I have been able to process my own pain, and find a way out of the darkness that often descends when cancer treatment has ended.

On the surface, this book might be about the heartbreak and rage of a woman who has lost her son and is dealing with a cheating, lying husband. However, at the heart of it is the idea that no matter what you have been through there is always room for reinvention, and reclaiming what you once believed to be lost – i.e. a writing career, and yourself. *The Other Mrs Collins* has been a hard story to write at times, but has also been incredibly healing. I am thankful for this book, and for the following people...

Thank you to Betsy, Fred, Ian, Tara, Hannah, Patricia and all of the Bloodhound team for your enthusiasm and support during the writing and publication of this book. I'd also like to thank Betsy and Fred for publishing my first two novels and giving me my start in the world of fiction.

My husband Richard has been by my side since 1988, and took care of me every day of my illness, and every day since.

Richard, you taught me how to walk again after chemo, how to believe in myself again, and how to live again. You will always be my person. I love you so much.

Thank you to my darling daughter, Daisy, for being my sounding board, my ray of light, my amateur therapist and best friend. Being your mum is my proudest achievement, and watching you become a woman, and meeting your soulmate, Harry, has been a blessing. I love you to the moon and back. Always remember that my dreams came true because of you.

Finally, I'd like to thank my family and friends, for their love and encouragement. Special mention must also go to my reader friends for supporting me over the years and buying my books. Your beautiful comments, messages and mentions mean more to me than you'll ever know. Because of you, I get to write my stories, and I truly cannot thank you enough.

A NOTE FROM THE PUBLISHER

Thank you for reading this book. If you enjoyed it please do consider leaving a review on Amazon to help others find it too.

We hate typos. All of our books have been rigorously edited and proofread, but sometimes mistakes do slip through. If you have spotted a typo, please do let us know and we can get it amended within hours.

info@bloodhoundbooks.com